MW01537414

SPEED KILLS

The yellow Mercedes pulled up in front of a duplex on Harper, just north of Sunset. Barry Ashford and Cynthia got out of the car at the same time, Cynthia not waiting for Ashford to be a gentleman and open her door. He never did.

Ashford had started across the street when he saw the headlights closing in at high speed. His eyes widened and he froze. The car hit Ashford head on. He slid over the hood, caromed off the windshield, and rolled to a bloody stop under the wheels of a car on the other side of the street.

Cynthia ran toward him, but by the time she could see his mangled form, she slowed to a dazed walk.

"Oh my God," was all she could say through her tears as she knelt next to her dead lover.

HOLLYWOOD HEROES

HAMILTON T. CAINE

BERKLEY BOOKS, NEW YORK

HOLLYWOOD HEROES

A Berkley Book / published by arrangement with
the author

PRINTING HISTORY
Berkley edition / June 1986

All rights reserved.
Copyright © 1986 by Stephen Smoke.
This book may not be reproduced in whole or in part,
by mimeograph or any other means, without permission.
For information address: The Berkley Publishing Group,
200 Madison Avenue, New York, NY 10016

ISBN: 0-425-09090-6

A BERKLEY BOOK ® TM 757,375
Berkley Books are published by The Berkley Publishing Group,
200 Madison Avenue, New York, N.Y. 10016.
The name "BERKLEY" and the stylized "B" with design are trademarks
belonging to Berkley Publishing Corporation.

PRINTED IN THE UNITED STATES OF AMERICA

For my father

PART ONE

BARRY ASHFORD OPENED the glass doors to the patio and the warm Santa Anas brushed across his face like a hot fist that just missed. He strolled out to the pool, walked around its turquoise luminescence, which rippled lightly as the Indian summer breeze skimmed across the lazy liquid. He plopped himself down in a white, crisscross-vinyl pool lounge chair and jiggled the cubes against the sides of his half-empty glass of real Russian vodka. The million lights of L.A. winked knowingly through the sparse manicured hedges that surrounded the pool. A lot of people had tried to find out what that seductive wink meant. Barry Ashford was one of them. He still didn't know.

"Fuck!" he sputtered half out loud, and took another swig of the socially acceptable, numbing liquid. He sat at poolside sputtering and sipping, sipping and sputtering, for about five minutes before the approaching click of high heels on cement captured what was left of his attention.

"Honey . . ." the woman purred, and sat down in a matching pool chair next to Ashford. "Everyone's asking for you, honey."

"Oh? Do they need some ass to pin a tail on?" snapped

Ashford, and squeezed another sip out of the ice cubes in the bottom of the glass.

"Hey," said the woman soothingly. "They like you, honey. You've just got to make an effort sometimes, that's all."

Ashford grabbed hold of what strains of untethered consciousness he could latch on to, swallowed, and said, "Cyn, that's a bunch of bull and you know it. I know what they think of me and, well, to tell you the truth, if I were in their shoes, I might feel the same way. But . . ." His head fell back clumsily against the chair and he lapsed into an elliptic stupor.

"But what?"

Ashford came around again and a vinegary smile split his face. "But I'm *not* them. I'm me. I'm an asshole, but it's a fucking asshole's world. I didn't make the rules. And I'll be damned if I'm going to lose at *any* fuckin' game."

Cynthia didn't say anything for a moment. She stroked Ashford's head gently as again it fell back against the chair and he stared off into the city lights.

Barry Ashford was a young man not much pleased with himself, or anything else, for that matter. This was not the first time Cynthia had sat alone at a party nursing her wounded lover back to relative sanity. But that was all right. Cynthia Walcott was not getting any younger, and in a town where important men, wealthy men, wore eighteen-year-old girls on their arms like flashy jewelry, a thirty-five-year-old woman, even one with a few bucks, felt good about having a good-looking guy in tow who had more going for him than a stiff cock. Of course, Ashford had that, too—when he didn't drink himself to sleep. All things considered, Cynthia Walcott, who was a looker herself, for her age, felt pretty good about the whole arrangement.

Her spirits, as well as her tits and ass, were beginning to sag more than a little just before she had met Ashford. She had gone to a party at a producer's house in the Hollywood Hills. Cynthia had a few dollars and the mid-twenties types she met at these parties usually could walk away with a reasonable day's wages if they did the right tricks. But that act was getting pretty old, and Cynthia was beginning to wonder if she would ever again meet a guy who would be with her for any of the right reasons.

Enter Barry Ashford, the lead actor in one of TV's hottest daytime soap operas, *Doctors and Lovers*. He had money. He had the right connections—at least, he had more than Cynthia.

And they hit it off for more than a one-night stand. It wasn't Romeo and Juliet, but then what was.

"I think I love you, honey," whispered Cynthia Walcott in a voice that Ashford couldn't hear—even if he would have been able to.

Ashford hiccuped and his head moved forward off the back of the chair. He blinked enough of the vodka stupor from his eyes so that he could tell where he was and looked drowsily at the woman sitting next to him. "Hi," he said, and smiled a pitiful, drunken smile at Cynthia.

"You wanna go home now, honey?" she said softly, and stroked a lock of hair off his forehead back up top where it belonged.

Ashford heaved a heavy sigh, dropped his head wearily onto his upraised palm, and massaged his temple, silently willing the pain, the craziness, to be exorcised from his whirling brain. "Yeah. I'd like to go, Cyn," he said just loud enough so that she could hear.

As the couple made their clumsy way back into the house and through the living room full of loud, laughing, animated guests, Ashford and his lady tried not to hear the whispered remarks as they passed. At first he thought it was his imagination, but even in his drunken state, Barry Ashford could feel the eyes on him as he moved toward the foyer to retrieve his hat and coat. His white fedora, an affectation to be sure, had become as much a part of his image as his brash, blunt, often rude manner.

Ashford easily found his coat—a satin athletic jacket with *Doctors and Lovers* written in white against a shiny purple background—but he had a little trouble finding his hat. He thought he had put it on the shelf just above his coat, but for some reason, even though it *was* on the shelf, it was much farther to the right than he remembered. I'm drunk, he thought to himself; it's a wonder I can even find the closet.

He put on his coat and made a stab at helping Cynthia on with hers. Then he picked up his hat and placed it firmly upon his head. Or at least he started to. The fedora was full of shit and it plopped onto Ashford's head and started to run down his face.

The eyes that Ashford had felt were on him now and they were full of laughter, uncontrollable laughter. Immediately Cynthia took the hat off Ashford's head, and, plucking a towel from a nearby bathroom, she began to clean him up.

Maddie Paxton, the party's hostess and director of *Doctors and Lovers,* raced to the scene looking genuinely surprised, and besides apologizing a dozen times or more, made some excuse about her cat, who liked to climb in the closet and was known to do such things from time to time. But Ashford and Cynthia knew it wasn't the cat. Everybody knew that it was a cruel practical joke played on the man everyone loved to hate.

Finally, after what seemed an eternity to Ashford, he was cleaned up, and he and Cynthia left the party, got into her yellow Mercedes 450SEL, and escaped down the hill to safer ground. Though he had been dead drunk before, the incident sobered Ashford up a little and he insisted on driving.

"You okay, honey?" asked Cynthia after she'd lit a cigarette, waved out the match, and thrown it out the window.

"It's a shitty world, baby," said Ashford in a cool, calm voice. "I shit on people, they shit on me. This is just a bit more graphic an exchange than I'm used to. I'll get over it. And when I find out who did it, I'll get him, or her, fired. That stunt was a cruel thing to do. But when it comes to cold, I invented the word."

Cynthia didn't say anything. She knew he was right. He could be very cold. He wasn't cold toward her, but she'd seen him do things that would have made her dislike him, if she hadn't needed him so much. She'd seen him fire a regular actor because he'd found out that the actor had said he didn't like the way Barry dressed. Cynthia knew that Barry had fired a writer because he and Barry were interested in the same girl, a supporting actress in the series. Ashford was cruel and swift with his cutting sword, but Cynthia knew that with him she'd experienced the closest thing to love she'd known in a long time. In spite of his cruelty. And when Cynthia was totally honest with herself, she admitted that she loved him partly *because* of it.

The yellow Mercedes pulled up in front of Cynthia's two-story house on Harper, just north of Sunset. They got out of the car at the same time, Cynthia not waiting for Ashford to be a gentleman and open her door. He never did.

Ashford checked the driver's door to make sure it was locked, thinking to himself for the hundredth time that Cynthia should have a garage to put the car in. A quarter-of-a-million-dollar house, you'd think there would be a garage. What the fuck, he thought, she probably paid enough for insurance on the car. He was thinking these thoughts when he saw the headlights closing in at high speed. His eyes widened and he froze. Cynthia turned around quickly—she was already half up the sidewalk to the front door. The car, which was just a blur of headlights and taillights to Cynthia, was going over forty miles an hour when it hit Ashford head on. He slid over the hood and caromed off the windshield into the street, where he rolled to a bloody stop under the wheels of a car on the other side of the street.

Cynthia ran toward Ashford, but by the time she could make out his mangled form, she had slowed to a dazed walk, wincing as she closed in on the grisly scene.

"Oh, my God," was all she could say through her tears as she knelt next to her dead lover.

ACE CARPENTER OPENED the unlocked door to the reception room he shared with his friend, Stephen Kagy. Kagy usually opened his doors to business about 9:00, while Ace opened his sometime after 9:30. How much after depended on how late he got to bed the night before.

The office was nice, a step up. It had charm. It was located in what was referred to as the Crossroads of the World on Sunset near Highland. The offices looked like two-story gingerbread cottages, each one a little different from the other. Together they formed what was known as a Hollywood landmark, the significance of which depended on whom you talked to about it.

The offices of Ace Carpenter were located on the second story of one of the buildings in the back of the courtyard-connected complex. Stephen Kagy had met Carpenter when he'd hired the detective to get him out of a jam. One of his clients—Kagy was in the talent agency business—had tried to put the screws to old Stephen. Maggy Tate, up-and-coming young actress, was the type who could always act as if she were coming. Maggy figured Stephen for a lot more money than he really had—but then Kagy never really expected anyone to *believe* all the bull he threw out—and decided that since they *had* spent a night in the sack together, she'd slap a paternity suit on him when she happened to get pregnant.

Carpenter unraveled the plot by discovering that Maggy had gotten an abortion shortly after she'd confronted Kagy. Armed with this information, Kagy dodged a bullet, as well as a settlement that would have just about wiped him out.

Kagy had kept in touch with Ace, and when the office had become available—basically Kagy couldn't hack the rent on both offices anymore—the two had worked out a mutually satisfactory arrangement.

"My dog can juggle," said an elderly woman who stood up when Ace walked into the reception room. The leash on the dog was a little short, and when the woman stood, the dog was lifted slightly off the floor by its neck and made a grunting sound.

"That's nice," said Ace.

"Balls," said the woman proudly.

"I beg your pardon?"

"Bill, my dog. He juggles balls with his paws while lying on his back. Isn't that something!" she said, her face aglow with pride.

"Your dog's name is Bill?"

"Why?"

"Oh, I don't know. It seems like a person's name."

"Mrs. Fido, this is not Mr. Kagy," said Bunny Aguirre, the blonde behind the desk.

"It's a joke, right?" Ace said.

"What's a joke?" asked the woman.

"The name. Yours, your dog's."

The woman gave him a stern look and sat down, mumbling something to her dog that sounded like, "Why didn't he just say he wasn't Mr. Kagy."

Ace took a deep breath and walked over to Bunny's desk and looked down at his message pad for anything interesting. "Morning, honey," he said to the blonde. She had come as part of the arrangement with Kagy. She was a real looker, whom Kagy had bragged about banging on the side. The way Ace had it figured, though, that was just one of Kagy's fantasies. Bunny was a class act from the tip of each of her firm breasts down to the toenails she'd had painted with pictures of her favorite movie stars. The job was better than waiting tables, and she was close enough to "the business" to be able to maneuver a *real* break for herself one of these days.

"Jenny called," said Bunny, handing Ace a piece of paper

with Jenny's name and a "call back" message on it. "Said she'd like to see you for lunch. Wants to talk to you about something important. I'd call her right away."

"Thanks. For the message *and* the advice," said Ace with a slight but noticeable edge in his voice. "Anything else?"

"Nope."

Ace took Jenny's message, went into his office, and closed the door behind him. The office consisted of a large oak desk with five drawers; two large leather chairs, beige, comfortable; and a couch that converted into a bed for those long nights or matinee performances. A bookcase with three shelves were filled with relevant law books, Carpenter's favorite mysteries, and the stereo receiver, which ran to the two speakers in the corners opposite the desk. On the walls hung posters of *Casablanca, Chinatown, The Maltese Falcon, Body Heat,* and *Double Indemnity.* There was also a framed cover of *Mystery Magazine,* in which Ace was one of several L.A. private investigators interviewed on the topic of what it was like to be a *real* PI. There was a knee-high refrigerator in the corner, which usually contained a bottle of Absolut vodka, some Perrier, low-fat vanilla yogurt, lettuce, spinach, hard-boiled eggs, croutons, pickled beets, Maui onions, and a bottle of homemade french dressing.

Carpenter didn't drive a Rolls-Royce, but then neither did a lot of people who were doing all right. He had paid his dues and the business was starting to pay off. He drove a new white Celica GT convertible with a beige top, was flush with all his creditors, and was willing to pick up the check for almost all his dates. He was on retainer to a couple of corporations to do various things, including deep background on people the computers couldn't thoroughly flesh out, as well as other things that sometimes crossed the line into industrial espionage. It wasn't all that exciting, but it beat the hell out of the suspense of whether or not he was going to be able to pay his rent.

He sat down in his swivel chair and looked at the message in his hands. Jenny Ling. Now that was a beautiful woman. She was a dancer at a club in Hollywood and . . . and the woman he loved. Not that he wanted to.

He had fallen in love with a woman he'd met on a tour of "Raymond Chandler's L.A." A woman who loved to see old movies and eat popcorn and snuggle up in bed at night. A woman who was an artist, a ballet dancer with aspirations of going all the way, with the kind of dedication it took to practice those long, grueling hours *every* single day of her life.

He hadn't known that she was a nude dancer, and she hadn't told him until he'd fallen for her hook, line, and sinker. "But I *never* go home with anyone I meet here, I swear, Ace," she had said. And he had believed her.

God, he'd wanted to believe her. Especially after he had brought himself to go see her perform and got sick outside in the parking lot. He had told her, told himself, that knowing what she did changed things. It *did*. Some things. But not others. He still loved her, but he didn't want to. She wasn't ready to get married, nor was he, for that matter. But he wanted *something*. Some kind of commitment. He couldn't stop feeling what he felt for her, but he knew that it was dangerous to feel so much for a woman unwilling to be committed and who was constantly in the sexual spotlight, so to speak.

It all would have been so much easier had Jenny not told him so often how much she loved him. She manifested all the traits he desired in a woman. She was affectionate, sexy, secure enough in herself to be willing to play a submissive role that made him feel like a king. She actively created their relationship, but she was too committed to her dancing to make any "romantic commitments," as she put it, to anyone, including someone she loved as much as she said she loved him.

In a lot of ways, Jenny had spoiled him for other women. She knew exactly how to make him happy in *and* out of bed. She could write the owner's manual to Ace Carpenter.

He tossed the message aside for the moment and sat back in his chair, his head resting against his clasped hands.

The phone rang on his desk. It was his line and he picked it up. "Ace Carpenter," he said.

"Hi, honey," said Jenny Ling.

"Hi, Jenny."

"Didn't you get my message?"

"Yeah. I just got in."

"Long night?"

"Hard night."

"But not as long and as hard a night as the ones you spend with me," she said playfully.

"Probably not," he said, not really in the mood for such banter.

"Look, honey, I've got a friend who's in trouble. I thought

you might, you know, listen to her, tell her the options, give her a professional opinion."

"What's the story?"

"I don't know *all* the details, but her friend, her lover, was killed a few days ago in a hit-and-run accident and the police don't seem to be coming up with anything. They're just writing it off as a drunk driver thing, you know. But my friend seems to think it was murder."

"Uh-huh."

"So anyhow, I told her that I would ask you to listen to her story and give her some advice."

"Free advice?"

"No. She's pretty well off. She'll be a paying customer. In fact, she's planning to pick up the tab for lunch today at the Brown Derby."

"Oh? I was counting on a salad here in the office."

"Give yourself a break."

"Okay. What time?"

"Twelvish."

"What time does that mean to a *real* person? In L.A. a half hour late is the same as on time."

"We'll be there at twelve-fifteen. I'll be the one without any panties under my slit-up-the-side skirt."

Ace's heart skipped a beat. He'd seen Jenny naked plenty of times—as had a lot of people. But he never, *never* took the sight for granted. She was an Oriental beauty with jet-black hair down to the middle of her back, a tiny waist, a tanned body with minuscule white marks where the top and bottom of a bathing suit kept her from getting arrested on public beaches, firm, natural breasts—not like some of the dancers Jenny worked with—and that sweet, sweet spot between her legs, which would be unadorned when they met for lunch. She would sit down next to him with that knowing, sexy smile on her face.

"Well? We on?"

"Yeah, that's fine," said Ace, coming out of his reverie. "Twelve-fifteen. Oh, and I don't believe for a minute what you told me about not wearing any panties."

"I'll prove it to you when I see you."

"That's my girl."

"See you in a couple hours," said Jenny, and hung up.

It was a few minutes before Ace could shake the heat that had begun in his crotch and which he could now physically feel in his head. He poured himself a very cold glass of Perrier and concentrated on figuring out how a dog could juggle balls on its paws while lying on its back.

"I'M REALLY TOO UPSET to concentrate on this menu," said Cynthia Walcott. "Jenny tells me that you and she have eaten here before. Could you recommend something light and tasty?"

"Sounds like you're talking about the Cobb Salad. You like blue cheese?" Ace asked.

She nodded her head and smiled helplessly at Ace, like a vicious animal playing dead.

"Then a Cobb Salad it is."

Ace ordered for the three of them. The trio sat in a semicircle around the semicircle booth table. Ace sat on one side, Jenny in between him and Cynthia Walcott. After the waiter had taken their order, Ace felt Jenny's left leg rub subtly against his right leg. He took the cloth napkin from the table, shook it once, and placed it on his lap with his right hand. Looking straight ahead at the would-be client, Ace placed his hand on Jenny's left knee and slowly slid his hand up along her toned thigh, the muscles of which she playfully flexed as he passed along them, up to the place between her legs, where he ascertained once and for all that Jenny was a woman of her word.

"I appreciate your meeting with me, Mr. Carpenter," said Cynthia Walcott.

"No problem. Glad to be of help. So, tell me what's going on."

"According to the police, nothing. But I'm sure that Barry— Barry Ashford—he and I, well . . ."

"Yes. You were very close friends."

"Very. Anyhow, three nights ago, he was run down out in front of my house about midnight."

"Did you see the car?"

"No. I was halfway up the sidewalk to the house by the time Barry was . . . struck. And all I saw when I rushed out into the street were two red taillights speeding away. In fact, it's hard to remember anything specific about what happened when Barry was killed. It's all just so . . ."

"Painful?" aided the detective.

"Yes. Very."

"So what makes you think Mr. Ashford was murdered?"

"Well, this might not be a very nice thing to say about someone who's dead, but Barry was not a very well liked man. In fact, there were a lot of people who had reason to wish him harm."

"Anybody have enough reason to wish him dead?"

"That's hard to say. The night Barry was killed we had just come from a party where someone put shit in Barry's hat."

"That's a long way from murder."

"That's true. But I've never known a man to have as many enemies as Barry had. And I got to know him well enough to know that he was the kind of person who really didn't give a damn what others thought of him."

"What do the police say about what happened?"

"Not much."

"But when they do say something, what do they say?"

The waiter delivered three Cobb Salads, two Perriers, and a glass of white wine. The wine was for Cynthia Walcott, who quickly wrapped her hand around the wineglass stem and sipped a healthy gulp of Chablis, then answered Ace's question. "Well, since I couldn't give them a description of the car, and they could find no other witnesses, they didn't have any leads to follow. I told them about what happened at the party and gave them a list of people who I thought might have it in for Barry."

"Did the police ask you for the list, or did you just volunteer it?"

"I volunteered it. Why?"

"Well, if the police really think this is a hit-and-run by some drunk driver, then they probably won't push too hard in any other direction."

"But I'm sure Barry was murdered."

"Oh?" asked Ace, using his napkin to wipe some excess blue cheese dressing off his lip. "What makes you so sure?"

"Woman's intuition. You can laugh. But mark my words, when this thing is over and done with, you'll find that Barry was murdered."

"Maybe."

"Can you help me, Mr. Carpenter?" said Walcott in her best woman-in-distress tone.

But it didn't faze Carpenter. He'd heard it from the best. He'd been conned by women much more beautiful than Cynthia Walcott. He just saved the words and threw away the wrapper.

"What would you like me to do?"

"Why, find Barry's killer, of course."

"It might just be some drunk, you know. In real life people are always getting killed by people with little or no imagination."

"Either way, I'll know the answer. And that's worth something."

"It's worth exactly two hundred per day plus expenses. At least that's what it's worth to me."

"Then two thousand dollars will buy me ten days of your time, is that right?"

"Basically. There will be some expenses."

"Very well, then," she said, and took out her checkbook, wrote Carpenter a check for two grand, and slid it across the table.

He picked it up and tucked it in his shirt pocket. "Do you suspect anyone in particular?"

"No, but I'm sure if you could just sit down with anyone in the know who works for the show who's willing to talk, you would get an earful."

"I think I'll start by talking to a friend of mine who's a cop in the West Hollywood division. He can fill me in on exactly what's gone down until now.

"There *are* a few things you could tell me, though."

"Anything," said Cynthia Walcott.

"What exactly *was* your relationship with Barry Ashford?"

"Well . . ."

"It won't make my job any easier if you hold back on me. And you never can tell what might be useful to me farther down the line."

"Barry and I were lovers."

"Did you replace anybody who might have taken offense?"

"No."

"You're sure?"

"As sure as I can be. I mean, Barry saw other people, but who doesn't, right?"

"Right."

"But there was nobody special. No engagements broken, no irate ex-wife, if that's what you mean."

"That's what I mean. Did you and Barry live together?"

"Not exactly."

"How exactly?"

"He stayed at my house four, maybe five nights a week. He kept some clothes in my closet. But he kept his place in the Hollywood Hills."

"A house?"

"Yes. But he didn't own it. He rented it."

"Maybe you could write down the address for me. You wouldn't happen to have a key to Barry's house, would you?"

"As a matter of fact, I do. But not with me," she said as she dug out a pencil and a note pad, scribbled down Ashford's address, and handed it to Carpenter, who put it to bed with the check.

"That's all right. I'll be calling you soon, probably tonight. We can set up a time for me to pick up the key and go up and take a look around."

After the dishes were cleared, and the after-lunch coffee downed, Cynthia looked into Carpenter's eyes and said sincerely, "I feel better already. Like I'm doing something. Do you know what I mean?"

"Yeah," he said. And he *did* know. Death was something that made lots of people feel helpless. And the vacuum caused by having someone close to you whisked away was usually a pretty hollow space, and the silence could echo forever. Or so it seemed at first. It didn't feel right just to accept such tragedy without doing *something*. This was what Cynthia Walcott felt she had to do.

"I think I'll run along, then, and let you two talk for a while," said Walcott, picking up the tab as she stood.

Carpenter stood, nodded politely, and Jenny kissed Cynthia on the cheek, after which Walcott turned and walked away.

"Hi," said Carpenter, turning and facing Jenny.

"Hi," she responded, a warm smile spreading across her face. "I really appreciate your taking the time to see Cyn."

"I should be thanking you," he said, patting the check in his pocket. "How do you two know each other?"

"She owns the ballet studio I study at. I've known her for about five years now. We really hit it off well. Being friendly with Cyn is how I managed to get to teach the beginner's classes last year."

"She pretty straight?"

"What do you mean?"

"She on the up and up? Can I believe most of what she tells me?"

"Oh, yeah. Sure. I mean, she's flighty sometimes, a little spacey, but she's got at least three wheels on track."

"That sounds like something I'd say."

"Maybe I've been hanging around you too long."

"Or maybe not long enough," he said, a silly grin taking a ride on his face. "How about your place. We're only a few minutes away."

"Honey, I can't. I've got a class in about a half hour. I'd love to, honest, but I just can't. What about tonight? I'm not working."

"Sounds like I'm going to be busy with this Ashford thing till well into the evening, and tomorrow morning is your early class, right?"

"Right. But Wednesday night for sure."

"Yeah. I'm not sure I can wait two nights for a lady who doesn't wear panties to lunch."

"Maybe I can give you a preview of coming attractions," she said, sliding toward Carpenter and making movements to get up. Ace slid out of the booth and stood facing Jenny, who slid over, turning her body toward him, keeping her legs slightly apart and her skirt just up above the knee so that Ace caught the flash of pubic hair as she glided out of the booth. Her eyes, lighted playfully, never left his, wanting to catch his reaction.

"Very nice. But that's kind of like showing a hungry man a picture of a great meal." He paused and looked at Jenny, who now stood next to him. "A *great* meal."

"Well, you've got the rain check, honey. Use it."

He walked Jenny to her car, kissed her good-bye, and walked across the street to his car.

EDDY PRICE WAS A LITTLE over six feet tall, about fifteen pounds overweight, and starting to show signs of a receding hairline. He wasn't doing his weight problem any good working on his third beer. He raised his hand, waved, and said in a loud voice, "Ace. Over here."

Carpenter saw his friend, nodded his head, and went over and sat down at Price's table. The two men went back a long ways. They had both come out from Ohio together about fifteen years before, and Eddy wound up being a cop, rising to his current rank of lieutenant, while Ace was still working on doing a sincere imitation of Philip Marlowe.

"Beer?" asked Price.

"Nah. Too early for me. I'll just take some conversation. A double."

"How's Esther?" asked Carpenter politely. He didn't want Price to think the only time he wanted to see him was when he wanted something from him. Although that's the way it usually worked out.

"Oh, she's fine. Her team won the league championships last night. She's in seventh heaven."

"Bowling, right?"

"Yeah. She had a perfect game going until the sixth frame."

"No kidding."

"That kid's a winner. How's Jenny?"

"She's fine," said Carpenter unenthusiastically.

"What's the problem?"

"Did I say there was a problem?"

"You didn't have to. Time was, I'd mention Jenny's name and your face would light up like Times Square."

"Yeah, well. Hell, I don't know. Maybe I'm just going through a stage. I guess I want something more out of our relationship than she does. But, like I say, maybe I'm just going through a stage."

"What does Jenny say?" said Price, lifting his beer mug to his lips and pouring down some ginger-colored brew.

"Ah, you know Jenny. Dancing is her life. She's got to give it the full shot. You know what I mean? The *full* shot."

"I think I know."

"She couldn't give me the kind of commitment I would like without diluting some of that burning desire to make it. Or so she says." Carpenter paused, took a deep breath, and let it out slowly. "It's kind of funny, really."

"How so?"

"In the beginning we met each other and became close because of our mutual interest in fictional detective characters; in books and movies, you know the kind of thing. Well, she was embarrassed because she had a job that, well—you know, dancing in a topless club—just didn't seem to fit in with the relationship we'd created. There I was, a real life detective, and she, well . . . it just didn't fit. But her motivation to achieve her goal of being a professional dancer—it was the reason she kept the bar job: to make good money and have her days free—was stronger than any motivation I had. She wants to be a dancer more than anything in the world. And that includes being my girlfriend."

"Want my opinion?"

"Sure," said Carpenter, though he really didn't.

"That Jenny is a rare bird. She's a good girl. She might not look it to someone who doesn't want to take the time to look, but she is. And Esther thinks so, too. In fact, when you two came over for dinner about a month ago, Esther was saying how she thought Jenny was a good influence on you. She's special, Jenny is. Don't throw her away for no good reason."

Carpenter sat in silence for a few seconds, then said, "I think I *will* have a drink," and waved a waitress over to the table and ordered an Absolut on the rocks.

The two made small talk until Ace's drink was delivered. He sipped at it, then said, "Eddy, what do you know about this Ashford killing?"

Price downed a little more brew, wrinkled his brow in thought, then, smoothing it in recognition, said, "Oh, yeah. That hit-and-run thing over on Harper. The guy was some entertainment type, right?"

"Right. Soap opera hero."

"That's right. In fact, Esther brought it to my attention one night when she read about it in the paper. She watches that stuff. Why, I'll never know. Although if it's anything like *Dallas,* I can see how you could get hooked. I try to watch that whenever I can."

"Yeah. You know anything about what happened to Ashford?"

"Not much. I could turn you on to someone who does, though. If it means something to you—and if you don't make a pest of yourself."

"Yes, it does. And I won't. I promise. Who do I see?"

"That would be Lafferty in West Hollywood division. He's a good guy. Tell him you and I are buddies from Ohio. He's from Ohio, too. Like I say, as long as you don't press your luck, he should be cooperative."

"Great. Why don't you tell me what little you do know about what happened?"

"Not much to tell, from what I hear. Pretty straightforward. Hit-and-run, no leads, pretty much a dead end."

"I understand there was a witness to the incident."

"You *understand?* Come on, now, Ace. You can do better

than that. Especially if you want my help."

"Okay," said Carpenter, sipping his Absolut. The first taste of the day always went down with just a trace of a burning sensation. After that it was like silk on ice. "I'm working for the victim's girlfriend. She was at the scene when it happened, but it's all a traumatic blur to her. You know the story."

"Sure. I also know that without a witness in a case like this, there's only so much we can do. *You* know that, Ace."

"Yeah, I know. Anything else?"

"Not really. Best bet is to talk with Lafferty. You in a big hurry?"

"Just to see Lafferty."

"He doesn't come on for another two hours, about seven. How 'bout you and me grabbing some dinner? Little place over here on Larabee treats the boys in blue extra special. We could walk outa there just payin' the tip. And the food ain't bad. Whatcha say?"

Carpenter thought about it for a few seconds and said, "Sure, what the hell."

It was about six forty-five when Carpenter shook hands with Eddy Price in front of the restaurant on Larabee, thanked him, walked to his car, and drove over to the West Hollywood division headquarters to meet with Joseph Lafferty. It was another two hours before Lafferty actually arrived. Carpenter kept himself busy by nursing several cups of coffee and reading the sports sections of the two major L.A. papers. He had just finished memorizing the statistics for the top ten hitters in the American League when a man sat down behind a desk on top of which was a name plate, black with white letters, spelling out the name Joseph Lafferty.

"Joseph Lafferty?" asked Carpenter, now standing in front of the desk.

The man looked up. He appeared to be in his middle to late thirties. His dark hair was cut short, his tie was loose and cocked to one side. He had the body of a high school wrestler, with the kind of muscle that one thinks will never go away, until it does, in a less than graceful manner. "Yeah," he said.

"Carpenter. Ace Carpenter," said the detective, extending his hand. "I'm a friend of Eddy Price. And a fellow Ohioan."

The cop let a cynical grin curl up one side of his lips and he tilted his head toward a wooden chair beside his desk. "Take a load off."

Carpenter sat down.

"Cigarette?" asked Lafferty after taking a pack of Camels out of his shirt pocket and tapping a few into sight.

"No, thanks. I don't smoke."

Lafferty nodded, withdrew one, lighted it, and returned the pack to his shirt pocket. "So how's Eddy? Haven't seen that son of a bitch in . . . hell, it must be two, three months. We work in the same damn building just a floor apart. Just never run into him."

"He's fine. Esther's bowling her ass off."

"And balling *his* ass off, if I remember my last conversation with Eddy."

"Yeah," said Carpenter. Obviously *he* knew Eddy better than Lafferty. "He's doing fine. Just fine."

"Glad to hear it. I gotta call his ass one of these days. So, what can I do for you, Carpenter?"

"I'm a PI," he said, and waited to see how that struck Lafferty. With cops the reaction could be anything from mild amusement to wanting to throw you down the steps. Lafferty just tapped the ash off his cigarette.

"I've been hired by Cynthia Walcott. . . ."

That got a reaction. "That crazy bitch. Yeah, yeah, yeah. . . . So she wants you to track down the killers of the stud she was shacked up with."

"Well, basically, yes. I told her that it could just be some drunk, but she seems to have other ideas."

"You don't have to tell me. I think the lady has played too many games of Clue. She gave me a list of suspects and pointed out that I already had the weapon, so . . ."

"She told me she didn't have anybody's name in particular, but that Ashford was the kind of guy who was just generally disliked by everyone."

"She told us about a party the two of them had just come from where somebody had shit in Ashford's hat. Can you believe that? Anyhow, if somebody did that to me, I'd make him eat it. Ah, hell, those entertainment types, they're something else, you know?"

"Yeah. I know. So what happened with the lead she gave you?"

"Not much of a lead. I took a couple of guys and we went up and checked out the party. Didn't do us much good. By the time we got there, most of the guests had left. And no one had any idea who put the shit in Ashford's hat. The hostess tried to lay some wise-ass tale on us about her cat doing his 'duty' in the hat, but I pointed out to her that I didn't drive over to her house in a covered wagon.

"Anyhow, the bottom line, Carpenter, is that without any idea of what the car looked like, we don't have diddly-squat to go on. And that's the truth. Besides, the chances are it *was* some drunk who ran Ashford down."

"So that's it?"

"I said that was the bottom line. We did some follow-up, asked around at the studio where Ashford worked, checked out a few cars, but we came up empty. I *will* say one thing. None of Ashford's coworkers seemed very broken up about his sudden departure."

"What's your gut feeling about this case?"

"Well," said Lafferty, taking a deep breath and filling his lungs with smoke, then crushing out his cigarette in a department ashtray, "let me put it to you this way. For me, it ain't no case anymore. Nobody—except for this space cadet, Walcott—is making any kind of a stink about what went down. We've got enough murders with real leads without running around in circles with something that will probably come to nothing anyhow. Honestly—now this is straight and definitely off the record, understand?"

"Sure."

"We went through the motions. My gut tells me we're not going to come up with anything, and after giving it a shot, I'm convinced that's what we'd get for our trouble. Nothing."

"Fair enough. Mind if I take a whack at it?"

"Hell, no. I'll get you the file," said the cop, and stood and walked into an adjoining room. A few minutes later he came back with a folder under his arm, handed it to Carpenter, and sat down.

"You can't take it out of here, though."

"I understand. And I appreciate the cooperation."

"No problem. I'm willing to cooperate as long as what you do doesn't get in my way. And as long you don't make any problems for me. You know what I mean?"

"Yeah, I know. Eddy and I have worked together on quite a few things. Don't worry. I keep in practice by walking on eggs."

"Just so we know where each other stands," said Lafferty,

taking out his Camels and going through the ritual again. "Look, I've got some things to do. Why don't you take the file in the other room and look at it. Make notes if you want. Just leave it on my desk when you're done, okay?"

"Great," said Carpenter. He stood, shook Lafferty's hand again, and went into a room that was about fifteen by ten, which had a large, chipped wooden table in its center and about eight chairs, none of which matched, scattered in various places around the room. Carpenter sat down in what looked to be the least uncomfortable chair and pulled up another to put his feet on. He took out a note pad and a pen from his sport coat pocket and settled in to look at some gruesome eight-by-ten glossies and read the various reports. He was yawning by the second page.

IT WAS ABOUT ELEVEN-THIRTY by the time Ace finished going over the Ashford file. He had dutifully taken notes, done his job, earned his $200, but the bottom line, as Lafferty had already said, was that there were no real leads.

Since it was still before midnight, Carpenter decided to swing by Jenny Ling's place on Havenhurst, which was less than ten minutes from the West Hollywood station. It would be nice, he thought as he drove through the unabated stream of Hollywood nighttime traffic, the radio supplying the background music to some of his favorite fantasies about Jenny, to feel that fabulous, round, smooth, toned ass of hers fit up against him. Maybe they wouldn't even make love tonight. Sometimes he would think that, but they always did. He liked being with her, holding her, feeling her warmth against him in the darkness, the silence. Ever since the first night, they had always held each other, or at least stayed in contact, their bodies touching, the whole night. They had never come to take that special shared closeness for granted.

He was thinking about these things as he turned off of Santa Monica Boulevard onto Havenhurst and pulled up in front of Jenny's duplex. He turned off the car lights and the radio but didn't get out. It appeared that Jenny was already occupied. She was walking up the stairs to her apartment with another man. She put the key in the lock, opened the door, and they both went inside. As the lights went on in Jenny's place, some brightness went dark someplace inside Carpenter. He wasn't sure exactly where that place was, but he *was* sure he knew the feeling. It had happened before. It had happened to everyone who is a part of this generation, he thought as he turned the key, started up his car, and pulled away from the curb. He fought the impulse to wait and see if the guy would leave before the lights went out and Jenny put her warm, beautiful body to bed.

He was sitting at a traffic light at Santa Monica and Gower when a horn blaring at him from behind mercifully woke him from a nightmare peopled with a mixture of characters and situations from his past, his present, and what he hoped would not be his future. "Dammit!" was all he said as he jerked the Celica into first gear and pulled through the green, that, according to the guy with the horn, wasn't going to get any greener.

THE FIRST THING he saw when he walked into his Hollywood Hills apartment was the telephone. He wanted to use it but didn't think he could take having Jenny not answer. Instead he went to the refrigerator, took a chilled bottle of Absolut from the freezer, poured himself a shot and a half, tossed in a couple of ice cubes and went to the piano in the living room.

The apartment had a nice view of the city. The Santa Anas had cooperated by blowing away the constant layer of smog that obscured what was a spectacular sight. Millions of lights—some were cars, some street lamps, some porch lights, some commercial signs—all glistening like a giant connect-the-dots puzzle. According to his moods, Ace saw lots of shapes in those lights. Sometimes they inspired him, made him feel a part of something very much alive. And sometimes they made him feel very, very lonely, a disjointed part of something he could no longer remember.

Tonight, for a reason he didn't understand, or question, he thought of Ohio, his family. A place where he was interwoven into part of a familial fabric that seemed endless and, when not stifling, comforting. Out here, in L.A., there were lots of acquaintances, lots of people with whom to do things. You didn't know how much they *really* cared, but you suspected they cared about you just as much as you did about them—

which wasn't all that much. Not really.

That's why the special people meant so much. Special people, Ace thought, and swigged down about half the liquid in his glass. Jenny Ling was his special person. And he had thought he was hers. Live and learn, he thought as his fingers began to search out an appropriate melody on the piano keys.

He was a decent piano player and could sing well enough to have made a meager living playing guitar, piano, and singing when he'd first come out west. But that was short-lived. Now he played often and had no ambitions of "making it" in the music business. Yet there was absolutely no bitterness about that. He loved music. This was his way to unwind, relax. He did this instead of punching people out. Instead of sitting in front of apartments all night waiting for guys to come out.

Or not.

"GOOD MORNING."

"Cynthia?" said Carpenter into the phone.

"Yes."

"This is Ace."

"Oh, Mr. Carpenter. How's it going?"

"Slowly, I'm afraid. I spent last night, or a good portion of it, at the West Hollywood division police station. I saw the file the police have compiled and, well, to be quite frank, they're going nowhere with it."

"I thought as much," said Walcott sharply. "But then, that's why I hired you."

"Right."

"So where do we go from here?" she said, her voice alive with a certain excitement.

"I'm going to go over to the studio today. I've got an idea. It'll be sort of an undercover job."

"Sounds exciting."

"Another thing. I'd like to get that key from you."

"No problem. When?"

"I'm going to be in the Hollywood area in about an hour or so."

"I've got to be over at the dance studio then, but I can leave the key under the front door mat."

"Fine. Then I'll call you tonight," he said, and hung up, not waiting for her response.

AFTER A SHOWER, some yogurt, vitamins, hot chocolate, and a perusal of the *L.A. Times* sports and entertainment sections, Carpenter dressed, in jeans, a long-sleeved Pierre Cardin shirt, a tweed sport coat, and banana-colored Frye boots, and descended from the Hollywood Hills in his white Celica. It was a nice-enough day to put the top down, which he did.

His first stop was Cynthia Walcott's place to pick up the key to Ashford's apartment. He pocketed the key, which was wrapped in a piece of paper on which Walcott had written Ashford's address. There was also a blue NBC pass wrapped in the paper, which the note said would get him past the guard at the back entrance.

The guard at the gate didn't give Carpenter a second look once he saw the pass. The detective parked his car in a lot marked "Visitors" and, once inside the main building, asked directions to Studio C, where *Doctors and Lovers* filmed five days a week.

"Yes? May I help you?" asked the pretty blond-haired, green-eyed girl, who couldn't have been many days over twenty-one, when Carpenter opened the door and walked in.

"I hope so," he said, giving the blonde his best smile.

She just stared back at him.

"Well, you see, I'm a writer—"

"For what shows?"

"Well, to be completely honest, none. Not yet. But I'm a great believer in ingenuity and personal contact. You know what I mean?"

"How did you get past the guard?" she replied.

"I'm ingenious. And I'm willing to start just about anywhere to get my feet wet, to get to know the right people."

"You look a little too old to be a mailboy."

"Do I really look that old to you?"

"Not *old* old. In fact, you look pretty good," she said, giving him a not-too-subtle smile. "But I don't think I can be of much help. We're not hiring anybody, especially not someone without any background."

Carpenter, thinking on his feet, played another card. "You an actress?"

The girl got a self-conscious smile on her face and said, "Well, not yet. But I'm studying. Three nights a week with Isaacson. You've heard of him, right?"

"Oh, sure. Hasn't everyone? You see that gives us something in common. We're both almost stars. I wish there was some way you could help me out."

"Well, maybe . . ."

"Yes?"

"There's a party tonight at Mr. Clark's house."

"Mr. Clark?"

"He's the producer. We're winding up another season today and he always has a party."

"Hey, that would be great if there were any way you could get me in. I wouldn't come on real strong or anything. I'd just mingle, you know."

"Well, I could probably ask you to come as my date. I wasn't planning to take anyone."

"Great. Where shall we meet and when?"

"Hey, I didn't say yes yet."

"You wouldn't say no *now*, would you? And break my heart?" he said with a big smile.

She laughed and said, "Okay. You know Burbank?"

"A little."

"Here's my address," she said, handing him a piece of paper on which she'd just scribbled her address and phone number.

Carpenter took it, pocketed it, and said, "Thanks. I really appreciate this."

"Seven o'clock," she said. "Don't be late or else I'll leave without you."

"I'm very punctual," he said, and turned to leave.

"Hey, wait a minute. What's your name?"

He turned back around and said, "Barry. Barry Lyndon."

"Okay, Barry. My name's Julie Wharton." She paused to give him a rather blatant sexual appraisal, then smiled broadly and said, "See you tonight."

Carpenter smiled back and left. Sometimes you just got lucky.

• • •

CARPENTER WAS AN HONEST guy, and when somebody was paying him two hundred a day, he felt guilty about not giving them their money's worth. So even though he knew his night was taken up with the party, he decided to swing by Ashford's Hollywood Hills house before going home and catching a nap. Besides, it might help take his mind off Jenny.

The house was long and yellow, with aluminum siding and a shingle roof. It wasn't one of those charming little castles so often portrayed in the coffee table magazines. The small asphalt driveway leading from the two-lane winding hillside road up to the garage was empty, and Ace pulled his Celica up in front of the garage door.

The key worked fine. The house was silent; the words "dead silence" kept running through his mind. There was a stack of dirty dishes in the sink, and a sack of garbage topped by a couple of beer bottles sat stinking next to the back door.

Ace went into the living room, which was richly decorated with a plush eight-piece sectional, deep-pile carpeting, and some Impressionist art on the wall. The detective went to the stereo, which was turned to the FM radio mode. He pressed the power switch, and country and western music emerged from the four speakers, one located in each corner of the room. That was a trick Ace always liked. Turn on the car and house radios. See what stations they were set at. It might not give you the name of the killer, but it told you something about the person whose radio you were listening to. From the very little he knew about Ashford, Ace had the actor figured for an all-news station, or maybe a hard-rock station. But not C and W. He switched off the stereo.

The bedroom was fairly large, and the king-sized bed had plenty of breathing space. It was raised slightly so that the head of the bed was just above window level, affording a magnificent city view.

The dresser drawers were stacked with underwear, socks, T-shirts, nothing too exciting or informative. The walk-in closet was full of expensive suits and shoes.

Ace walked through the living room and out to a small breakfast nook that was just big enough for a white wrought-iron table and four matching chairs. The sports section from a week-old *L.A. Times* lay folded on the table. The chubby face of Fernando Valenzuela stared up at the detective. Ace picked up the paper and something fell out onto the floor. He bent over and picked it up. It was a snapshot of a younger Barry Ashford dressed in cut-off jeans and a white tank top standing with his arm around a pretty blonde who was doing great things for a small bikini. But there was something wrong with the picture. Someone had used a pen to draw an "X" across the girl's face. Though the blonde's face was still recognizable, the intent seemed clear—whoever marked the picture up didn't seem to care much for the girl.

He turned the picture over. "Boulder, 1977" was written in ink on the back. Ace pocketed the photo, held his nose going past the garbage, and let himself out.

COREY EASTLAND MOVED the feather duster carefully, almost caressing the old Carole Lombard poster on the wall. His favorite Gable poster was right next to it, to the right. But then, where else would it be? At least that is what Corey had told customers on more than one occasion.

The dusting chores finished, Corey checked his watch, and sure enough, it was now exactly 10:00 A.M. He walked to the front of the store, unlocked the door, and turned the "Closed" sign so that it faced toward the inside of the shop and the "Open" sign now faced Hollywood Boulevard.

The coffee had finished brewing and was just now ready to drink. Corey *knew* this, just as he knew that his first customer on Tuesdays, which today was, would be Eric. And he would be in before eleven.

Corey poured himself a cup of coffee, sipped it to confirm what he already knew—that he made the best coffee in Hollywood—then returned to the front of the store. The counter, upon which sat the cash register and impulse items such as movie star biographies in paperback, all under $5, ran about twenty feet along the right side of the store, as one faced the street. Although the shop was only about thirty feet wide, it was almost a hundred feet deep. The walls were lined with thousands of books, eight shelves high, all categorized for easy reference. If it had to do with the movies or a movie star, Corey had it.

Even though he didn't own the store, he was the person the multitude of Hollywoodophiles associated with the place. The real owner was in his eighties. He had tried to make a go of it for years and had built up a modest clientele. Corey had started working there about two years ago. He'd made some suggestions, all of which had worked out. Then he'd made more and more suggestions, which had led to changes that had led to more profits. The owner was ready to call it a life's work, and he had faith in Corey and his judgment.

These days the store was doing better business than it had ever done, and everyone was happy with the arrangement. In fact, Corey rarely saw the owner. Most transactions between Corey and the owner were handled over the phone or through the mail.

"Eric," said Corey, looking up from his comfortable old chair behind the counter as he was just about finished with his second cup of coffee.

"Good morning, Corey," said the man. Eric Mayfair was in his early fifties and didn't look a day over sixty. He was gray, and time had weighed heavily enough upon him to have put a visible bow in his back. He walked slowly, but that was all right. He hadn't had to be anywhere for quite some time.

"And what can I do for you today, Eric?" said Corey, getting out of his chair and standing up against the counter.

"Let me see, let me . . ." said Eric, his voice trailing off as he set his paper bag with the handles on it down on the counter. He pulled the bag open and searched inside for something. "Ah, yes. I'm looking for a used copy of Southerland's John Barrymore biography. You think you can lay your hands on it, son?"

"We'll take a look. Okay?"

"Sounds good to me," said the old man.

And that's exactly what they did—look. Corey seldom had what Eric Mayfair was looking for. And even when he did, he didn't stand to make much on the item. There had been times when Corey had known exactly where to find an item the old man was looking for but had taken his time leading Mayfair to it. The motivation was simple. They had a great deal in common. They shared a passionate obsession. They were collectors. Not of memorabilia, though to most it appeared that way. But rather, they were collectors of dreams. The dreams of anyone who ever believed in make-believe. The dreams of those who felt more at ease with the reality of celluloid projected upon a screen than with the one that always came back to life when the lights came back up. Dreams that were, finally, very much their own.

"See *Double Indemnity* last night?" asked Corey as he stopped at a row of books near a sign marked "Biographies." Corey had made the sign himself out of wood and had painstakingly wood-burned the likeness of Clark Gable on the upper-right-hand portion of the sign. He had thrown away his first two attempts—the ears hadn't been just right with the first, and the lips were wrong in the second. "It wouldn't be right to display an imperfect likeness of the 'King,'" Corey had said at the time to a customer who hadn't discerned the flaws as readily as Corey had.

"Wouldn't miss it for the world," replied Mayfair. "The dialogue in that film, for what it is, is unsurpassed as far as I'm concerned. And it's so, well, camp; some of it, that is."

"I love that film. I've seen it eighteen times. Each time I catch something I missed before. Yes, it's certainly in my top ten. How about you?"

"Oh," Mayfair said, drawing it out, raising his gaze as though the answer were written somewhere on the ceiling. "Top twenty, definitely. Not sure about top ten, though."

Someone coughed. Corey turned in the direction of the sound. A man stood at the front of the store, near the register. He wore jeans, Jordache, rust-colored loafers, a tweed sport coat, and a long-sleeved green shirt. His dark hair was showing signs of making a rather hasty retreat. He wore glasses and adjusted them further up the bridge of his nose with the middle finger of his right hand as he spoke to Corey. "Can I get some help here?"

Corey turned back to Mayfair and said quietly, "I'll just take care of this. You're in no hurry, are you?"

"Nah . . ."

"Good. Then I'll be with you in a few minutes. Browse, okay?"

Mayfair smiled and nodded.

"May I help you?"

"Well, if you can't, I'm just about out of options. I've been to a couple other places like this in Hollywood and no one has exactly what I'm looking for. But both places recommended that I try here."

"That was nice of them."

"Yes. Well, I'm looking for a picture of Marilyn Monroe where she's dressed up in one of those dresses that makes her look real skinny at the waist and big in the hips and chest. You know. I think the dress was kinda shiny."

"Hmmm, I think I might have something for you."

"But she's got to be sticking her butt out and making one of those kind of faces where she's sticking her head up. It kinda looks like she's kissing the air. You know what I mean?"

"I honestly can't say that I do."

"Kinda like this," said the man, and wrinkled up his nose, puckered his lips, winced, and raised his chin in what appeared to be an extremely uncomfortable, if not unnatural, position. "See?"

Corey coughed—it was that or laugh—and turned toward the back of the store. "Follow me, please."

The young man followed Corey to a section designated "Pictures." Thousands of eight-by-tens were neatly cataloged in bins similar to the ones in which records are displayed in a record store.

"Here's Marilyn," said Corey, stopping at a bin bearing the star's name.

"Great."

"A beautiful woman," said Corey as he leafed through the photos. "But so tragic. She deserved better."

The man said nothing. Then, "You have any of the calendar pose in color? You know, the ones with her tits and ass showing?"

Corey removed a photo from the bin, turned, and looked at the man incredulously.

"That would just be for me personally. Not for the film."

"Film?" asked Corey.

"Yeah. This is for a film. I'm . . ." Then he saw the picture Corey had removed. "Hey, that's it! That's it! Yeah, that's great. Thanks."

"Just what kind of movie is this?"

"It's a spoof. You know, kind of like a National Lampoon of Marilyn Monroe. Hey, you know, since you're into all this nostalgia stuff, I bet you'd really get a kick out of it."

"What are you planning to do with this picture?" asked Corey, ignoring the man's remark.

"Oh, well, it's gonna be used in a fraternity house game. It's kind of like pin the tail on the donkey, but instead of a donkey's tail, we use a picture of this cock, see. It's ten points

if you pin it on her ass and five points if you pin it on her lips
... her *mouth* lips, that is," said the young man, getting a shit-
eating grin on his face and taking the photograph from Corey's
hand. "The chick had knockers, I'll say that," he said.

"What did you *think* she had?"

The man was taken aback by the sharp-edged remark. "Well,
naturally, I mean I *knew*... hey, what's the problem?"

"The problem is, young man, that I just don't think I can
permit you to buy this photograph," said Corey, taking back
the picture.

The man made a grab for the photo, but Corey held it out
of reach.

"Come on, man. What is this? The lady's dead. What's the
harm?"

"Because she *was* a lady, I cannot allow you to *use* Marilyn
this way. At least I refuse to be a party to it."

"That's crazy."

"Crazier than pinning a 'cock' on the picture of a beautiful
lady who is deceased?"

"What's with you, anyhow? She wasn't a friend of yours
or anything like that, was she?"

"I never had the honor of making her acquaintance, if that's
what you mean. But yes, Marilyn and I are very close. As she
is very close, in a way that I'm quite sure you are incapable
of understanding, with millions of others throughout the world.
Why anyone would... how anyone *could* even think of doing
what you propose... well, it's simply out of the question."

"Look, are you the owner?"

"No, sir. But I run this establishment."

"Let me speak with the owner."

"He never comes in."

"Look," said the man frustratedly, "you're open for business. I'm a customer who wants to buy something you've got
for sale. What I do with it after I buy it is of no concern to
you. Do you understand?" he said, his voice becoming louder
as he spoke.

"I don't think *you* understand," said Corey. Picture in hand,
he started walking toward the front counter. The young man
followed after him and finally confronted him when they both
arrived at the counter.

"Look, I've been all over town and spent all morning looking
for that picture, and I'm not leaving here without it," said the

man, and reached for the photo still in Corey's hand.

In an instant Corey had the sharp, cold steel of the letter opener blade pressed up against the soft, vulnerable flesh of the man's neck, backing him up against the opposite wall. Gone from the man's eyes were the looks of impudence, bluster, and condescension. They were replaced with a single look of abject fear. His eyes widened and his lips tried to move, but he could not speak.

"You will leave here, without Marilyn, without any further argument. Do you understand?"

The man answered and nodded his head slightly, ever wary of the blade against the soft skin on his neck.

Corey withdrew the steel blade and let the hand with the weapon in it fall to his side. The man swallowed hard, put his hand to his neck, wiped the tips of his fingers across the place where the blade had been, checked his fingers for blood. There was none.

The two men stood looking at each other for a moment. Corey seemed calm, cool. Very cool. His eyes were cold, unblinking. And that seemed odd to the man. Corey's eyes were not ablaze with hysteria or wild, uncontrollable passion. He appeared totally in control, relaxed, at ease, comfortable with the experience of putting a knife against someone's throat.

Slowly the man moved away from Corey, at first almost sliding along the bookcase against which he had been pushed. Then, when he was several feet away from Corey, he moved quickly to the door. He turned before he darted back out to the boulevard and said, "You're one crazy motherfucker!" That said, the man was off like a shot, not bothering to see Corey's response to his remark.

Eric Mayfair had been startled by the man's parting shout and, for the first time since the other man had entered, turned his attention away from his browsing. Corey walked over to him.

"How's it coming, Eric?" asked Corey.

"Fine, fine. Did I hear somebody yell?"

"Oh, that. Yes. Just some boulevard crazy coming in to try and cause trouble."

Mayfair turned and looked into Corey's eyes and said seriously, "Lot of those crazy people around these days. This city, this part of town, draws 'em like a magnet."

Corey put his right hand—the one still holding the letter

opener—around Mayfair's shoulder. "The world's getting to be a crazy place, my friend. A damned crazy place. And it's getting harder and harder to tell."

"To tell what?"

"The sane people from the crazy ones."

"That's for sure."

"Yes, that's for sure."

JENNY LING TOUCHED her fingers to the side of the glass coffeepot to see if the brew was hot enough to drink. It was more than hot enough, and, her mind elsewhere, she left her fingers on the pot a few seconds before she realized that she was burning her fingers. She jerked her fingers away, shook her hand, and instinctively brought the wounded fingers to her lips, opened her mouth, and licked the sensitive tips lightly. "Dammit!" she muttered to herself.

"Jenny? You say something?" said a voice from the living room.

"No. Nothing. I'll be right in." She removed the coffeepot from the brewer, took it to the counter by the sink, where two coffee cups and saucers sat ready for use.

"Cream or sugar?" she called out.

"Cream," came the reply.

Jenny went to her refrigerator and, leaving the door open while she poured the cream, fulfilled the request, then returned the cream to its place and closed the refrigerator door. She took a deep breath, then let it out slowly, closing her eyes as she did so. She stood silently in front of the cups and saucers for a moment. She was thinking. Again. Still.

"Here you are," she said, trying to be cheerful as she handed Jack McMann the coffee with the cream in it. "Careful; it's kind of full."

"I'll be careful. Thanks," he said, taking the cup and watching Jenny as she sat down on a stack of pillows opposite him, about ten feet away. She curled her legs up under her. Her back was straight, though she wasn't leaning against anything. Jenny's posture, a characteristic that had been commented upon many times by many people, was perfect, erect; the way one would expect a ballerina to carry herself.

"Good coffee," said Jack, sipping from his cup, making small talk, breaking the ice.

Jenny just smiled, nodded her head, then stared at her coffee.

"Something wrong?"

Jenny looked up and started to say, "No, no. Of course not," but stopped herself, looked sincerely into Jack's eyes, and told the truth. "Yeah. Something's wrong."

Jack put down his coffee, stood up, moved toward Jenny, and sat down beside the pillows she was sitting on. "I like hardwood floors," he said, rubbing his hand against the floor, still slightly ill at ease. "Hey, look, we're friends, right?"

Jenny nodded her head.

"Come on, then, Jenny. You can talk to me. After all, we shared the same bed, we ought to be able to share a few thoughts."

Jenny set her coffee on a nearby end table, sighed deeply, dropped her head forward into her hands, and began massaging her temple with her fingers. "This is so hard," she said, just loud enough for Jack to hear.

"What is?"

"What? What do you think?" she said, suddenly looking up at him, confused; angry, but not angry; hurt, but not feeling like a victim.

"I'm not sure, Jenny. That's why I asked. No need to bite my head off."

"I'm sorry," she said, getting up and walking to a chair a few feet away, turning it toward Jack, and sitting down. Her back suddenly felt in need of some support.

"You mean you feel bad about my spending the night here last night?"

"That's part of it."

"How about because we had sex last night?"

"That's a bigger part of it," said Jenny, managing a little smile.

"We've been friends a long time, Jenny."

"I know that, Jack. But that's just it. We've been friends, not lovers. That's something very different and . . . very special for me."

"For me, too, Jenny," he said sincerely. "You know, I—"

"Don't," she said, interrupting him. "This just isn't right. You shouldn't be here now. I should be here alone, doing my exercises, drinking my tea." She laughed to herself. "When I lose control I go all the way. This is the first cup of coffee I've had in a few months. I gave it up over Easter. Shit," she said, looking away from Jack, her eyes starting to fill with tears.

"What is it, Jenny? Is there somebody else?"

She looked at him a moment before she spoke. "Yes. And I don't know what in the hell I'm doing sitting here having morning coffee with you. Last night when you asked me to go to the show at UCLA, I just thought that, well . . . I just thought we'd go to the show at UCLA."

"So did I, Jenny. But—"

"Please, don't say anything until I'm through. Look, I'm no prude, but I'm just not used to doing this—hopping into bed with someone when . . . especially when I've got something going with another man. It means a lot to me—what I think of me—and this just doesn't fit the image I have of myself." She paused for a second, closed her eyes, and sighed deeply.

"I think a great deal of you, Jenny. In fact, I've been wanting to get to know you a lot better for a long time."

She looked at him and said, "That's very sweet, Jack, but I honestly don't see much of a future for us."

"Who knows? We could give it a try. I'm willing."

"I'm not. Not now."

"Then what was last night? If it didn't have anything to do with me?"

"I don't know, Jack. I honestly do not know."

"I think you do, Jenny," said Jack, overcoming his own feelings of rejection and sincerely trying to focus his attention and words on helping a friend. "I have a theory that people *really*—I mean *really*—always know when they say they don't know—when it's about themselves. 'I don't know' saves a person from taking any responsibility. It's a cop-out."

"So you're a philosopher, too?"

"No. Just a friend, Jenny. Maybe I'm not the one you have to talk to about all this. Probably I'm not. But maybe this other guy should hear what you've got to say."

"Maybe I've got nothing to say. He'll never find out about what happened here last night if I don't tell him."

"Maybe it goes back to what you said earlier about self-image. There are some things that you just can't hide from yourself."

"Thanks, Jack, really, but I guess I'm just not in any mood to be philosophical."

"Sounds like you're in the kind of mood to be alone."

Jenny smiled a little at him. "Is that being too rude?"

Jack gave her an understanding smile. "Nah." He stood up, went to Jenny's chair, bent down, kissed her warmly on the forehead, and said, "See you in class?"

"*Some* things are sacred," she said, managing a slight laugh.

Jack nodded, went to the door, opened it, and let himself out.

Jenny heard the door close and listened as McMann's footsteps got farther away. A car door slammed. An engine turned over, a gear kicked in, then another, then the engine's sound faded. Jenny closed her eyes. Her mind filled with thoughts of Ace and their relationship. At first the memories were warm, real, comforting, close. But something about the pictures she saw did not seem quite right, and gradually they lost their clarity and slowly disappeared in a misty haze, which kept getting brighter and brighter until Jenny realized that her eyes were now wide open and she was crying.

ACE CARPENTER WALKED into his reception room just in time to see Stephen Kagy quickly pull his hand out from under their secretary's skirt. Kagy looked startled. The blonde looked bored.

"Any calls?" Carpenter asked, putting everyone at ease.

"Not really," said the blonde.

"What do you mean, 'not really'?"

"Some chick called to see if you'd be interested in leasing a copy machine."

"That's it?"

"Uh-huh."

"Hey, Stephen, you doing anything—besides taking your fingers for a walk."

Kagy got an embarrassed look on his face—his tan turned a darker shade. Bunny made a strange look appear on her face. Ace decided it was something like an invitation with teeth. But then, Bunny sent that to everyone, so he didn't take it personally.

"Whatcha got in mind?"

"Lunch. And I'm buying."

"Throw in a game of Asteroids and I'm yours."

"One game," said the detective firmly. The last time they'd gone to lunch at a local restaurant, they'd gotten waylaid in the bar playing an electronic table game. Ace had played a couple of games, then Kagy had taken on challengers for the next two hours. Ace had never gotten hooked on video games, though many of his friends had; many he never would have expected to fall prey. He had a doctor friend and a lawyer friend who were hopelessly addicted to the video voodoo.

"Okay. One game."

"I mean it, Stephen. One game. Then we eat. I've got things to do. And I want to talk to you about something."

"Ah, so that's it. Bribing me with lunch."

"So say no."

"It's the best offer I've had today."

"So let's go."

Kagy turned back to Bunny and said, "We'll be back in about an hour and a half. And Bunny . . ."

"Yes?"

"Save my place."

One game turned into two, but Ace was successful in his second attempt at dragging Kagy away from the madness. Ace had the salad bar, Kagy a burger combo with fries and slaw. It was that kind of place. After Kagy's order was served and Ace had begun to whittle away at his salad, Kagy said, "Okay. So I'm ready to sing for my supper. Whatcha need, pal?"

"I'm going to a Hollywood party tonight."

"That can mean a lot of things. It's like saying you're going to get laid. It could be you're going to a massage parlor, or it could mean Loni Anderson's got the hots for you. Lots of room for interpretation, if you know what I mean."

"It's a party for the soap opera *Doctors and Lovers*. You ever hear of the show?"

"Are you serious? Has a butcher heard of sirloin? I'd kill to get somebody on that show."

"No kidding," said Ace, legitimately impressed with Kagy's reaction.

"Yeah. You know, soap operas aren't what they used to be. I mean, they used to be a joke. You know, forced drama and organ music. But things have changed. There's soap opera mania out there, my boy. And it's not just housewives. College kids watch in their dorms—not just the girls, either. Businessmen stay in their offices for lunch or take breaks in the afternoon and turn on the Sonys in their offices to watch this stuff. People with video recorders tape their favorite soap operas and watch them at night while they're eating dinner. I'm telling you, it's big. Very big."

"You ever watch them?"

"No. But I read about the rating points in the trades. So, you're going to a *Doctors and Lovers* party, eh. How's come?"

"Have you always said 'how's come,' or is that something new?"

"Huh?"

"Nothing. I just hustled myself an invitation. I'm going with one of the secretaries. Lied a little and said I was an aspiring writer."

"Aren't we all."

"I said it was only a little lie."

"So what's the attraction? Why do you want to crash a soap opera bash?"

"It's not important. Just something I'm working on."

"I *know* that," said Kagy, picking up the napkin from his lap and wiping some ketchup from his mustache. "Come on, Ace. Be a sport. Tell me. I'd really like to know."

"I'm sure you would."

"Come on. What's the harm?"

"Do you realize that you're almost whining?"

"Am I? Come on, tell me."

"Pull yourself together, Stephen. We sound like a couple of kids trying to pry sex secrets out of one another."

"Oh? I hadn't noticed. Sounds like most of the lunches I have with casting people."

"You're a caricature of yourself, Stephen. You know that?"

"Sure. Now give. I won't tell anyone."

Ace sighed deeply, exhaled, and said, "I'm trying to find out a little about the Barry Ashford incident."

"Ashford, Ashford . . . Oh, hell yes. He was one of the daytime heroes on *Doctors and Lovers,* right?"

Ace nodded his head.

"You know, I've made kind of a personal study of actors."

"Oh?"

"Being in the business and all, I meet a lot of actors and actresses. And you know, it's crazy, but a lot of the actors who play nice guys, hero types, are really schmucks in real life. And the guys who play the villains, the guys who really look tough, are pussycats. Same thing with the actresses. Those real sweet goody-two-shoes types a lot of times are real bitches when they're reading their own lines. So, Ashford was a good guy, eh. I'll bet he was an asshole in real life. Am I right?"

"Tell you the truth, I don't know. Never met the guy. But a few of the people who *did* know him seem to think he wasn't too well liked."

"What did I tell you?"

"You're right, Stephen. You're a genius in the entertainment biz. Why do you think I came to you for guidance?"

Kagy smiled contentedly at Ace. He wasn't completely certain whether his friend was putting him on or not but decided to take the remark as a compliment. "Let me give you a few tips about this party you're going to. First of all, unless it's a masquerade or a black-tie formal, you can always get by with a pair of dress jeans, one of the YSL shirts I see you wearing now and then, a sport coat, and those white jazz dance shoes of yours. That way you're dressing, but not really. You know what I mean?"

"I think so."

"Well, the shirt, jeans, and sport coat shows that you *could* dress if you wanted to. The lack of a tie gives a more casual appearance, and the jazz dance shoes exude an air of individuality. Makes you look a little arty, you know?"

"Yeah."

"As far as a patter goes, when some chick gets into earshot, say something like 'Oh, *Steve* told me that he was rejecting this story about some fish and I said, "Hey, why not make the fish a shark?" And the rest is history.'"

"Steve?"

"Spielberg. He did *Jaws*."

"But isn't that lying?"

"Kind of. But you've got to remember that no one expects anyone else to tell the whole truth at these parties. If you want to be honest, talk about things or projects you're just *thinking* about as though they've already happened. *Everyone* does that."

"I see."

"You've got to think of conversation at these things in quantitative as opposed to qualitative terms. A certain amount—say, oh, twenty percent—will be the pure, unadulterated truth."

"So I've got to talk with five people before I can figure I've talked to a whole truthful person."

"Something like that," said Kagy, missing Carpenter's irony. "What can you tell me about *Doctors and Lovers?*"

"What do you want to know?"

"I'm not really sure. So *Doctors and Lovers* is one of the top soaps?"

"One of the top three, that's for sure. Used to be number one by anybody's count a few years ago. It came on about ten years ago and experienced tremendous immediate success. Been that way up until about two years ago. It still holds its own. Hey, nothing can go on forever, right? At least not on TV."

"Who's the grease that makes things go?"

"That's hard to say, being an outsider. Owen Clark is the producer. He's a real heavyweight; big name in daytime TV. Used to do some of the late-fifties, early-sixties game shows. Made a few George Harris comedies. But even though *Doctors* was Owen's baby, I don't know who rides herd over things now. Could be Owen, but I just don't know."

"Anything juicy you can tell me about the show? Any gossip? You're good at that kind of thing, Stephen."

"I *do* have my sources. Let me see," he said, raising his eyes to the ceiling, searching through the mental records. Ace sipped his water while Kagy flipped through the files. Finally Kagy leveled his gaze back in Ace's direction and said, a little dejectedly, "Nothing real juicy. I seem to remember—and this was, oh, maybe a year or two ago—that one of the major characters on that show was killed off—on the show—suddenly."

"Nothing peculiar about that, is there?"

"It was a big deal at the time. I mean, this character was beloved by millions. He was the patriarch of the show and had been with the soap since the beginning. I think he played the part of one of the doctors. He was a hero—yeah, yeah, it's starting to come back to me; I remember trying to get hold of casting over there to find out if they were looking for another strong male lead to replace him. Anyhow, this guy played a real straight, ethical doctor who was dating the show's popular female lead. They never got married; they only dated each other. Everybody came to this guy—what the hell was his name?—for advice. Then one episode, out of the blue, they had some nurse run into the room and say that Dr. Daniels—

that's the name: Dr. Daniels; his real name was Corey Eastland—had just been run over by an ambulance. Kind of corny,
eh? But the audience bought it."

"What choice did they have?"

"None. But anyhow, the mail that came in was unbelievable.
You know, now that I think about it, the Dr. Daniels killing
was probably the point at which things began to turn around
for the show. Lots of viewers refused to watch the show anymore. Life's crazy, eh? I mean, who the hell knows why they
killed him off, right? He might have been holding out for heavy
money and they just gave him the axe."

"This Corey Eastland, he doing anything these days?"

"Haven't thought about the guy since it happened, but come
to think of it, he's not. Haven't heard the name since that
fiasco."

"Think you could check around a little and see what he's
doing nowadays?"

"Sure. No sweat."

"While you're at it, see what you can find out about Barry
Ashford. There's another lunch in it for you."

"I'm too easy."

"You're just too hungry."

"Yeah."

"Don't feel too bad. Most of us are."

CYNTHIA WALCOTT SAT BEHIND her desk in her office catching
up on the correspondence and miscellaneous paperwork that
had begun to pile up since her lover's death. The wall directly
opposite where she sat was glass from the ceiling down midway
to the floor, as was the door that was set to the far right in the
wall. As she looked up she saw Jenny Ling walking past in
the hallway. "Jenny!" she said rather loudly. Jenny turned, saw
that Cynthia was waving to her, and went inside.

"Got a minute?"

"Just," said Jenny.

"Sit down," said Cynthia, motioning toward a leather couch
that ran along the outside wall of the office. Jenny sat down
and put one of her feet up under her. She was dressed in a
white Danskin top, black leotard, black jazz dance shoes, and

she carried a bag with street clothes in it. She usually had a sweet disposition. Although not consciously aware of the fact, she now wore her unhappiness like a neon sign. "Something wrong, honey?" asked Cynthia.

Jenny shook her head, looking up just briefly at Cynthia.

"Hey, come on, honey. I know I haven't been very perceptive lately, what with Barry's death. . . . Maybe I missed something. That a new mask, or do you have to cry a long time to get it that way?"

Jenny looked at Cynthia and frowned. "Is it that obvious?"

"To a friend."

"I didn't know."

"Jenny, honey, I'm here if you need someone. God knows you've been my shoulder to cry on lately. Without your help . . . well, it was good to have a friend like you around."

"It's nothing. Really. It'll pass."

"I know you like to keep things to yourself, honey, and sometimes that's the best way. But sometimes it isn't."

Jenny just looked away and nodded her head.

"Okay," said Cynthia, changing her tone to one of forced cheerfulness. "You hear anything from Ace?"

Jenny looked quickly back at Cynthia, then just as quickly away again. Cynthia got the message.

"I *meant* about finding Barry's killer. But I saw the way his name made you jump more than a little. You two having some problems?"

Jenny put her right hand to her forehead and rubbed it several times, closing her eyes as she did so. "Nah. Not really."

"Not really. I don't have to be a detective to read between those lines. Tell me if I'm getting too nosy. That's a real problem with me."

Jenny took her hand away from her forehead, but the look on her face indicated that the massage hadn't done any good. "I don't *know* what's wrong, Cyn. I really don't. Things *should* be fine. I mean, Ace has adjusted to my working at the club; we've gotten through a lot together. But . . ."

"Yes."

"But he wants more. He wants a commitment from me."

"What kind of commitment?"

"He wants me to move in."

"How do you feel about that?"

"Not good. Dance is my life. *You* know that. Nothing can come before that. Why can't things just stay the way they were?"

"A wise man once said that if a thing is not growing, it's dying. Living things can't stay the same. Maybe you've reached a point in your relationship with Ace beyond which you just don't want to go."

"And if I have?"

"You tell me."

"What you're implying is that I should cut it off."

"I'm not here to give you permission, honey. I'm just listening. I think you've got to do an honest evaluation of your priorities and find out what's important and what isn't. Is there another guy?"

"What?" Jenny looked startled.

"Don't look so shocked. A couple students mentioned seeing you at the concert last night at UCLA. Jack McMann, wasn't it?"

"Yes."

"Jenny . . ."

"Don't ask, Cynthia. Okay?"

"Okay, honey. But this guy, Ace, besides being a real looker, he seems to be a bright guy. You know better than I, but don't sell him short."

Jenny didn't say anything. After a while, the silence started to become uncomfortable for both women. Looking up, Jenny said, "Hey, Cyn?"

"Yeah, honey?"

"I think I'm going to call it a day."

"Sure. You run along. Take some time to relax, think things out. It'll be all right. One way or the other. You'll see."

"Yeah," said Jenny unconvincingly. She stood, curled a half smile in Cynthia's general direction, and walked out.

The phone rang as Jenny pulled the door shut. Cynthia picked up the receiver and said, "Walcott's Dance Studio."

"Cyn?"

"Yes."

"Ace Carpenter."

"Oh, hello. How's it going?"

"All right. I just thought I'd check in. No big news. However, I am going to a party tonight at Owen Clark's house. If I keep both ears open and my private eye peeled, I might catch something. You never know. I just wanted you to know that I'm in there pitching."

"Thanks. I appreciate it. Say, are you free for lunch tomorrow?"

There was a silence as Ace thought about his schedule. "Seems open right now. But I'm not certain. I might come up with something tonight that might take precedence."

"Well, barring such an occurrence, why don't we plan to meet for lunch."

"Okay."

"Can you pick me up here at the studio?"

Ace paused. They both knew why Ace didn't want to stop by the studio, but neither knew that the other knew. Cynthia decided to make things easier. "I could meet you somewhere if that would be more convenient for you."

"How about the Melting Pot, say around noon?"

"Fine. So unless I hear from you I'll see you there at noon tomorrow."

Ace hung up the phone, got up, and put on a Pat Metheny album. The soft riffs of a good jazz guitar seemed like the medicine he needed most now. Or at least the remedy most readily available. He lay down on the couch as the tasty electric guitar licks caressed the air with their sophisticated sanity. Ace closed his eyes, took a deep breath, then another, and tried to center himself. His mind filled with pictures of Jenny Ling and a man whose name he did not know. Even though he was trying to keep himself cool, drain the tension, the anxiety, by breathing deeply, he felt his jaw muscles tighten, his teeth grind. Occasionally, when a particularly unpleasant thought occurred to him, he felt pangs in his stomach, as though some invisible demon had just run up and kicked him in the stomach. He considered whether or not to ask Jenny if the man he'd seen her with last night had spent the night. He and Jenny had always been honest with each other. In this case, he was afraid she wouldn't lie. And he didn't know whether he could deal with the truth.

Sure, he'd go on. He wouldn't go off the deep end. Certainly no veteran of the modern battle of the sexes had escaped the inevitable confrontation during which one is told that one's mate has been—what's a good word? he thought—disloyal. What it meant, of course, was that one's lover was fucking someone else.

Ace got off the couch and went into the kitchen. He opened the refrigerator, then the freezer door, and took out a chilled bottle of Absolut vodka. He poured himself a small glass, returned the bottle to the freezer, and came back into the living room. Jazz by itself was not enough this afternoon.

He sat back down on the couch, sipped at the vodka—the first sip burning a little—and looked at the phone. He put his hand on the receiver, then pulled it back and wrapped it around the vodka. He decided that his date with Jenny the following night would be soon enough. Or would it?

He wanted to know the truth, and the not knowing was killing him. But then, he thought, maybe not knowing would ultimately save him. "If I weren't so damn nosy," he said aloud. When he did, he felt a warm moistness nuzzling the palm of his right hand. For the first time since he'd arrived home this afternoon, Ace became aware of his sandy-colored cocker spaniel, named Marlowe—for fairly obvious reasons.

"But then I wouldn't be much of a detective if I weren't nosy, would I?" he asked the dog. Marlowe responded by licking some vodka off Ace's hand. "Want to go for a walk?" Marlowe's tail began to wag rapidly. He was a smart dog, or so Ace was given to saying. "Maybe that's what we both need. A walk. A little space and a little exercise and we'll see if we can clear your bowels and my head. Right now they both seem to be full of shit."

Marlowe had stopped wagging his tail during Ace's little speech, thinking that Ace might have changed his mind. Ace said, "Outside," and the tail started up again.

Ace stood up, turned off the stereo, and went outside, almost tripping over Marlowe. Just as he was about to pull the door closed, his eyes focused again on the phone. He paused; Marlowe barked for Ace to follow him. The detective took a deep breath and closed the door.

"HOW MUCH TIME we got?" asked the brunette sitting on the couch. She wore orange terry-cloth short-shorts. Her tanned legs were tucked up under her. She wore a white tube top that came down to about four inches above her navel.

"Oh, about an hour. Plenty of time," said the man. He had

just finished pouring two drinks from a wet bar and was now walking across the room toward the woman. "Here," he said, handing her a glass. She took it without acknowledgment.

The man sat down opposite her on a wood-framed chair that had a stuffed dark blue corduroy pillow at the back and on the seat. He loosened his tie and unbuttoned the top button of his expensive-looking shirt. "You coming to the party tonight?" he asked.

"I don't know yet."

"You're welcome, of course."

"Naturally. I'm just not sure whether I *want* to go."

"There's no need to feel uneasy just because—"

"I don't. It's just that I may have other plans."

"I see," he said, taking a sip of his whiskey.

The woman shook her long, dark hair, lifting her chin elegantly as she did so. Then she leveled her gaze at the man, her eyes hard, unsympathetic. Absently, slowly, she slid her hand across her left thigh, then sipped her whiskey with her other hand, always looking the man in the eye. "No need to wait, is there?" she said.

"No," said the man, setting down his drink on the end table to the right of his chair. The hint of a smile started to play on his face but faded into an uncomfortable curl of his lips. He swallowed hard, licked his lips, took a deep breath, all the while looking his unflinching companion directly in the eye.

"How have you been the past few days?"

"Fine," said the man nervously. "Things have been—"

"You *know* what I mean. How have *you* been?"

"I . . . I've been . . . bad."

"I thought so. Tell me about it. And don't forget who you are talking to. Do you understand?"

"Yes, mistress."

"That's better. Tell me how you've been bad."

"I've had unclean thoughts, disloyal thoughts."

"Disloyal to whom?"

"My wife, mistress. I've fantasized about . . . about you. And others."

"Others? Well, well. You've been *disloyal* to *two* women then, haven't you?"

"Yes, mistress."

"How do you feel about this?"

"Guilty. Like my thoughts are out of control. Like I'm just being led around by my cock. Mistress," he added as an afterthought.

"You are an unworthy man. As are most men," said the woman, now uncurling her long, tanned legs and standing up, legs spread apart, arms akimbo. "You are a slave to that pitiful excuse for manhood that hangs—barely, I might add," she said, her mouth turning into a sneer, "between your legs. You disgust me."

"I do not wish to disgust you, mistress."

"What shall I do with you, you sniveling dog?"

"Whatever you will, mistress."

"You deserve to be punished, slave."

"Yes, mistress."

"Get down on your knees," she said. The man got off the chair and onto his knees and crawled to a place directly in front of the woman.

"Follow me," she commanded.

She walked into the bedroom; the man crawled along behind her. One wall of the bedroom was covered with two floor-to-ceiling mirrors. Against the opposite wall was a contraption that consisted of two vertical two-by-fours, securely anchored to the floor, and a third two-by-four that ran horizontally across to the tops of the other two. Two chains were suspended from the horizontal two-by-four, at the ends of which were padded wrist restraints. Attached to the right vertical two-by-four was a crank that raised and lowered the wrist restraints.

"Stand up!" commanded the woman.

The man stood and the woman strapped him into the restraints, turned the crank until his arms were totally vertical pointing toward the ceiling and his toes were an eighth of an inch off the ground. The man's heart raced as he caught sight of the image in the mirror opposite him. The woman had pulled off her orange shorts to reveal black string bikini panties. She had slipped on her high heels. Her more than ample breasts heaved rapidly now as the man and woman neared the inevitable climax. The climax they both knew so well. Her nipples were fully erect and were pointed slightly upward by her firm breasts. She approached him now. In the mirror he saw her beautiful tanned legs and buttocks move slowly, sensuously, toward him. He saw her long hair falling halfway down her back, shining, sliding across her smooth tanned back, a back unmarked by a bikini line.

He saw that look in her eyes that told him she was riding the top of the wave. And from the soft light that lit the room, he could just see the knife.

"Look at this!" she commanded, grabbing the man's genitals. "What kind of man are you?"

"None at all, mistress."

"You are led around, made to do bad things, humiliated, all by this . . . this thing," she said contemptuously.

"Yes, mistress," said the man, his anxiety evident in his voice.

"Well, I've got the cure for that," she said, bringing her knife up against his genitals.

"But mistress—"

"Hush!" she commanded, her attention centered on the blade against the man's penis. "You won't want to see this," she said, removing the knife and picking up a blindfold from a nearby chair. She wrapped the blindfold around the man's head, silently picked up a bucket of ice from under the chair, and set it down next to the man's dangling feet.

"Now we'll take care of the problem. Once and for all," said the woman slowly, wickedly.

"No! No! Mistress, no!" cried the man.

"Shut up!" commanded the woman, picking up the knife again and pressing it against the man's genitals.

A few minutes later there was a loud scream.

"That was the best," said the man, lying back in bed, an arm placed casually under his head, a cigarette in the other hand. The woman, her black string bikini panties discarded upon her high heels next to the bed, just purred as she rested her head on the man's chest. She toyed idly with the man's pubic hair, twirling it around her finger.

"It felt, well, almost like the real thing."

"But I would never do anything to hurt . . . him," said the woman, referring to the man's genitals, which she now caressed gently.

"Don't say that," said the man in an irritated tone. "It erodes the fantasy."

"I'm sorry," she said.

"Shit," said the man, catching the time on the face of a

nearby digital clock. "I'm late. Helen is going to read the riot act. I'm supposed to be there when the caterer arrives. And he'll be there in forty minutes. Shit," he repeated, then stubbed out his cigarette and got out of bed.

The woman got to her knees in the middle of the bed and said, "When will I see you again, Owen?"

"You're whining again, Arlene. I hate that tone of voice. You're not a child," said Owen Clark, pulling on his trousers.

"I'm sorry. It's just that..."

"Don't play games, Arlene. If you have something to say, say it. I'm late." Clark pulled on his shirt and started buttoning it.

"It's just that sometimes we don't see each other—like this—for a while. And I really enjoy doing this, Owen. Regular sex just doesn't do it for me anymore."

"That's very flattering, dear," said Clark, pulling on his socks and slipping on his shoes. "But let's not get carried away here, all right? We do this because we enjoy it. But let's not get heavy with each other. No demands, real or implied. Do I make myself clear?"

"Yes, Owen. But it's just that it's getting to be like a drug for me. I think I'm beginning to need it."

"Don't be silly," said Clark, standing up, checking his pocket for his tie. "We're both adults and these are adult games. But they *are* games, Arlene. Don't let them get under your skin. Or else..."

"Or else what, Owen?"

"Or else I think we should put a stop to things before they really *do* get out of hand."

"No," she said, her eyes alive with a strange desperation.

"Very well, then. Let's not hear any more of this kind of talk. We get together when it's convenient and have a good time. No one gets hurt. No one gets hung up. Let's keep it that way."

Clark now stood at the end of the bed looking down upon Arlene, who had moved toward him on her knees. She reached up, gently pulled the lapels of his jacket, brought his lips down to hers, and kissed him passionately. When she had finished, Clark raised back up again, straightened his jacket, and turned to leave.

"Owen?"

Clark turned back toward the kneeling girl. "Yes?"

"I love you," she said.

Clark smiled at her and said, "Maybe I'll see you at the party," and walked out.

WHEN ACE CARPENTER PRESSED the doorbell, his watch read exactly 7:00 P.M. Julie Wharton opened the door.

"You said you were a very punctual person. I figured you would admire that quality in other people."

Julie smiled and ushered Ace into her apartment. "I'll just be a minute," she said, and disappeared into a room off the living room. Before Ace had a chance to leaf through the current *People* magazine she had returned, a light brown coat in hand. "I'm ready," she announced. She was dressed in beige high-heeled shoes, a beige blouse that had gold sparkles flecked throughout the material, and skintight white slacks, the smooth, form-fitting curves of which left no doubt that they were the only thing between her and some lucky admirer. Her shoulder-length hair was pulled to one side and flatteringly showed off her "aspiring actress" profile. Her lips were on fire with an inviting shade of lipstick, and her green eyes were highlighted in a way that made Ace think of a cat.

"You look great," he said sincerely.

"Thanks. You look pretty good yourself," she said, giving him a slow once-over from head to toe. "You a dancer?" she asked, indicating his white jazz dance shoes.

"No. I just like the feel. I had street soles put on so they'll last. They're really comfortable."

"They look good. Kind of suits a writer."

"Really?" said Ace, getting up and opening the door for her.

"IT'S THE PLACE with all the cars in front," said Julie as Ace guided his white Celica convertible up the small, winding canyon road. He pulled the car in behind a Rolls-Royce Corniche, curbed his wheels, and parked. They walked up a long semicircular driveway to the front entrance.

"Julie," said a woman who was about to shut the door after letting another couple inside.

"Mrs. Clark," said Julie, and embraced the woman perfunctorily.

Helen Clark looked up and saw Ace standing in the doorway. She looked directly into his eyes, smiled in a way that he didn't quite understand, and said, "And your young man?"

Julie turned to Ace and said, "Barry, this is Helen Clark. Helen, this a friend of mine, a writer, Barry Lyndon."

"Barry," said Helen Clark, extending her hand.

"Mrs. Clark."

"Call me Helen, please."

"Helen."

"Well, come in, you two. The party's in full swing. Get yourself something to drink—or whatever—and have a good time."

Ace and Julie thanked Helen Clark and went inside. Just inside the foyer were the entrances to several of the large house's rooms. To the right was a large sunken living room with a fireplace. The entire living room, now occupied by about thirty people either standing or sitting on the large white sectional, was visible from the foyer. Directly ahead was a fully equipped wet bar, around which dozens of men and women gathered, trying to get the Mexican bartender's attention. To the left of the bar was the doorway to the kitchen. Although they were not entirely visible from where he stood, Ace could see a stove and a dishwasher. Directly to the left of the kitchen was a small open room that contained a large dining room table full of snacking foods. A large punch bowl filled with something red sat at the far end of the table.

"So, what do we do?" asked Ace.

"Mingle," Julie said. "Come with me. I'm going to put my coat in the back bedroom."

"You've been here before?"

Julie gave Ace a "who hasn't" kind of look and said simply, "Uh-huh. Come on."

Ace followed her through a labyrinth of hallways until they came to the largest bedroom he had ever seen. There were mirrors on literally every wall as well as on the ceiling. There were two bathrooms directly off the bedroom, presumably one for Clark and one for his wife. The plush pile felt knee deep to Ace as he walked through the bedroom.

"Follow me," said Julie, tossing her coat on the bed. She walked to a door to the right of the bed and next to one of the bathrooms and opened it. "Oh, excuse me," she said, but took her time closing the door, allowing Ace to see. Inside was a sauna. And two women and three men acting out some of the advanced passages from the Kama Sutra.

"Interesting," said Ace as he followed Julie back through the hallways to the main party area.

"You ain't seen nothing yet. It's only seven-thirty. The night is still young."

"I'll save my strength."

She stopped just before they got back out to all the hustle and bustle, looked him in the eye, and said, "Good."

After about a ten-minute wait wading his way through people stacked against the bar pawing for free booze, Ace returned to a small patch of couch saved for him by Julie and handed her the gin and tonic she'd asked for.

She sipped it and said, "What kind of gin is this?"

Ace gave her an impatient look and said, "I don't know. Somehow it didn't seem important at the time. The bartender wasn't taking requests."

Julie raised her eyebrows and nodded her head in an accepting fashion.

"Julie," said Ace, bringing his straight juice to his lips— he had seen that the only vodka they were serving was domestic, and he had a firm rule against the partaking of such vodka— "I'd appreciate it if you would point out some of the movers and shakers from the show and tell me a little bit about them."

"Sure. No problem." She scanned the room, sipping her drink as she did. "There," she said, raising her plastic cup in that direction, "by the fireplace is Owen Clark. The guy with the curly hair. He's the host. And the producer of the show. *Doctors and Lovers* was his idea."

"He still run things?"

"He's still in charge. His name is at the top of the credits."

"But does he still *run* things, make the decisions in the trenches. You know."

"Well, that would probably be Maddie's job. She's on the set every day. All the writers report to her. She was Owen's first director. That's her over there next to the potted palm talking to the black guy."

"She's still got her figure," said Ace admiringly.

"What?"

"You made her sound so old. I mean, you said she started

working for Clark as a director ten years ago."

"She started *very* young," said Julie meaningfully.

"Directors usually have to work their way up."

"Oh, Maddie paid her dues."

"How old would you say she was when she started directing for Owen?"

"I'd guess about twenty-two."

"That *is* young."

"Let's just say she had influence with Owen."

"She had his ear?"

"And a few other precious parts."

"I see."

"I'm not telling tales out of school. It's all common knowledge."

"Was Owen married at the time?"

"Yes. He and Helen have been married twenty-five years. I know that because we threw an anniversary party for them a few months ago. As far as I know, Owen and Maddie are just friends now—actually more business associates than anything else."

Ace looked at Maddie, who had just thrown her long blond hair back in animated laughter. "She seems the likable sort. Maddie, that is," he said, tilting his head in her direction.

"Maddie? Oh, yes. Maddie gets along with everyone. She's the strength of the show, its backbone. She's great."

"Did she get along with Barry Ashford?"

A frown made an appearance on Julie's face, and she turned to Ace. "Why do you ask that?"

"Just curious. I heard some things about him; you know, like he was hard to get along with."

"Now that's an understatement. The guy was a real creep. And to answer your question, no, Maddie didn't get along with Barry. But then no one did."

"Why didn't they get rid of him, kill him off with some disease? I could have written a perfect exit scene."

"I don't know *why* he stuck so long."

"Did Maddie have the power to let him go?"

"I don't know."

"Was he that popular?"

"He was popular, but the show is more popular than any of its stars. It could survive the loss of any of its characters. I really don't know why he wasn't canned. Barry and Maddie had fights like you wouldn't believe. I mean, I'm not usually on the set—although occasionally I am—but the things I hear from other people . . . wow! He tore up the pages of his scene one day and threw them in her face. He told an interviewer that the reason the show was slipping in the ratings was because of her. I mean, there was a real feud going on."

"And still she didn't let him go. That's interesting."

"That's stupid. Or gutless, if you ask me."

In the distance Ace could hear the keys of a piano being tickled. He turned to see a bushy-haired man, tanned, mid-twenties, launch into the opening chords of the Stones' "Honky-Tonk Women." "Who's that?"

"That's Jerry Russo. He's the new heartthrob."

"New?"

"And lucky. He was originally just a walk-on type character—in for a week or so and then out. In fact, Barry's character was supposed to kill him—accidentally, of course. In the show he and Barry were after the same girl. Well, naturally Barry, the good guy, was supposed to win the girl's favor and this guy was supposed to die in a construction accident on a job he was working on for Barry's construction company. The story was supposed to get complicated in that there was supposed to be some suspicion that Barry killed Jerry to get the girl. Well, when Barry was killed in real life, the script was rewritten so that Barry's character was killed in the accident and Jerry's character got the girl. The initial feedback with Jerry as a regular has been so strong that he's being written in for at least the foreseeable future. And everybody seems to like him. Funny how things work out sometimes, isn't it?"

"A million laughs."

"How about another drink?"

"Sure," said Ace. He stood up and made his way through the ever-increasing sea of swaying humanity toward the bar. He managed to retrieve another plastic cup of juice and a gin and tonic for Julie.

"Thank you," she said, taking the cup from him.

"Were you at the party that Barry Ashford attended the night he was run down?"

"Yes."

"I understand someone pulled a prank."

Her brow furrowed slightly and her eyes looked toward the ceiling, then back at Ace in recognition. "You mean the shit in the hat thing."

"Yes. Never found out who did it, did they."

"Oh, everybody knew. It was Willy Dodd."

"Is he here?"

"No. I haven't seen him. But he still might show."

"Who is he?"

"He's one of the writers."

"Why did he play that prank on Ashford?"

"He and Barry had had one of the more blatant, out-front feuds in the show's history. From what I understand, hardly a single day passed that Barry didn't hold Willy's work up to ridicule on the set. You know, he'd take some line Willy had written and say it in some stupid way that would make it sound totally inane. Like I said, Barry was a real creep."

"How did Willy manage to hang on?"

"He's the show's best writer. In fact, he's got more Emmys as a soap opera screenwriter than anyone else in the business. Some people say the idea for *Doctors and Lovers* was really Willy's. He used to be with one of the big soaps in the sixties and made a name for himself there. Then Owen wooed him away from the competition when he presented the network with the idea for *Doctors*. Owen and Willy had been tight for a couple years before the show started. Anyhow, Willy's a character and he just wouldn't take Barry's harassment lying down. Tell you the truth, I thought the shit in the hat was a nice touch. It suited Barry just fine."

"Kind of if the hat shits, wear it, eh?"

Julie winced a little when she heard what Ace had said and turned toward him. "That a joke or something?"

"More or something."

"Julie!" paged a voice in the distance. Julie and Ace turned their attention toward the voice. "Julie," said a tall, tanned young man standing several layers of humanity away from Ace and his companion. Julie waved and turned to Ace. "That's a friend of mine. I'm going to talk with him. You mingle, have a good time. If I see anyone I think you ought to meet, I'll come find you. Okay?"

"Sure," he said, and got up and plunged into the chattering, sipping multitude.

Just outside the large living room, through sliding glass

doors that were wide open, was a pool, beyond which was a steep mountainside and below that the city lights of L.A. Ace swirled his drink around in its glass and moved away from the party din closer to the steep drop of the mountainside.

Looking down upon the million flickering lights, he thought how far away from home, from his roots, from Ohio, he was. He thought about his mother. And his father. He thought about how much of a disappointment he had been to them. Being a detective was something one read about in cheap novels, certainly not something to waste a life doing—or so he had been told many, many times.

There was just a trace of a chill in the air and some of the trees that weren't palms were starting to change color—just like in the real world, thought Ace as he took a sip of juice. He filled his lungs with the cool air, and for a moment he was at a high school football game huddled under a blanket with a girl in a plaid skirt, a fuzzy sweater, and a white blouse. Her face was unpainted, her soul untarnished, her body unravaged. And she was holding his hand, tightly, and looking into his eyes as if she thought he had some answers. He didn't, not then. But he had them now and was glad that he hadn't been the one to break the bad news.

He turned back toward the sound of a thumping bass drum and repetitive bass lines. People were prancing about wildly, and bodies were strewn in various positions on the floor and on cushions that lined the walls of the living room. One young woman, dressed in high heels and a Danskin top only, began to peel down the shoulder straps of her Danskin. A crowd started to gather around her and urge her on. Soon her top was down around her navel and two of the most luscious, upturned breasts money could buy were on display, bouncing playfully to the disco beat. About this time Ace's point of view was cut off by an ever-increasing crowd of observers. A few seconds later a Danskin came flying out of the center of the circle to be caught like a bride's bouquet by a drunken man. A cheer went up. Ace turned back toward the city lights. He felt very far away from home.

Out of the corner of his eye he saw a woman walking slowly along the opposite side of the pool toward a group of chairs looking out over the mountainside. He could tell from her hair, from the way she walked, that she was Oriental. It was a sixth sense Ace had about such things. And that sense had become more acute since his relationship with Jenny.

He walked over to where the woman was now sitting sipping a drink, looking into the distance. She was wearing a white dress with a blue vent up the front, black stockings, and blue high-heeled shoes. Her hair was jet black and fell softly upon her shoulders. He could tell from her round face that she was either Chinese or Korean.

"Hi," he said.

She turned toward him, slightly startled, as though he had awakened her from a light sleep. She smiled warmly at him and looked as though she liked what she saw.

"Hello."

"Mind if I sit down?"

"No. Go right ahead."

Ace pulled a chair around so that it was facing her, his back to the mountainside, and sat down. "You with the show?" he asked.

She smiled and said, "No. My sister cuts Helen Clark's hair. I happened to be in the shop today—I'm in town from Dallas— and she invited my sister and me to the party. Are you someone famous?" she asked, only half-kidding.

"No. I'm just a friend of a friend of an underling. My name is Ace. If you hear anyone call me Barry, don't be surprised. But everybody calls me Ace."

"My name is Connie."

"Nice to meet you. How do you like the Hollywood party?"

She hesitated, then said, "Oh, it's all right, I guess. I'm just not used to some things."

"Like girls doing strip shows in the middle of the dance floor."

"Yes."

There was something about this woman that Ace liked very much. She seemed quite genuine. In such a context as Clark's party, it was like discovering a diamond in a pile of crushed ice.

"How long you going to be in town?"

"About a week. I just came out to visit my sister. I haven't seen her in a couple of years."

"What do you do back in Dallas? You one of the Dallas Cowboy cheerleaders?"

"Nothing quite so glamorous," she said, taking another sip from her glass. "I'm a computer programmer for a bank. I work mostly nights. Money's good, but it can get tedious. I've been doing pretty much the same job now for about five years."

"Chinese," said Ace without explanation.

"I beg your pardon?"

"You're Chinese, aren't you."

"Yes. Very good. Lots of people think I'm Korean. Once when I was stopped at a traffic light, some man jumped out of his car and ran up to my window and yelled at me, 'You Korean?' I said that I was Chinese. He turned around and went back to his car, got in, and drove away. I wondered what would have happened if I'd been Korean. Maybe he fought in the Korean War and would have killed me. You weren't in the war, were you?"

"Which one?"

"Any one."

"Only the war on poverty. And even then, I'm a conscientious objector. I don't think people should be killed just because they're poor. Oh, sure, I know it sounds crazy, but I really believe it."

Ace smiled at Connie and she smiled back.

All of a sudden the music stopped and was replaced with loud screams, cries, and shouts.

"What's that?" Connie wondered aloud.

"I don't know. But just to be on the safe side, don't put on any hats."

"What?"

"Nothing. Private joke." Ace stood and Connie did the same. Their hands brushed against one another as they walked. Ace hesitated, then took her hand in his. There was no resistance, and in fact, he was certain she had squeezed his hand just a little harder than she had to. Contact. It felt good.

Inside, Ace and Connie pushed their way through the crowd to see what all the shouting was about. In the middle of a large circle of people were two women, Arlene and Helen Clark, rolling around on the floor.

"What's happening?" asked Ace of the man standing next to him.

"Beats me. Maybe it's the entertainment. Personally I like it with mud better."

Meanwhile Arlene, who was probably twenty years Helen Clark's junior, seemed to be getting the best of things. Helen Clark, an attractive, early-fortyish redhead, was close to being

pinned by Arlene, who was on her knees on Helen's chest.
Helen's blouse had been ripped, her beige bra exposed. Her
legs were flailing, her skirt was up around her thighs, and her
stockings were snagged in several places. Arlene's blouse was
ripped and the knees of her stockings were torn.

Helen managed to get a hand free and grabbed a handful of
Arlene's long hair. The brunette followed the pain and fell
backward off Helen. With her other hand now freed up, Helen
delivered a powerful fist to Arlene's stomach. The brunette
doubled over and gasped. Helen got to her feet and kicked
Arlene in the ribs, sending her sprawling on her back in pain.
Helen, now standing over Arlene, grabbed the brunette's ankles
and spread her legs apart. Arlene's dress fell to hip level to
expose garter belt, stockings, but no panties. Helen, poised
ominously between Arlene's legs, suddenly dropped to one
knee, which landed with all her weight right on Arlene's pubic
bone. Arlene let out a loud scream and doubled up in pain.
Helen got to her feet and kicked Arlene in the butt and said,
"Now get the fuck out of here, you bitch!" and kicked her
again.

At that moment several people, apparently satisfied with
enough blood sport and humiliation, moved in. Some com-
forted Arlene, others tried to calm Helen down.

"I would have bet on the brunette," said the man Ace had
spoken to when he'd arrived on the scene. "But that old broad's
got something."

"Spunk," said Ace.

"Yeah. That's it."

Then, just as quickly as it had begun, it was all over. The
music started up again in earnest, the bar was recaptured by
thirsty heathens. Everyone went back to dancing or talking
about how they wanted to meet people, not just make lurid
propositions—but to make the right connections.

Ace felt a hand on his shoulder. He turned to see Julie
standing hand in hand with the guy who had called to her earlier.

"Hi, Barry. This is Bo," she said, indicating the man whose
hand she held. Introductions were made all around. Connie
nodded politely at the couple.

"What was that all about?" asked Ace. "Helen Clark didn't
seem the type."

"Oh, she's sweet all right," said Julie. "But not when it
comes to her husband playing around."

"From what you told me earlier, she must get into a lot of fights."

"Most of the time she doesn't find out. You know that old male bullshit game—if she doesn't find out, it's okay."

"Yeah, I've heard of it. Next to Monopoly, it's my favorite."

Continuing as though she hadn't heard or understood his remark, Julie said, "I told you I'd let you know when Willy Dodd got here. Since he's the head writer, he might just be the guy who you want to see. Want me to introduce you?"

"No, thanks. I think I'll approach him my own way. But it's a big help now that I know who he is. By the way, who is he?"

Julie pointed to a man who looked to be in his early forties, had a receding hairline, a neatly trimmed beard and mustache. He stood about five feet ten or eleven, wore a blue plaid shirt that looked as though it might have been tailored to fit his slender, but lightly muscled body, jeans, and what appeared to be a new pair of tennis shoes.

"Just thought you might like to know."

"Thanks, Julie. I appreciate it."

"No problem. Oh, hey, I've got my own way home, okay?" she said, not quite sure whether or not it would offend him, but in the short run not really caring one way or the other.

"Sure. I appreciate your help getting me in here. Thanks."

Julie smiled politely, then led Bo back to the dance floor, where they proceeded to start shaking in a rhythmic, lewd fashion.

"She come with you?" asked Connie.

"Jealous?" Ace asked playfully.

"Couldn't be very much since she just told you she's going home with someone else, now, could I?"

"Guess not. No. I just met her today. I told her I was a writer who wanted to get to meet some people on the show; you know, to break in."

"You say that's what you *told* her. Is that the truth?"

"Kind of."

"I'm not sure whether I like that or not."

"Why don't you give me a chance to convince you fully one way or the other?"

Connie looked at him, puzzled.

"You come here with your sister?"

"Yeah. Why?"

"Well, I'm over sixteen and I've got my very own car. There's a little place down the hill called Mirabelle's. I know the bartender there pretty well. Ever have a Carpenter?"

"A what?"

"Great. Then it's settled."

"Hey, wait a minute. My sister..."

"You want to come with me, don't you?"

Connie started to put up at least a perfunctory show of resistance, but it all melted away into an acquiescent smile.

Ace and Connie sat down on two stools at the bar. Spike, his red hair combed perfectly, his mustache trimmed properly, stood in black vest and white shirt, drying the inside of a large brandy snifter.

"Who's the dame?" he asked Ace.

Connie, taken slightly aback, turned to Ace for clarification.

"He likes to talk that way," said Ace. Then to Spike, "Spike, this is Connie. Connie meet Spike." The bartender and the girl shook hands.

"Pleased to meet you," they both said at about the same time.

"Connie tells me she's never had a Carpenter," said Ace with a smile on his face.

"No kidding?" said the bartender in mock surprise.

"Now come on, you two," said Connie. "Let me in on this little private joke."

"Allow me," said Spike to Ace. "You see, it's a drink named after a famous Hollywood PI—detective. Guy by the name of Ace Carpenter."

"Ace, eh? Now I get it. So you're 'kind of a writer,' but more like a private eye. And this is your bartender, who makes potent drinks which aid in the seduction of unwitting young women."

"Now, it isn't all that bad. There is, in fact, a drink called the Carpenter which Spike and I invented. It's great. And though it is potent, it's not lethal. Let's have Spike mix up one and you can taste it. If you don't like it, I'll drink it myself. Fair enough?"

Connie, who was taking all this in the spirit of fun in which it was meant, smiled and said, "All right. I'll *try* it."

Spike took out some Baileys Irish Cream and poured three shots into an old-fashioned glass. Then he took a bottle of chilled Absolut from the freezer down below and poured in a

shot and a half, tossed in a few ice cubes, and stirred. He set
the concoction down in front of Connie on a cocktail napkin.
"A Carpenter," he said simply.

Connie picked up the glass and cautiously took a sip. Her
face did not betray an opinion immediately; then a very pleasant
smile spread across her face.

"Another convert," said Spike.

"This is delicious."

"I wouldn't steer you wrong," said Ace. "Make it two,
bartender."

A couple of Carpenters later, Ace and Connie adjourned to
a corner table, where they told each other the kinds of things
one tells a likable stranger; the kinds of things one is initially
impressed by. He believed everything she told him, and she
everything he told her. They both wanted to believe and be
believed; to impress and be impressed.

"About that time," said an intruding voice they both traced
back to Spike, who was now the only person left in the bar
besides themselves.

"Okay," replied Ace.

The two were silent for a moment while they both fidgeted
a little and prepared to leave.

"You want to come home with me tonight?" asked Ace.

"Yes. But I'm not going to. Not the first night. I've got a
policy about that."

"You sound like an insurance salesman."

"Don't spoil it, okay?"

"Spoil it?"

"You sound testy. I'm not rejecting you. I'm going to be in
town for another week. I'll be spending a lot of time with my
sister, but apart from that I'm pretty free. And if you'd like,
I'd like to spend some of that time with you."

Ace let out a deep sigh. He was considering arguing, pushing
his case, but he actually felt she was right.

"It'll keep." She slid her hand across the table and took his.
Ace looked up into her eyes and she said, "Believe me, if it
would have felt good tonight, it'll feel twice as good tomorrow
night." She smiled a contagious smile and Ace felt the tingle
of acute infection.

"You won't try to sell me any more policies tomorrow night,
will you?"

"It's up to you to find out what I'm selling tomorrow night.

If you want to," she said coyly.

"Let's get out of here," he said, standing and moving toward the door. With Connie in tow, Ace gave Spike a good night wave and walked out onto the nearly deserted Sunset Strip.

"YOU'RE IN A GOOD MOOD," Bunny Aguirre accusingly said from behind her desk as she looked up from polishing her nails a blood-red color.

"Oh? How can you tell?" said Ace, trying to wipe some of the grin off his face.

"You don't often whistle."

"Was I? I hadn't noticed. Any messages?" he said, changing the subject.

"Just one. Jenny called. She wants you to call her right away. And Stephen wants to see you. He says he's got some information for you. You got him playing Sherlock Holmes again?"

"Not exactly."

"Well, he loves it. He's in if you want to talk with him now."

"Okay," said Ace, picking up Jenny's message from Bunny's desk, looking at it as though it had some inherent power. He hadn't thought about Jenny since he'd met Connie the night before. Seeing her name now on the piece of paper he held in his hands brought everything back to him, and the pain of those memories washed over him like a bad dream.

"You want me to buzz Stephen?" asked Bunny.

"Pardon?"

"You're just standing there. Are you waiting for me to buzz Stephen?"

"No. I'll just go on in," said Ace, and walked toward Stephen Kagy's office door, opened it, and went inside.

"Ace!" Stephen said, getting up from behind his desk.

"Good morning, Stephen."

"Hey, what's wrong? You look like you've just been run over by a tank."

"Oh, it's nothing. Bunny said you wanted to see me." Ace took a seat in a brown chair opposite Kagy's desk.

"Yes. I think you might want to buy me a few lunches after

you hear what I've got to tell you."

"Skip the sales pitch. We're both on the same side here, okay?"

"Sure. Well, you know you wanted me to find out what I could about Corey Eastland, the lead on *Doctors and Lovers* who was suddenly killed off on the show a few years ago? Well, I hit the jackpot. I made a few calls, and as it turns out, the woman who used to do some casting work for the show is now working for a friend of mine. I went over to her office, took her to dinner—out of my own pocket, buddy—and she rattled on and on for about two hours. Most of what she said is pretty useless to you, but I did write down a couple things. Maury's. Does that name mean anything to you?"

"Can't say that it does."

"It shouldn't."

"I hate it when you play stupid games like that, Stephen."

"Okay, okay. Anyhow, Corey Eastland couldn't get arrested in this town for shooting the president on national TV. The guy's become one of the greatest nobodies of all time. I mean, the guy was *known*. I remember seeing his pictures in the trades every once in a while and thinking that I'd give my left nut for a client like that. Of course, those were the lean days."

"Of course."

"Now it would just be a minor part of my anatomy," joked Kagy.

Ace bit his tongue instead of opting for the obvious demeaning line. After all, Kagy still had more information to relate.

"Guess who replaced Eastland in the show?"

"Who?"

"Barry Ashford," said Kagy as though revealing the payoff to a magic trick.

"That *is* interesting. But that kind of thing happens all the time and it was probably just the luck of the draw. Certainly Ashford wasn't the one with the clout."

"Maybe yes, maybe no. According to my friend Eileen, this whole Eastland episode was a turning point in the show. She left shortly afterward, partly because of that incident, and partly because of others very much like that one. Also because she was fired," he said with a cruel smile.

"What are you getting at?"

"Just this. According to Eileen, there was nothing special about Ashford and no real reason to nudge Eastland out. Except for one."

"Yes?"

"The word came down from Owen Clark to do so. Eileen said that Clark was irrational about the move. He wouldn't listen to reason and threatened to fire anyone who openly opposed him on the matter. When Eastland heard about what was going down he supposedly went to Clark and literally begged him to reconsider. When that didn't work, Eastland went to a friend of his who was a columnist for *Variety*. Even though the columnist was a friend of Eastland's, he was no fool. Rather than print a column testing Eastland's popularity, as the actor had asked him to do, he took the information to his editor, who in turn called Owen Clark. Clark told the editor not to run the column. The next day Clark upbraided Eastland in front of the entire cast and told him that he would never work in this town again.

"It sounded more like a 'this town isn't big enough for both of us' kind of threat, but looking back and seeing what happened to Eastland, it kind of rings true."

"Do you have a line on what Eastland's doing now?"

"Oh, he's still in the business. In the most indirect kind of way. He manages a Hollywood memorabilia bookstore down on Hollywood Boulevard called Maury's."

"This is good information, Stephen. I appreciate it."

"I'm free for lunch today."

"Well, I'm not. I've got to meet a client. Maybe tomorrow. Don't worry, I won't forget. Tell me, this Eileen, did she have any idea why Clark went to bat so heavily for Ashford?"

"No. I asked her about it. She said she'd heard stories, but then none she felt were on the level. But it *was* damned strange. One day nobody's ever heard of Barry Ashford, the next day bam! Usually the casting people keep pace with who's hot, who's ready to pop, that kind of thing. Nobody, but nobody, had any idea where Ashford came from."

"Can you give me Eileen's number? I might want to ask her a few questions."

"Sure. No problem. But I warn you, she eats even more than I do for lunch." Kagy took a pen from his drawer, wrote down Eileen's phone number, and slid the paper across the desk to Ace.

"Thanks," he said, picking up the paper as he stood and turned to leave.

As he punched the last digit of Jenny's number, Ace's pulse was racing and he felt as though his heart had fallen into his stomach. The phone began to ring. He took a deep breath.

"Hello."

"Jenny?"

"Ace. Good morning."

"Morning. I got a message from you this morning. Said to call you right away. Something wrong?"

There was a slight pause. "No, nothing's wrong. I just wanted to make sure we were still getting together tonight."

He had forgotten. It was Wednesday, Jenny's night off. They had planned to get together, go see a movie, watch TV together, go out and have a drink, something. And he had also planned to see Connie.

"Ace?"

"Yes."

"You still there?"

"Yeah, sure. It's just that I'll have to let you know a little later. Something's come up."

"With the Ashford case?"

"Yes. I don't know whether it's anything or not, but I've got to give Cynthia her money's worth. You know."

"Sure, I know. You can always come over whenever you're through. I can leave the key in the usual place."

"I'm still going to have to let you know. You going to be at the studio this afternoon?"

"Till about four-thirty."

Ace had always been one to, if not meet a thing exactly head on, at least approach it from an angle. "You know, I got through a little earlier than I thought I would the other night." Ace paused and let the silence fall where it might.

"Oh?" she said noncommittally.

"Yeah. I cruised by your place about ten and didn't see any lights on. You go to bed early?"

Again there was a pause. Ace's heart beat more rapidly. Jenny had been caught off guard. She was thinking on her feet, not wanting to say the wrong thing. And not wanting to say the truth.

"You there?" asked Ace.

"Yeah. I went to a concert at Royce Hall. The New York

Academy was in town. I told you I wanted to go. Anyhow, a girlfriend at the studio offered me a couple tickets and I used them. Too bad I didn't know sooner that you were available, or else we could have arranged to get together."

"Yeah. You say you got a couple tickets?"

"Uh-huh."

"You go alone?"

After a shorter pause than the last one, Jenny said, "No. I took one of my students."

There was a temptation to go further. Ace was now almost biting his tongue. Finally he decided that this was enough for now.

Jenny said nothing. She waited. Would he ask? What did he really know? She told herself that he couldn't know whether or not she and Jack McMann had slept together unless he had bugged her apartment, and she considered that unlikely. Nervously she bit her lower lip while she waited for Ace to call the tune.

"So, I'll give you a call at the studio before four."

"Great. I'd really like to see you, honey. I miss you."

Ace thought of Jenny's long black silky hair, her perfect, toned thighs and calves, her flat stomach, her tight butt, her sultry lips that always seemed to be just wet enough to glisten whenever light struck them. He thought of the comfort, the safety, and yes, the love he felt when they lay awake in each other's arms into the early morning hours. But as strong as those feelings and pictures were, they were all steamrolled by a painful knot in his stomach that he couldn't shake.

"I'll do my best. I've got to go," he said.

"Try. Hope to see you tonight."

"Bye," he said, and hung up.

Ace took a deep breath, picked up the phone again, and punched out Cynthia Walcott's number.

"Hello."

"Cynthia?"

"Yes."

"Ace Carpenter."

"Oh, good morning. We still on for lunch at the Melting Pot, I hope?"

"Yes. I'm just calling to confirm."

"Excellent. See you in about an hour."

• • •

THE MELTING POT was located on Melrose, just off La Cienega in West Hollywood. On warm days, the outside patio area was full of enough people you'd "like to know better" to keep a jeans manufacturer working overtime for a month. The waffles were great, the rest of the menu, depending on what you ordered, was more than adequate, and the bar was full and well beyond adequate—an observation Carpenter had made on more than one occasion.

"So, do you have any leads yet, Mr. Carpenter?" said Cynthia Walcott after they were both seated at a corner table in the back room.

"Feel free to call me Ace anytime. And no, I don't have any strong leads yet. The reason I asked you here is to have you give me as much background on Barry Ashford as possible."

"Does that mean that you haven't come up with anything at all yet?"

"No. But you've got to understand my position. I'm starting to pick up a lead here, a piece of gossip there, and all of these things start to create a picture. They might lead to something, they might not. It's important in my business not to form any conclusions before I have all the facts."

"Just like Sherlock Holmes."

"And Jack Webb. I'm sure you understand the importance of my not giving you every half-baked idea I come across just to make sure you think I'm doing my job."

"I appreciate that."

Ace took the snapshot of Ashford and the crossed-out blonde out of his sport coat pocket and handed it to Cynthia. "Recognize the girl?"

Cynthia squinted, held the picture closer, then farther back, wrinkled her mouth into a puzzled expression, then lifted her eyebrows, puckered her lower lip, shook her head, and said, "No. Never saw her before. Looks like it was taken a few years ago."

"It says Boulder, 1977, on the back."

"That's where Barry's from. He told me that much about his past. Not a whole lot more, I'm afraid. Must have been his 'hippie' period," said Cynthia, handing the photo back to Ace.

"Yeah."

"Where did you find it?"

"It was on his breakfast table. I found it when I went by his place."

"Do you think it has any significance?"

"I have no idea."

"Anything else?"

"I went to a party for *Doctors and Lovers* last night. I kept an ear open and came up with a few things. First of all, you seem to be right in your opinion that Barry wasn't very well liked. And he seemed to work overtime earning that lack of respect."

"It was just Barry's way."

"Well, I guess the same could be said of Jack the Ripper, but being nasty to people over a long period of time is just asking for trouble you're bound to find. Did you know any of the people Barry worked with?"

"Some. I have a very dear friend who works at NBC. She and I occasionally work together doing choreography for variety specials and things like that. So I know some production people who work out of Burbank Studios. That's where *Doctors and Lovers* shoots. Other people I know only through what Barry told me about them."

"Okay. I'm going to give you a few names, and I want you to tell me what you know about them. Anything at all will do. What might seem inconsequential to you, might mean something to me. Okay, you ready?"

"Fire away."

"Willy Dodd."

"I've never met him. I know that he's the show's head writer. He and Barry rarely saw eye to eye on anything. They had some very ugly run-ins on the set, from what Barry said."

"Owen Clark."

Cynthia smiled knowingly, took a cigarette out of her purse, lit it, blew out some smoke, and said, "Now Owen is someone I can tell you a little about. Owen's knocked around this town for years. I met him in the early sixties when we were both working on an NBC Christmas special. He was the associate producer or some such thing, and I was a dancer. Suffice it to say that Owen Clark has a reputation as an insatiable sexual personality."

"Let's not have that suffice. At least not for my purposes.

What exactly do you mean? Was he a real ladies' man?"

"I mean if it had to do with sex, Owen had done it. Some people collect rare stamps and aren't satisfied until they've got every one they want. Some people are that way about wine. Owen is that way about sex. Women, men; the kinkier the better."

"How do you know all this?"

"How important is it that I answer that?"

"Maybe very important. Maybe it won't mean shit. I can't say. I can tell you whatever you tell me is confidential, if that's what you're worried about."

"Lots of confidential things have ruined lots of lives."

"I can't make you tell me. It would just make my job easier if you didn't hold back."

"Well, all right. It's no big deal, really. Owen and I used to date each other for about a year in—let's see . . . oh, I think it was maybe sixty-eight. It was the year Bobby Kennedy was killed. I remember because Owen was at my place watching TV when the news came across."

"That *was* 1968. Clark was married at the time, then."

"That's not a question, is it?"

"No."

"Look, I'm not proud of the fact that I was seeing a married man, but there's something you've got to understand about Owen. If it's not one woman—or man—it'll be another. That's just the way he is. It was never serious between Owen and me. Just sex. I still had a dancer's body and he was the horniest bastard in a pretty horny town. Excuse my language."

"I've heard worse. You'll pardon my saying so, but you haven't revealed anything all that indiscreet. Especially for this town."

"Yes, well, I'm not finished."

"You ready to order now?" asked a young man who looked as though he might have been a *Playgirl* poster boy.

The couple ordered, the waiter retreated to the kitchen, and Ace turned back to Cynthia.

"You were saying . . ."

"Well, Owen showed me a side of life I'd never seen before. I'm from Philadelphia originally and, well, the fast lane back there was usually closed for repairs, if you know what I mean. Owen and I were introduced through a friend, and we started going out. We became lovers. And he was a lover like I've never had before or since. Owen—how shall I put this?—is kind of a sexual pioneer. He's fascinated by the unknown, by pushing himself to the limit, by putting himself into dangerous situations."

"Could you possibly be a little more explicit?"

"Okay. First of all—and I don't know whether you already know this or not—his wife, Helen, is one jealous lady. But instead of this being a deterrent to Owen's promiscuity, it's more like a challenge. Do you know what I mean?"

"I've seen Helen in action with one of Owen's lovers. She doesn't pull any punches."

"That's for sure. Helen is one tough cookie."

"So why does she put up with him?"

"That's a whole other story. Let's take one thing at a time. Shortly after Owen and I had started seeing each other, he took me to a party at this mansion in Beverly Hills. I mean, this place had the winding staircase, the whole thing. I was impressed. And I was impressed by some of the other people who were there that night—a couple minor movie stars and directors. Anyhow, Owen had failed to tell me that the purpose of the gathering was to engage in various types of, shall we say, offbeat sexual behavior.

"Let me explain by saying that in my relationship with Owen I played a rather submissive role to his dominant one, and he felt—rightly so, as it turned out—that I would do whatever he asked, or demanded, that I do. This party was exactly the kind of situation he reveled in. There I was, in the dark about what was to happen. Then I was forced to do several things with other members of the 'club' that I had never heard of, let alone considered. Now, if you want explicit details about what those things were, I'm afraid you're going to be disappointed. That was a crazy time in my life. I'm the kind of person who's willing to try anything—just about anything—once. I was much younger then, infatuated with a very powerful, handsome man. I've outgrown the behavior of that time and do not wish to dredge those memories up.

"Owen and I still speak when we see each other, but we haven't been lovers for over a decade. We still occasionally see the same people. From what I understand, the portrait I've just painted of Owen is as true today as it was then."

"That's very interesting. And I appreciate your telling me. I understand that when Barry was hired for *Doctors and Lovers* he was an out-of-the-blue choice. I also understand that the clout came from Owen himself. Would you know anything about that?"

"That was before I met Barry."

"You didn't answer my question."

Cynthia smiled. "Sorry. I'm not trying to be evasive. It's just that it never came up—why he got hired. Why does any actor get hired over another?"

"You don't think there was anything between Barry and Clark?"

Cynthia made a face and said, "Sexually, you mean?"

Ace nodded his head.

"No. Definitely not. Barry was as straight as they come. And I ought to know."

"Just asking. Tell me about Helen Clark."

"I don't know much about her. But what I do know is that she can be hell on wheels when she gets angry. She comes across as being a real bitch when she's threatened—which she usually is whenever she finds out about the latest chapter in Owen's sexual escapades. Owen used to tell me some things about her. When they're alone, she's his slave. And I'm not talking about bringing him his pipe and slippers. I mean the real McCoy. They've got a little dungeon in their basement with whips and chains, everything. Anyhow, apparently in the beginning Helen tried to leave Owen. But to be blunt, she was hooked on Owen's brand of sex. She couldn't get off on straight sex anymore. So she came back. For his part, Owen likes the sexual play of their relationship, but more important is the fact that Helen is the sole heir of a former major studio founder and has close to half a billion dollars in the family account. Now that's financial security. It gives Owen all the clout he needs with the networks. He can afford to lose now and then, but he usually doesn't because he knows how to grease the right wheels."

"Not exactly Ozzie and Harriet we're dealing with here."

"Not exactly."

"How about Corey Eastland?"

"Never heard of him."

"He's the guy Barry eased out in *Doctors and Lovers*."

"Barry never mentioned the name."

"Okay. Jerry Russo."

"Now that's a name I've heard. He's the guy Barry was

supposed to kill off on the show just before Barry was killed. I don't know much about the guy, except that I seem to remember Barry saying they weren't hitting it off too well. But for Barry, that isn't saying much. It *is* strange that on the show Jerry was supposed to die. Then Barry's real-life death saved Jerry's life in the show. Jerry benefited directly from Barry's death. That's the kind of thing detectives are supposed to look for, right?"

"One of the things. Was Jerry at the party the night of Barry's death?"

"Yes. So were Owen and Helen, for that matter. Most of the cast and crew were there. That's the only reason Barry went—out of social obligation. He didn't like parties much."

"Was Maddie there?"

"Maddie Paxton?"

"Yeah. The show's director."

"She was there," said Cynthia. There was a definite coolness in her tone now, which had not been present before.

"Tell me," Ace said simply.

"Tell you what?"

"You didn't like Maddie. Why?"

"That's ridiculous," she started to protest, but then decided it wasn't worth the effort. "That's good. I'm glad I hired you."

"It's nothing, really. So, what did you and Maddie have between you?"

"Nothing that should concern you. But I'll tell you anyhow. Maddie and Barry used to date before Barry and I started going out."

"Was it serious?"

"I'd say it was more terminal than serious."

"How so?"

"She was stifling him. She was very possessive. For a man like Barry, that's the worst possible type of relationship."

"How long had they been seeing each other?"

"Since right after he came on the show."

"Was she aware that Barry had left her for you?"

"It wasn't exactly like that. He was splitting up with her anyhow. He was looking and so was I. But I'm afraid Maddie thought I had interfered. We didn't get along too well."

"Did she ever threaten Barry or you?"

"Heavens, no. After all, we're all adults."

"I keep forgetting. The world is a terribly civilized place these days.

"You know a brunette with long hair and legs; a real looker named Arlene who is probably Clark's latest addition?"

Cynthia wrinkled her brow and repeated Arlene's name a couple of times. "I think I know who you're talking about. She has some job on the production staff. I've seen her at a couple of parties, but I don't know her and I've never talked with her.

"You know, several of the people you mentioned had reason to wish Barry harm."

"Yeah, them and half of Hollywood. I don't mean to be a wet blanket, but we're still in the starting blocks. Also, until we establish once and for all what happened to Barry, be a little extra careful."

"Why? What do you mean?"

"I'm not trying to scare you, but there is always the possibility that Barry *was* murdered. If he was, then you were the only one at the scene of the crime. And we still don't have a motive. It's just a safety measure. Better safe than . . . you know."

"Well, I don't think that it's necessary, but I'll take extra care until this thing is wrapped up. After all, I might as well take your advice. I'm paying for it."

OWEN CLARK TOOK A DEEP breath as he stuffed a script into his attaché case. He closed the case, pushed the lock, and it clicked shut. It had been a long day. As usual, he was the last one out of the office. The digital clock on his desk read 6:34. As he turned the key and locked the office door behind him, Clark thought about stopping by Arlene's on his way home.

It was already dark outside. The light in his car went on as he unlocked and opened the door of his Porsche 928. He got in, sank into the seat, and listened to the real leather pop as it fitted around his body. He loved his car and never tired of driving it full out along Mulholland Drive on his way home. With the radio blaring, the engine roaring, and the city lights glistening below him on either side of the mountain, he became rejuvenated. Some people needed booze, a needle, a guru. For Clark it was his car, speed, music, sex, and the city.

By the time he hit the NBC gate, which opened out onto a

side street, Clark had decided he didn't have enough time to stop and see Arlene. He chuckled to himself when he thought of Helen beating up Arlene at the party the night before. He and Helen had had great sex after everyone left. He had made her recount the fight several times while they were having sex.

He pulled the Porsche out onto Cherry Street, an unlighted road that led to the freeway the producer took home every night. He pulled up to the stop sign at the end of the street. Another car pulled up next to him. He recognized the driver, who was motioning for him to roll down his window.

The other driver's window was already rolled down. Owen rolled down his and said, "What are you doing out here so late?"

But the only answer he got was a rude spit from a silencer leveled at him by the other car's driver. The bullet hit Clark in the forehead. His head jerked backward, and then he slumped forward, dead in his front seat.

The other car pulled away onto the freeway, into the tail end of the rush hour traffic.

PART TWO

"ANY CALLS?" asked Ace.

"Some chick named Connie. Sounded Oriental to me," said Bunny Aguirre.

"You're getting pretty good."

"So I'm right."

"Chinese," he said, tearing the message off the pad on the desk.

"You should try some non-Oriental girls sometime."

"Got anybody in mind?"

"Maybe," she said, her face becoming one cute invitation with teeth.

"I've got a rule about dating employees."

"So do I. Never date a fellow employee unless he's real good-looking."

"Sounds a lot like mine. I'm going to have to get back to you on this, Bunny," said Ace. He walked into his office, but not before appraising and appreciatively noting the fine curve of Bunny's right leg, which was revealed to midthigh in a tight-fitting, beige, slit-up-one-side skirt.

• • •

"Connie?"

"Yes. Is this Ace?"

"Yes. I'm returning your call."

"I see. I was actually expecting a call from *you* earlier today."

"Yes, well, I've been really busy. A murder case I'm working on, actually."

"I subscribe to the theory that people make time for what they really want to do."

"Is this a scolding?"

"No, just a little philosophy. Are you still feeling rejected about last night?"

"No. That was all right. And I really had a great time. Honestly. I was going to call you, but things really have heated up around here."

"Okay. I just wanted to let you know that I can't get together with you tonight. My sister has us committed to dinner at some distant relative's house. But I wanted to confirm a time for tomorrow night if you want to see me."

That was a load off his mind. Now he could see Jenny without making any lame excuses to Connie. "That should work out fine. How does eight o'clock sound?"

"Great."

"Dinner and whatever. Okay?"

"Fine."

"I'll just pick you up at the place I dropped you off last night."

"Right. I've got to go now. My sister is expecting a call. But I'm looking forward to seeing you tomorrow."

"I'm looking forward to seeing you. Bye."

"Jenny?"

"Ace, I was wondering if you were going to call."

"It's been a madhouse around here. Anyhow, I just wanted to confirm tonight."

"Good. I'll make dinner at my place. How does eight-thirty sound?"

"Fine."

"Good. Hey, I've got a class in about a minute and a half. I gotta go. See you tonight, hon."

"Bye."

ACE GOT HOME about seven-fifteen. Marlowe went through his nightly paces: wagging his tail for all it was worth and jumping up on Ace's legs. After a five-minute walk, during which Marlowe did his best for the local greenery, Ace dumped a can of Alpo into Marlowe's red dish, chopped it up, and slid it under Marlowe's wet nose. Then he poured out the now tepid water in the green bowl and filled it with cool water from the bottled supply he had delivered once every ten days.

Ace poured himself a shot and a half of Absolut over ice and went to the Baldwin. He set down the drink on top of the piano on a coaster his mother had made for him. By the time Ace was into the refrain of "Desperado," Marlowe had assumed his position: head, now moist with water drippings, resting on Ace's feet. Luckily Ace rarely used the foot pedals.

About a half hour of bluesy ballads later, Ace turned on the TV and retired to the couch to watch the news, Marlowe's head now resting on his lap.

"Think I should just come out and ask her?" Ace said to his cocker spaniel companion. The dog looked up at him with sad eyes, looking as though he genuinely would have liked to answer. But of course he didn't. Not really.

The phone rang. Ace leaned forward and picked up the phone from the coffee table. "Ace Carpenter," he said.

"Ace. Eddy."

"Hi, Eddy. What's up?"

"Something I thought you might like to know about," said Lt. Eddy Price.

"I've been watching game shows all day, Eddy. My mind's tired. Just tell me, okay?"

"Owen Clark has been shot."

"Is he dead?"

"Couldn't get any deader. A thirty-eight in the forehead."

"Where?"

"Just about a block from NBC."

"You there now?"

"I'm on my way. Corner of Cherry and Riverside."

"See you there. And thanks."

AFTER CALLING JENNY and saying that he would be late, Ace made tracks for the murder scene. When he arrived, it was like a pinball arcade in the middle of a nightmare. There were dozens of swirling, flashing red, blue, and white lights.

"I'm looking for Eddy Price," he said to a cop standing by a wooden horse barricade that had been set up to keep out curious passersby.

The cop turned around and looked for Price, spotted him, and turned back to Ace. "Stay here. I'll be right back." The cop went to Eddy, pointed back toward Ace, then motioned for Ace to come into the cordoned-off area. As Ace moved toward Eddy, the cop returned to his post by the barricade.

Behind Eddy, Ace could see Owen Clark's body being taken out of his Porsche and being put into a plastic bag.

"Got anything yet?" asked Ace.

"Not a damned thing except for the fact that Clark rolled his window down for his murderer. That much we can surmise. It was too cool to be driving with his window down, especially if he were planning to go on the freeway, as we suspect he was. But that doesn't help much. He might have known the person—that might have been the reason he rolled down the window. Or he might have just rolled it down because the motorist next to him asked him to. Maybe Clark thought the murderer was asking for directions or something. Put yourself in Clark's position. Somebody pulls up next to you and they ask you to roll down your window. As long as they don't look like Hell's Angels, most people would oblige."

"Yeah, I guess so."

"You come across anything with this Ashford thing that might help us here?"

"Nothing that comes to mind. I've found out a few things about Clark, but nothing that adds up to this. I was at a party last night at Clark's house. His wife had a catfight with one of the guests—some brunette named Arlene. I heard rumblings that Clark had been getting it on with her."

"The irate wife bit, eh."

"I don't know. It's a little like picking the Yankees to beat the Taiwan Little League champs. It's too easy, too predictable."

"But the Yankees would probably win. That's the way these things usually end up. Very predictably. You know that just as well as I do."

"Yeah. Well, go with the percentages."

"Anything over fifty percent makes you right most of the time, right?"

"And it saves a lot of work."

"That's not fair."

"It's a bitch if you happen to be on the short end of a percentage like that, Eddy. And you and I have seen it play that way too many times to slide by on the numbers game."

"I wasn't going to 'slide by,' as you put it. You know me better than that. But I will check out Mrs. Clark first."

"That makes sense," said Ace assuagingly. "How long has he been dead?"

"Guard at the gate saw him leave a little after six-thirty. I figure his lights went out a minute or so after that."

"Sounds like the killer might have known Clark's habits."

"Maybe, maybe not. At least he knew Clark's whereabouts today."

"And then it could have just been some nut who would have killed anyone who drove up to that stop sign when Clark did."

"Could be. I tell you, Ace, the life of a cop ain't easy these days. Nope, ain't easy at all."

"Probably never was."

Eddy and Ace talked a little while longer, and each promised to keep the other informed. Ace left and drove over to Jenny's. The FM station Ace had on when he pulled up in front of Jenny's was playing "Heartbreak Hotel." It was that kind of a night.

WILLY DODD SAT next to a tabletop version of the video game Asteroids, fidgeting with the small leather bag in which he kept his wallet, credit cards, and other small personal items. He looked at his watch and pursed his lips in irritation. Dodd was dressed in tight-fitting, straight-legged blue jeans, T-shirt, ivory-colored canvas shoes, and a sweater tied around his neck that hung loosely down across his back.

Though it had been less than a minute since he'd last checked, Willy Dodd looked again at his digital watch. It read 7:45. Again he wrinkled his lips and fidgeted.

The door to the Japanese restaurant opened. Willy turned around expectantly. A smile spilled across his face and he stood up to greet his friend.

"Willy, sorry I'm late. I had another customer at the store who was just fascinated with Marilyn—as we all are, of course—but he just would not quit. What could I do? I'm sorry."

"No harm done, Corey. Oh, miss..." paged Willy. "My friend is here."

Corey Eastland and Willy Dodd were led to a table in the back corner of the back room. It was the table, or at least the general area, where they usually sat on Thursday night. They each ordered a serving of sake, which was brought immediately, and tried to relax before they ordered.

"What's the matter, Willy? Did it really upset you so much that I was late?"

"No, that's not it."

"What is it, then? I demand to know what's bothering you before this evening progresses another moment."

Willy played with his water glass for a few seconds, then took a drink from his sake cup. "Did you hear about Owen?"

Corey frowned a question back at Dodd.

"He's been shot; killed. I just heard it as I pulled up in front of the restaurant. It was a news bulletin. Not many details."

"My Lord," said Corey, his eyes growing large, then back to normal size. "Do they know who did it?"

"They said no suspects were in custody."

"It's so shocking. I mean, I haven't seen Owen in a long time, and God knows I hardly wish him well, but... it's just so... strange to know someone who's been murdered."

"Yes," said Willy, looking away from Corey and taking another drink of sake.

"Is there something more you want to tell me, Willy?"

"What do you mean?" he asked defensively.

"Hey, this is Corey you're talking to. I know you, your

moods, when you're upset, when you're anxious about something. There's something going on with you and I would like to know what."

Dodd took a deep breath, let it out, and said, "I'm pretty sure I'm going to be a suspect."

"My Lord. Why?"

"I didn't do it, if that's what you mean. But Owen and I had an argument this afternoon."

"So what? Owen has arguments with people every single day of his life. That doesn't mean anything."

"Yes, but this was a highly visible argument, in front of several witnesses, and . . ."

"And?"

"He fired me. After more than ten years that bastard fired me. I created the damn show and he has the audacity to fire me," said Dodd, his voice cracking on the last word.

"My Lord, that's awful. But as far as murder is concerned, you're still in the clear. After all, losing a job is one thing. With your reputation, you'll get another, probably better, job right away. But murder, that's an entirely different matter. After all, you didn't kill him."

"Of course not."

"So there you have it. If you didn't do it, you've got nothing to worry about."

"But the publicity, the ordeal. I just don't think I could bear it. I really don't."

"Look, the world is full enough of *real* problems without going around creating ones that don't exist. You didn't kill Owen and therefore you have nothing to worry about. If and when the police question you, just tell them where you were at the time of the killing and you'll be off the hook."

"That could be a problem."

"Why?"

"Owen fired me around two this afternoon. I went to the Cavalier across the street from the studio and had a few drinks. I guess I got a little loud talking to Edgar, the bartender. Anyhow, I stayed till about four, then went back to my place and went to sleep until about forty-five minutes ago when the alarm woke me up and I dressed and came over here."

"So you've actually got no alibi," said Corey Eastland, tilting his head toward the ceiling, apparently lost in thought.

"No. No one saw me except for the people at the bar, who heard me call Owen the worst kinds of names."

"I've got an idea."

"I'm open to just about anything," Willy said desperately.

"First you've got to swear to me that you did not murder Owen. I've got to know the truth. It could be my ass if you're lying."

"I swear, Corey. Not that I didn't want to, but I swear that I did not kill Owen Clark."

"All right, then. I will be your alibi."

"What?"

"It's simple. I'll say that you were with me at the shop at the time of the murder."

"But I thought you said you had a customer. He could testify that I wasn't there."

"*I* know that. But I could just as easily tell the police that I had no customers at that time. Even if I say I did have a customer, I could just say that he didn't buy anything. How am I to know how to contact *any* of my customers. After all, they don't sign in and leave their addresses."

"I don't know, Corey," said Dodd warily.

"It doesn't sound like you've got much choice. And the alibi is foolproof. As long as I say you were with me at the shop at the time of Owen's murder, no one can dispute it."

"Unless someone else was at the shop at the same time."

"I'm telling you, Willy, that's not a problem. Even if someone were at the shop at that time, who's to say that you weren't in the back room getting something for me or behind a bookshelf unseen by my customers? I'm telling you, as long as I say you were there, you're in the clear. After all, it's only a small lie. Who knows what could happen if the police don't find the killer and come after you—the man who had the most clear-cut motive for killing Owen? And within hours of the time he fired you and humiliated you in front of your peers."

"I appreciate the offer, Corey. Honestly. But maybe I won't have to lie."

"From what you tell me, that doesn't sound very likely. You will undoubtedly be one of the first people the police interview. And one of the first questions they will ask you is where you were at the time of Owen's murder. You've got to be consistent in what you tell them. No, I think you've got to face facts."

Willy Dodd slumped back in his chair and exhaled deeply, resignedly. He looked like a man who had just received his draft notice and an IRS audit notice in the same batch of mail. "I suppose you're right."

"Unfortunately, I am right. It really was fortuitous that we happened to be eating dinner together tonight. It was fate, Willy. And I'm glad to be able to help you," said Corey, sliding his hand across the small table, placing his hand gently in Willy Dodd's cold, moist palm.

Willy looked up slowly, sadly. "Thanks."

"Shall we order now?"

"I'm not very hungry."

"Suddenly I have an appetite. I'll order for both of us." He raised his hand from Willy's and waved a waitress in a blue kimono over to their table. Just before she arrived, Corey said firmly, "Don't worry, Willy, everything is going to be all right."

And for the first time since he had heard the bad news, Willy Dodd was beginning to think it might.

JENNY LING WAS just putting the finishing touches on some spiced carrots sautéed in garlic. The red snapper was ready, the French Colombard was chilled. Ace had called about fifteen minutes ago and said he was on his way from Burbank. Everything was ready. Everything, that was, except Jenny. She was looking forward to seeing Ace, but she wasn't sure why. She wanted everything to be ready, but she wasn't sure for what.

On the phone earlier in the day, she had been certain that Ace knew something about the other night. She had hoped he wouldn't ask her. Even now she didn't know what she would have said then, or what she might say tonight, if he pressed the issue. She rarely lied, and almost never about anything important. But then, she was almost certain that if she told Ace she had slept with another man, he would stop seeing her. He would want to know why and she would have to tell him she didn't know why. The whole thing sounded crazy, but she knew enough about herself to know that somehow—maybe in a way that defied logic—it had happened for a reason.

The doorbell rang. Jenny's heart skipped a beat. She took a deep breath, went to the door, and opened it.

"Ace," she said, a smile on her face.

"Hi, Jenny," said Ace with what looked like a forced smile making an obligatory appearance.

Jenny's apartment was sparsely, but aesthetically decorated. Green plants hung or sprouted from everywhere. Two posters in metallic frames depicting ballet dancers adorned one white wall. Hardwood floors, regularly polished by Jenny, a white couch and matching chair, a nonworking fireplace, a small color TV, and a blond wood coffee table made up the living room. In the kitchen, where Jenny had led Ace and seated him, were more plants and a round oak butcher-block table with matching chairs.

"Delicious," said Ace after sampling both the carrots and the snapper and washing it down with a sip of wine.

"It's not bad, if I do say so myself."

They ate in a somewhat strained silence for a few minutes, then Jenny said, "So, what took you to Burbank tonight?"

"Owen Clark has been murdered."

Jenny stopped her fork on its way to her mouth and a look of genuine astonishment flushed her face. "My God! Isn't that the producer of the show Barry Ashford was working on?"

"Yes," said Ace, continuing to eat his meal.

"That's incredible. Do they have any idea who did it?"

"Not as of the time I left a few minutes ago. That's one reason Eddy called me over—to see if I could give him any help."

"Did you?"

"No. Not really."

"Isn't this a bit of a coincidence. First Barry, then Owen?"

"A coincidence, yes. Anything more in terms of a connection, I just don't know. I still don't know whether Ashford's death was an accident. It might have been. I just don't know."

"Have you turned up anything interesting yet?"

Hearing Jenny ask him these questions reminded him of how he enjoyed solving mysteries—the big ones, the little ones—with Jenny. She was a great audience—genuinely interested, not just listening to be polite as most people did. "I've turned up a few things, but nothing that leads directly to murder. Cynthia was right when she said Barry wasn't well liked. But that doesn't mean a whole lot; especially in this town. I've got quite a list of desperadoes I wouldn't want to buy a drink for under any circumstances, but nobody I'd even consider rough-ing up, let alone killing. No, it's usually more than casual hate that leads to murder.

"Lust, sex, passion, that's the stuff a good murder is made of. Some guy comes home to find his wife with another man. That's the kind of thing we're looking for. Remember our Hammett and Chandler," Ace said, lightening things up a bit. He had come close to the subject both of them knew would come up sooner or later, though hopefully in not so tragic a context.

"The movies," said Jenny, sipping the wine.

"I beg your pardon?"

"The old detective movies. That's how we met. That seemed like all we did in the beginning. Combing the old revival houses for the classics."

"We did a couple of other things, too."

"That's true," she said, smiling, acknowledging her lover's obvious reference. Again, more than just politely. She *did* re-member.

"Those were good times," said Ace, leaning back in his chair, slowly raising his glass, taking a measured taste of the excellent wine. "What about these times, Jenny?"

"What do you mean?"

"What about our relationship these days? It was wonderful then. If it isn't wonderful now, or at least pretty good most of the time, we're cheating each other, don't you think?"

She didn't answer immediately; then she said, "I suppose so. What do you think?"

"You still haven't answered me. And I asked you first."

Jenny took a deep breath, her brows furrowed, then looked away from Ace. "You know I've felt pressured ever since you asked me to move in with you."

"I know. But I can't say that I totally understand why. Then again, maybe I just don't want to. Explain it to me again."

"Dancing is my life, honey. I've dedicated my body and soul to it since I was fifteen years old. I just can't give it up now."

"I'm not asking you to give it up, Jenny. And you know that. I have a life's work, too. Sure, maybe being a private eye isn't the same as being a dancer, but I like what I do and I wouldn't give it up for almost anything. But I don't think that's the point. I don't want to shrink your world, I want to expand it."

"But can we really share with each other so intimately without giving something up?"

"I think the key to this whole conversation is in the answer to that question. Sure, life is full of choices, trade-offs. I know what I was willing to give up, and it all seemed like excess baggage when I looked at what I was getting in return. I was giving up nothing I wasn't willing to part with. What was it that you felt you were giving up you couldn't do without?"

"Ace, I don't think it's that simple."

"Jenny, I don't think it's that complex."

"I want to maintain my freedom. That's all. I told you that. I'm used to living on my own. That's just the way I am. I need my own space. Do you understand that?"

"I've lived alone all my life. Certainly I understand. But you talk about freedom. What I want to know is, freedom to do what? What exactly?"

"I don't know what you're getting at."

"I think you do."

"You might have to lead me along."

"What could you do living alone that you couldn't do if you were living with me?"

"It's just that it wouldn't be my own space. It's hard to explain."

"It's not hard to explain. But maybe it's just hard to be honest."

"And what is that supposed to mean?"

"Part of the kind of commitment we were talking about precludes sexual activity with other people. If not by formal, spoken agreement, at least logistically."

"You know that I never go home with anybody I meet at the club. I swear to you, Ace. It's the truth. I have offers every single night of my life there and I've never followed up on a single one. Not just out of an unspoken agreement with you, but out of respect for myself."

"What about guys you meet outside the club?"

"You know that I see other people socially. Especially guys from the studio. We just all go out together, a few guys, a few of us girls. We don't pair off and hit the sack, if that's what you mean."

That was exactly what he meant. He also had the vague impression that his question had been only partially answered. And Jenny was doing some mental gymnastics trying to figure out whether she had just lied or not. She convinced herself that she had not and took another sip of her wine. "This is good," she said, finishing it off. "Would you like a little more?" she asked as she stood up and moved to the refrigerator.

"No, I'm fine." But he wasn't fine. He had been to the brink and had come back unfulfilled. Why not just come right out and ask her? he thought. After all, it's a simple yes or no answer. But he knew better than that. These things were not simply explained and, God knows, not simply understood.

"What about you?" asked Jenny as she sat back down at the table.

"What do you mean?"

"Have you dated other people since we've been seeing each other?"

"No, I haven't dated other people," said Ace, choosing his words carefully.

"Let me rephrase that. Have you had sex with other people since we've been seeing each other?"

"What do you mean?"

"Get off it," said Jenny, suddenly turning angry. "You know exactly what I mean. You know the words; you don't need a dictionary."

"Why are you doing this?"

"You started it," she said, tears filling her eyes. "You're the one who was sitting there playing grand inquisitor. I'm not going to just sit here and roll over. I give you a lot, I care for you. I love you. What more do you want from me?" Jenny was now in tears.

Ace melted a little at the sight of Jenny's tears. He knew her well enough to know that she didn't turn them on and off to make points. They were real. She was in pain.

"Come on," he said, getting up and going around the table to her chair, putting his arm around her and comforting her. "Let's go into the living room and sit down," he said, taking her hand and leading her into the other room and to the couch. He sat down next to her, propping her head on his shoulder. Her makeup was running down her cheeks; the dam had burst.

While she cried, the hot emotions played for their turn on

stage inside him. Anger, jealousy, compassion, and love grappled with each other for the spotlight, but compassion seemed to be getting the upper hand. He realized that neither of them had admitted to any indiscretions, though both were now fairly certain the other had been "unfaithful." As he sat there stroking Jenny's hair, she continued to cry. Ace wasn't sure whether it was maturity, sophistication, not caring, or just plain fear that kept him from pursuing the audible, outright answer to his question. He thought back to when he was a teenager and had believed that life had some type of recognizable symmetrical justice to it and that that justice could be found in romantic relationships. The gut-wrenching sickness that accompanied the demise of that fairy tale had been a revelation, a psychic and emotional scar he would carry with him forever, haunting him when he least expected, or wanted, it. But as bad as it was, such things become easier to accept, if only slightly, the more they happened. So, he told himself, what if Jenny *had* slept with the guy? He'd slept with another woman or two during their time together, and it had meant nothing. It hadn't changed how he'd felt about Jenny at all.

It was good to accept it all theoretically, philosophically, he thought as he sat there on the couch listening to Jenny sob. But he caught himself silently hoping that she wouldn't say the words or make it any more real than it was now. He wasn't sure if his maturity and sophistication would carry him much further.

Finally Jenny stopped crying and looked up, mascara running, at Ace. "Would you mind getting me a Kleenex?"

Ace got one from the bathroom, came back, and handed it to her.

"Thanks," she said as she wiped away the liquid sadness from her face.

"You love me, Jenny?"

She blew her nose first, laughed at herself blowing her nose just as he asked the question, then said, "Yes, I do. Do you love me?"

"I think so. It's hard to explain. There is distance between us now that didn't use to be there. When you had reservations about taking what I considered to be the next step in our relationship, I pulled back a little. I felt a little at risk. You know what I mean?"

"Sure. Nobody wants to get hurt."

"Exactly. No matter what, I think our relationship is due for a change. It's been so good that it can't weather a very long season of mediocrity."

"Why can't we just go on like we have been? That's not mediocre."

"No, it wasn't. But things change. I changed. I've lived with a few women in my time, and I have this theory. I believe I could have stayed with a couple of them for a long, long time. But we had completely open relationships with little if any spoken commitments to each other. I think you've got to strike when the iron's hot. Otherwise it's too easy to just walk away. Every time there's an argument, you just say, 'Well, why don't we split up?' "

"Sounds like you're talking about marriage."

"Hell, maybe I'm just going through a rotten period in my life and I need to spread the misery around." He smiled, lightening things up. Jenny smiled, too.

"So, I think we've both got a little thinking to do," he said finally.

"About me moving in?" asked Jenny, a little confused.

"No. We've got some repair work to do first. We've got to work our way back to mediocre. I mean, coming over here, eating dinner, and listening to you cry is not exactly my idea of a fun evening."

"Mine, either," said Jenny, a narrow smile finding its way to her lips.

"I think we ought to take a step back and look at our relationship first. On our own. Let's spend a little time going over things, reevaluating, then let's get together again and see how long we can go without one of us breaking into tears."

"Okay," said Jenny in a voice just above a whisper.

"So, I think I'm going to call it a night."

"You sure?"

Ace hesitated longer than he wanted to but finally said, "I'm sure."

"Call me?"

"Or you can call me. We don't have to be totally out of communication with each other. But I just think we need some time to think this thing out."

Jenny walked Ace to the door, opened it, and kissed him

passionately on the mouth. It was the kind of kiss that made the rest of the world disappear, and he had second and third thoughts about passing up this ticket to paradise, but he figured if the trip were going to be worth it, it could wait until he could travel lighter than he felt tonight.

"Good night, honey," she said.

"Good night," he said, and trotted down the steps before he could change his mind.

"THIS IS MY LUCKY night," said Ace as he sat down in an armless side chair next to Eddy Price's desk in the West Hollywood division of the L.A.P.D.

"Ace," said Eddy, looking up, surprised. "What brings you down here at this time of night?"

"An urge to feel superior."

"Uncontrolled urges can get you into trouble."

"Yeah. I should have a sampler made of that and hang it over my bed. Then again, maybe not. The wrong people might read it."

"So, what can I do for you?"

"Nothing much. I was just over at Jenny's and I thought I'd stop by since I was in the neighborhood."

"Kind of early to end an evening with Jenny, isn't it?"

"I wore her out and she fell asleep."

"That'll be the day. I've seen that lady dance. No foolin', Ace, something wrong between you and Jenny?"

"We're just going through some changes, that's all. I'd rather not talk about it if you don't mind."

"No problem."

"You bolted to the desk or are you free to grab a brew or two?"

"Give me about ten minutes and I'm all yours."

"I can't make any promises. I'll need time to recover from Jenny."

"There's a room in the back for smart guys like you, pal. Nothing fancy, but it makes a point, if you know what I mean."

"I'll get us a table at Figaro's," said Ace, getting up out of the chair.

"See you in about ten minutes or so."

Ace nodded and left.

AFTER ACE'S SECOND beer and Eddy's first was delivered by a blonde wearing a peasant's blouse that revealed two areas in particular where she was abundantly blessed, Ace tried to start the ball rolling. "So, what do you have on Owen Clark's murder?"

"Did you see the set on that waitress? I'll bet her knockers sleep in a different time zone than the rest of her body. Hell, I almost asked for a glass of milk."

"You're pretty easily distracted."

"At least it's by healthy diversions."

"Eddy, you're a healthy man in a sick world."

Ignoring Ace's comment, Eddy continued, "I look at her breasts as a kind of health food for a demented mind. You know what I mean?"

"I can honestly, and gratefully, say that I do not."

"Simply put, they're good, clean, all-American sexual stimuli. Not bizarre shit like people pissing on each other or worshiping a pair of soiled panties. I mean, what could be more natural and healthy than being turned on by a nice pair of tits?"

"Probably nothing, Eddy. This kind of thinking could make carrot juice and push-ups obsolete. Remember, they laughed at Fulton."

"Sometimes you're such a shit, Carpenter. You know that?"

"No, but then sometimes I'm a little slow."

"You know, you should open yourself up a little, listen to other people. After all, you don't have a corner on intelligence."

"Maybe I've just got the fire hydrant on the corner of Intelligence and Vine, and that's why I'm always getting wet from the reign of ignorance that's sweeping the land."

"Laugh if you want. Sure, I was kidding about that girl's tits, but there was also a grain of truth in what I said. You know—and I can tell you this from lots of personal experience with Hollywood crazies—simple, straight sexual stimulation is an endangered species. Personally, I attribute it all to stress and a compulsive desire for more stimulation. I mean, if more guys were satisfied with the good old all-American turn-ons—like a nice pair of tits or legs—we wouldn't have all this kinky shit that litters up my desk day after day. People are going crazy trying to get their rocks off, and the old standbys just don't cut the mustard anymore."

Ace took a long sip from his frosted mug. The cold German beer tasted good going down. "Eddy, there *is* a grain of truth in what you say. But what can you do about it?"

"I don't know what you do about it, but I try my best not to lose interest in Esther's tits. Sure, they're starting to droop a little, but what the hell, right? She's what I've got and I love her."

"Sounds a little territorial to me, Eddy."

"I don't give a shit how it sounds to you. But it's one of the ways I stay sane and keep most of both feet on the ground."

"Whatever works," said Ace, raising his glass, toasting Eddy.

"Whatever works," Eddy said, raising his glass and touching it lightly to Ace's.

"So, anything new on Owen Clark's murder?"

"Since it just happened a few hours ago, I don't have anyone in custody or anything like that, but we know a few things. First, Clark was killed with a thirty-eight slug in the head. I just got done crossing our number-one suspect off the list, which didn't exactly make my night."

"Helen Clark?"

"No. Guy named Willy Dodd. Ever hear of him?"

"I've never met him, but I saw him at a party last night. Didn't look the murdering type."

"They never do."

"Who clued you to him?"

"After a couple calls to some people with the show, it came out that Clark and Dodd had had a big, yelling, screaming argument in front of the whole cast and crew this afternoon. To top it off, Clark fired Dodd. Sound good so far?"

"A dream."

"Yeah, but it turns to shit. We went over to see Dodd, who had just gotten home from dinner. He was scared shitless when we saw him, but then most people are when you flash a badge. So we go in, talk to him, and he tells us he was at a bookshop on Hollywood Boulevard at the time of the murder. We get hold of the proprietor, and sure enough, the guy corroborates Dodd's story."

"Who is the proprietor of the bookstore?"

"Guy named Corey Eastland."

"No kidding," said Ace, a sly smile growing on his face.
"What?"

"Probably nothing."

"Come on. I've been doing all the talking."

"Corey Eastland was fired once by Owen Clark. He used
to be an actor on the soap opera Clark produces. He's never
worked in the business since. Quite a coincidence."

"Quite. That bears a little more looking into. Thanks for
the info. That's good."

"We'll see how good it turns out to be."

"We're running a check on anyone associated with the show
who owns a thirty-eight. Anyone you might suspect more than
anyone else? After all, you've been sizing up this crowd for a
few days."

"You might check out a brunette named Arlene who works
for the show. She and Helen Clark had a catfight last night at
Clark's house. I saw it. Arlene got the worst of it. Naturally,
Clark's wife has got to be looked at pretty closely. The other
prime players, though I wouldn't even guess at their motives,
would be Jerry Russo, the new lead who took over as the show's
main heartthrob when Barry Ashford was killed, and Maddie
Paxton, the show's director."

"Do you think there's any connection between Ashford's
death and Clark's?"

"Tell you the truth, I have no idea. First of all, I'm not
totally convinced that Ashford was murdered. Also, if it was
murder, we can't rule out Owen Clark just because someone
killed him."

"That's true."

Ace and Eddy had another round, and by this time they
were talking about their experiences back in Ohio. "I remember
it as plain as if it were yesterday," said Ace, laughing. "You
under the hood looking for the horn, telling Bob that you were
trying to find the noise in his car. You found the horn, pointed
Bob toward it, Bob put his head under the hood, you gave me
the sign, and I laid on the horn. Shit, his head came out from
under there like it was shot out of a cannon."

Both men laughed at their childish prank. They had relived
it many times before, at least once a year. It was a link to a
past, a much less complicated past. Though the jokes may have
been somewhat crude and a little cruel, they were far less

painful than many things both men encountered now on a daily basis. Today's routine occurrences brought with them a certain numbness of life. Feeling and sensation hadn't died. They had just been crippled.

The two old friends swapped a few more stale tales before Eddy said that he ought to be getting home to the wife. Ace picked up the tab and the two walked out together.

"Keep me posted, okay?" said Ace as he shook Eddy's hand good night.

"Right. And you, too. Sounds like you might have some leads I might not."

"Sure." With a final wave, Ace turned his back to his old friend and all of a sudden the world got very still and lonely. The bar noises were gone, his friend's laughter—as well as his own—were gone, and Jenny's door was closed to him tonight—even if he had pulled it closed himself. He listened to the rhythmic scrape of his leather on the cement as he walked the two blocks to his car.

His loneliness seemed to echo through the steel-and-glass canyons of the city that night. The palm trees seemed to be swaying in slow motion, shadows against a gray sky, and the Ohio boy felt even more like a stranger. He was thinking about snow, a warm fire, and eggnog when he got into his car, thankful for the music that filled his car and his thoughts at the flick of a switch—background; it was a connection to something else alive. He heard the opening chords to Bob Seger's "Night Moves," and the tone and mood of the pictures in his mind changed. It would be all right, Ace told himself. Others had been there before and came back. It was just a bad night.

"*DOCTORS AND LOVERS*," said a voice.

"Hello. Is this Julie? Julie Wharton?"

"Yes," said the voice noncommittally.

"This is Barry Lyndon, the writer you went to the party with a couple nights ago. Remember?" said Ace, sipping his morning coffee.

"Sure. How are you?"

"Oh, I'm fine. But I guess things over there must be pretty up in the air."

"Oh, yeah. Sure," said the secretary, assuming the proper amount of despair expected of her at a time like this.

"I was just wondering if you're free for lunch."

"Why?"

"Well, I met some people at the party and I just wanted to know how things stand now. And besides, I wanted to show my appreciation to you for getting me into the party."

"I've got a boyfriend, you know."

"No sweat."

"Okay, sure."

"When do you take lunch?"

"It's pretty flexible today. The show's closed down for a couple of days because of, well, you know."

"Yeah. It must be a time of great sadness for the people over there."

"Uh-huh. Twelve would be good."

"Okay. See you at noon."

"Meet me in the lobby."

ACE MET JULIE in the lobby at the appointed time and took her a few blocks to the Studio Restaurant, which was a rustic, contemporary place with lots of salads with sprouts, juices, and waiters and waitresses who were all "members of the Academy"—or close to it.

Ace and Julie each ordered salad—Ace a Caesar salad, Julie a mung bean salad with Russian dressing.

"So, how is everyone taking Owen's murder?"

"Okay. You know, it's strange, but it's just like a soap opera. I've never known any real-life person who was murdered. Everyone seems to be taking it all in stride, though. What can you do, right?"

"Right."

"So, you mentioned you met some people at the party."

"Yes. It seems Willy Dodd would be the main person to contact, me being a writer," said Ace, even though he knew Dodd had been fired. He wanted to get the story from a fresh point of view.

"No. Not anymore. Willy was fired yesterday."

"You're kidding."

"No. Some coincidence, eh. I think the police ought to find out where Willy was at the time of the murder."

"Do you really think he did it?"

"I don't know. But it makes sense, doesn't it? I mean, he had a motive and all."

"Just because he got fired? People get fired all the time and don't kill their bosses."

"The show was Willy's life. He helped create it. And besides, it wasn't just that he was fired, it was the way Mr. Clark did it," said Julie, stuffing some mung beans into her mouth.

"And how was that?"

"He humiliated Willy in front of the whole company."

"Were you there?"

"No, but I talked to lots of people who *were*. They were all embarrassed for Willy. Everybody liked him. He's a nice guy who does his job and doesn't make waves. For some reason, Owen just went off on him yesterday. Then, to everyone's surprise, Willy stuck up for himself. I guess Willy's probably stored up lots of anger at Owen over the years. I mean, Willy wasn't rude or anything to Mr. Clark, it's just that he refused to back down about some change that Mr. Clark wanted. Willy pointed out the merits of leaving the script as it was and Owen just, like I said, went off."

"What did he do?"

"He started yelling at Willy. He took Willy's script, tore a page out of it, and pretended like he was wiping his ass on it. Then he told Willy that he was a no-talent parasite who wouldn't be anywhere without hanging on his—Mr. Clark's—coattails. It was ugly. Then Mr. Clark told him to clean out his desk and get out of the studio immediately."

"Why would Clark go off the deep end like that?"

"I don't know. I've only been with the show for about a year and a half, but I've been there long enough to know that Mr. Clark can be a little crazy. And he seems to be firing people left and right these days."

"Oh?"

"I'm really not supposed to say anything."

"Who would I tell? I'm not even a member of the Writers Guild. Who would care what I say?"

"You've got a point."

Ace let the comment pass and pressed on. "Who else did he fire?"

"Well, she was fired, but then she wasn't. It's hard to explain."

"Who?"

"You remember Maddie? Maddie Paxton, the director?"

"Sure."

"She was given a bullshit job with a bullshit title and relieved of her duties as the show's director. The title sounds hot, but she's basically just been sent to the showers."

"How's she taking it?"

"Not any better than Willy, I'm afraid. But of the two, Maddie is by far the most dangerous. You know, I've just changed my mind about who the killer is. Forget Willy, Maddie's the one. She can be one cruel mother. The show was her whole life, like with Willy. But with Maddie it was something more. She loved the spotlight, the importance, the significance, the power that went with being the director of a big show. She loved being the center of attention. Now that her power's gone, her identity is gone. She looks kind of lost to me. But that's just my opinion," said Julie, sucking in a mung bean.

Ace and Julie chatted a while longer, but Ace could not glean anything else of even minor importance from the secretary. However, he was able to get Julie to phone Maddie's address to him in the lobby after she had returned to work. He promised not to bother Maddie—that is, he promised not to try to push his scripts on her, which was an easy promise to keep in that he had never written a script. Ace told Julie he just wanted the director's address to send her a résumé. And he promised never to tell Maddie where he got the address.

THE AFTERNOON SKY was clear blue even though a brown smudge of smog was starting to leave its dirty fingerprint on the horizon. Ace pushed his Celica through its paces as he rounded the undulant curves along Lookout Mountain Drive to Maddie Paxton's house.

Ace pushed a lighted doorbell just to the left of the two white doors, both of which were about twice as tall as Ace. A black woman opened the door.

"Yes, sir?" she said, tilting her head slightly.

"Is Maddie in?"

"Is she expecting you?"

"Yes. I met her at a party a couple of nights ago and she asked me to stop by," he lied.

The black woman looked as though she'd heard that one before and moved to one side to let Ace in. "Who shall I say is calling?"

"I'd like to surprise her. Anyhow, I don't think she'd remember my name." Out of the corner of his eye Ace caught a glimpse of Maddie Paxton standing beside her pool. "Oh, I see her. I'll just go say hello."

"But . . ." said the maid, but it was too late. Ace was already past her and walking in the direction of the pool. Maddie looked up and caught sight of Ace just as he passed through the open glass doors. Her eyes didn't show any surprise or fear at the sight of a strange man in her house. Her eyes turned sultry as Ace approached. Her left hip cocked aggressively to one side.

"Hi, Maddie," he said.

"Hi," she said in a throaty voice that would have done Bacall proud. She got a funny look on her face. Ace couldn't quite place it. But it was the kind of look that would be at home at the business end of a gun. Or any weapon, for that matter. "Do I know you?"

"Not the way I'd like," he said, getting into the spirit of things.

"And just what way would that be?"

"I'm an imaginative guy. I like it lots of ways."

Maddie paused a beat, then said, "Me too. Are you a drinking man?"

"Not yet."

"I've got everything," she said, shifting her weight slowly to the other leg, then turning and walking like the pendulum of a fine clock to a wet bar next to a table with a large yellow umbrella over it.

"I can see that."

"I beg your pardon?" she said after she'd positioned herself behind the bar and was now facing Ace again.

Ace walked toward the bar. "I said I'll bet you've got some vodka on ice back there."

"What kind of odds do you give?" she said, turning those sultry eyes on him again.

"Looks like a pretty sure thing to me," he said, meeting her halfway.

Maddie used some metal tongs to grab two ice cubes from a leather-covered bucket, dropped them into an Old Fashioned glass, and poured some Absolut over them. "Here," she said, handing him the glass. "To your health."

Just then Ace heard a splash in the pool behind him. He turned to see a bronzed-bodied young man, who couldn't have bought a six-pack legally by himself, sliding gracefully through the water. The swimmer got out at the other end of the pool and positioned himself on a lounge chair so that he could take best advantage of the afternoon rays. The only thing he'd have been overdressed for would have been a nudist club pot luck. A drugstore jock strap would have covered more.

"Danny!" Maddie called over Ace's shoulder.

"Yes?" said the pretty young man.

"Be a dear and bring me some suntan lotion."

Danny got up and dutifully retrieved a small brown plastic bottle for Maddie.

"Thank you, honey," she said, and kissed him on the cheek. He accepted the gesture as though someone had just handed him last week's *TV Guide* and went back to his leisure post.

She held out the lotion for Ace.

"Drink's fine as it is."

Maddie smiled coyly and said, "You wouldn't want me to peel, would you?"

"How many layers?"

"Be a dear, won't you?" she said, mixing a pouty grin with a subtle firmness in the tone of her voice.

"Only one dear to a pool."

She looked at him without acknowledging his comment.

"Oh, all right," he said. He took the lotion and Maddie led him to a nearby lounge, where she lay down on her stomach. "Unbutton my top. I don't like to have a line. Too many backless dresses."

Ace did as he was told and gently smeared the hot liquid on her even hotter, smooth, tanned body. He noticed her breathing becoming heavier. As was his own.

"Now the other side," she said, and turned over, doing a poor job of covering herself with her top. He started with the feet and worked his way up to her chest. He could see that her nipples were erect through the bikini top. Somehow he got around those dangerous curves, trying to keep business in his mind. He finished with her face and she sat up, this time doing an even poorer job of covering her ever-so-slightly sagging breasts. She propped the back of the lounge up a couple of notches and relaxed. "So . . . I don't imagine you came here to put lotion on my body."

"No, but it was probably better than what I *did* come here for."

"Which is?"

"I'm a private investigator."

That didn't seem to sit too well with her, but then it never does with anyone. At least Maddie didn't immediately try to have him thrown out, like some people had done.

"So why do you want to talk to me?"

"Couple things, really."

"Don't tell me. This is about Owen's murder, isn't it? That bastard. He deserved to die."

"That's not the kind of thing you're supposed to say."

"I'm an unpredictable woman."

"I'll buy that."

"You could have, real cheap, a few minutes ago. But you didn't. You're a dedicated soul."

"That's not the reason I didn't make a play."

"Oh, you on the rag?"

"Nice mouth."

"I'm not overly proud of the way I act, but on the other hand, I don't apologize for it, either. So let's stop exchanging dirty jokes and get on with this."

"Have the police been here to question you?"

"No. Why should they?"

"They're going to find out sooner or later that Clark bounced you upstairs. It gives you a motive."

"It's reaching."

"Not too far."

"You can't be serious."

"I am. But don't panic. Just take it as a friendly warning."

"Are you a friend?"

"I can be."

"So what's your piece of the action here?"

"I represent someone who's interested in finding out if Barry

Ashford's death was murder or just some hit-and-run drunk driver."

"It's murder either way."

"True. But if somebody actually set out to do it, that's the kind of dime-novel stuff that makes my business worthwhile."

"I get it. So you're working for Cynthia Walcott." It wasn't a question.

"I'm not at liberty to give out my client's name."

"Who else could it be? Barry didn't have any other friends. And she would have grown to hate him before long, just like the rest of us did. He was balling everything that moved there toward the end."

"Maybe my client wouldn't have minded."

"Every woman *minds*. You never get too damn sophisticated to stop 'minding.'"

"So, was there anyone in particular in Barry's lust-life; anyone he was balling any more than anyone else?"

"Some brunette named Arlene something-or-other. She worked for the production company until a few days ago. Then Owen decided to give her a small part in the show. He was probably balling her, too. God, men are animals. And in this society they have the privilege of unbridled lust. Don't you just love it?"

"It's not everything it's knocked up to be."

"Men do it and it's just something they've got to do. Women do it and they're whores. But things are changing."

"And it looks as though you're leading the charge."

"I get in my licks, if you know what I mean."

"I don't need a translator for that one." Ace steered the conversation back on track. "Do you think Clark and Ashford could have had an argument over this girl Arlene?"

Maddie laughed a throaty laugh. "It wasn't their style. She was a plaything, nothing to be taken seriously by anyone. She was just this sneeze's Kleenex."

"What about the party you had here the night Ashford was killed?"

"That's old news."

"Who put the shit in Ashford's hat?"

"I don't know. Honestly. But that was a stroke of genius, don't you think?"

"Sounds like it might be kind of rough to be on the receiving end."

"I would imagine so. But then it was pretty bad to be on the receiving end of some of the shit Barry dished out every day."

"Was he really the bad guy everyone made him out to be?"

"Worse."

"What made him that way?"

"What makes anyone that way? Maybe he felt guilty making all that money, being so famous and having so little talent."

"Is that jealousy or the truth?"

"I was never jealous of Barry. The fact is, Barry was not a good actor. He had clout. He was connected. But then that's half of this bullshit business, anyhow. Always was, always will be."

"Where did Barry get his clout?"

"Now that's a good question. I pondered it more than once myself. No one seems to know where it came from, but there was no doubt it was there. One day Barry wasn't there—wasn't anywhere, for that matter—the next day he's dominating the show. I never came up with any answers. But it *is* a good question."

"Thanks. What do you think happened to Barry?"

"I don't know. And I don't care."

"I understand your feelings, but if you had to take a guess, what would you guess?"

"Hmmm . . ." She squinted her eyes, looked away from the detective, and contemplated her answer. "I'd bet somebody murdered him. Or had it done. Something like that. Bad *accidents* never happen to the right people. It's always some good guy who never hurt a flea. Yeah," she said, turning her gaze back toward Ace. "I'd have to vote for murder."

"Any guesses at who?"

"There you've got me. Too many suspects. That's one for Agatha Christie. Everyone hated the guy. It was just a question of time until somebody reached a breaking point."

An alarm went off on Maddie's wristwatch. She pressed a tiny button and it stopped. "Well, I'm afraid I've got something to attend to."

"I appreciate your talking with me."

"Not at all. I enjoyed meeting you. Give me a call sometime.

My number's 555-9995. It's easy to remember."

"And you'd be hard to forget."

"Nice combination."

"Very nice. Remember what I told you about the police. Sooner or later they're going to find out about Clark firing you. By the way, where were you last night about six-thirty?"

"Here."

"Alone?"

"At that time, yes. But I was expecting company later."

"What about your maid?"

"It was her night off."

"Not exactly a foolproof alibi."

"Why should I need one? I didn't do it."

"Well, I'll be running along."

Maddie just fluttered her eyelids a little and said, "See ya."

Ace let himself out. At the door, just before he was about to pull the door shut, he turned back and saw Maddie take the boy by the hand and lead him into the house.

IT WAS ABOUT FOUR P.M. when Ace pulled his car up to a meter with time on it in front of the West Hollywood division. He didn't have to pick up Connie until about eight, so that gave him plenty of time. He figured that Eddy ought to have some hard leads by now, if any were going to come the easy way.

"Why don't I get you an office with your name on the door?" said Eddy when he returned to his desk with a cup of coffee and saw Ace waiting for him.

"I don't like the doughnuts here. But thanks anyway."

"So, how does the leisure class spend its afternoons these days?"

"Contemplating murder, suicide, or just an occasional harmless affair. Some things never change."

"Well, I wouldn't know, I just clean up the mess."

"You're the garbage men of humanity, you cops," said Ace glibly, then reached for a doughnut in a box on Eddy's desk.

"I thought you didn't like the doughnuts around here?"

"All this talk of garbage made them look better to me."

"Look, I'm busy. You want something special?"

"Just checking to see what's cooking with Owen Clark's murder," said Ace in between bites of the coconut-sprinkled pastry.

Eddy got a satisfied smile on his face. "As a matter of fact, we did get a break."

"I'm all ears."

"We found the gun that killed Clark. The murderer apparently dumped it about a hundred yards away in a ditch."

"Any prints?"

"We'll know in a few hours. But we do know whose gun it is."

"Yeah?"

"Maddie Paxton's. She's the director of the show."

"You talk to her yet?" asked Ace, playing dumb.

"No. But we'll change that later this afternoon. After we get the prints back, we might do more than talk; we might just bring her back with us. There's more."

"There's another doughnut in there, so I'm not going anywhere," said Ace, reaching across the desk and picking up the last doughnut from the box.

"I was saving that glazed for later."

"Sorry," said Ace, and broke the doughnut in half and put the smaller half back in the box.

"And we're supposed to be friends."

"I wouldn't have put anything back if we weren't. So, you were saying that there's more."

"We've been interviewing some members of the show's cast and crew, and it seems that Willy Dodd wasn't the only person Clark fired recently."

"Let me guess. Maddie Paxton."

"Bingo. Now I'm not one to look for the easy way out, but this case is looking more like a lock every minute."

"I don't want to rain on your parade, but why would she throw the gun out so close to the murder scene?"

"Inexperience, lack of cool. Who knows?"

"It does seem strange to me. Why not throw it out in some field twenty miles away? Or in a body of water where it would *never* be found? Or just take it home and bury it in the backyard? Throwing it out a hundred yards from the scene of the crime seems like just about the least attractive of all possible options."

"People who don't kill people all the time have a tendency

to lose their cool when they commit a murder."

"I've met Maddie Paxton and she doesn't seem to be the kind of person who would ever lose her cool. She could chill an ice cube."

"Well, what you and I think doesn't really make any difference when it's put up against the evidence. If her prints are on that gun, she's going to jail."

"And if they're not?"

"There's still a good chance she'll be arrested."

"Anything else?"

"You're never satisfied."

"Just curious."

"No, nothing else."

"Well, then I think I'll be running along. Thanks for the doughnuts and the information."

"Sure. Don't forget, I don't mind information coming my way sometimes."

"I'll see what I can do."

The red "Expired" sign clicked up on the meter just as Ace walked out to his car. A meter maid was writing a ticket for the car in back of his. He got into his Celica and pulled away. Sometimes your timing was just right.

MARLOWE GREETED ACE dutifully at the front door, and Ace went through the ritual with him—the walk, the food, the water. Ace poured himself a finger of chilled Absolut and went to the piano. As usual, not long afterward, Marlowe deposited his moist chin on Ace's feet, relaxed, and took in the concert.

After putting a dent in the Jackson Browne songbook he kept inside the piano bench seat, Ace adjourned to the sofa, as did Marlowe. Dog and master settled in for a well-deserved, end-of-the-day snooze.

Ace was filled with ambiguities about his date with Connie. He was attracted to her, and after his conversation with her the night he'd dropped her off, he had reason to believe that she was also attracted to him, and there would most likely be the opportunity for sexual adventure this evening.

The thing was, he was still filled with unanswered questions and anxieties about his relationship with Jenny. Ace was looking forward to his date with Connie, and then again he wasn't. He wanted to have sex with her, and he *didn't* want to. "This is going to be some date," Ace said aloud. Marlowe sleepily opened his big brown eyes and turned to look Ace directly in the eye. "What do you think I should do, Marlowe?" asked Ace.

The cocker spaniel licked Ace on the face with his wet tongue, then turned away and went back to sleep.

"Thanks for the advice."

"Hi, Ace," said Connie after she'd opened the door. "You know, it still sounds funny to call you that. What's your real name?"

"Stephen. But I prefer Ace . . . or master, or honey, or Jim Bob."

"I'll stick with Ace. Come on in while I grab a wrap."

Ace walked inside and closed the door.

"I'll just be a second."

"No hurry."

Ace was dressed in a tweed sport coat, jeans, a pink Ralph Lauren shirt, and white jazz dance shoes. He smelled good, too, but not as good as he'd noticed Connie did. She wore a lavender dress with thin shoulder straps and a slit up one side that came to midthigh. She wore black stockings and black high-heeled shoes. Her jet-black hair was shiny clean and fell softly just over her bare shoulders.

She picked up a white scarf/shawl, draped it over her shoulders, and walked over to Ace.

"You look very handsome tonight," she said, and kissed him lightly on the mouth.

"You don't look so bad yourself."

"You could turn a girl's head."

"Only if I could turn the rest of her at the same time."

"You can turn me any way you want, as long as you turn me on."

"You sure you want to go eat?"

"I'm sure. I might need my strength."

•   •   •

ACE AND CONNIE were seated at a table next to the window of Mary Ann's, a medium-swank West Hollywood restaurant at which Ace was well known, more for his appearances at the bar than in the dining room, although he managed to eat there about once a month.

"I'll have a Carpenter," she told the waiter when he asked if they wanted cocktails. The waiter did not know Ace and frowned puzzledly at Connie's request.

"Is Alex working tonight?"

"Yes," replied the waiter.

"Just tell him. He'll know what it is. I'll have Absolut on the rocks."

"Yes, sir," said the waiter, and disappeared into the hallway leading to the bar.

"You must have quite a reputation here as a drinker."

"I don't brag about it. But it's better than having a reputation as a politician."

"You know," she said, pausing, searching for the right words, "there's something I'd like to ask you."

"Shoot."

"You're a nice-looking guy, and . . . and I was just wondering if you're as available as you appear to be."

"You mean am I married? No, I'm not. Satisfied?"

"That's only half an answer. Do you have a girlfriend? A steady girlfriend with commitments and all that?"

"It's hard to give you a straight answer."

"It'll probably get even harder as the night goes on—to answer the question, I mean."

"Why do you want to know?"

"I'm just curious."

"Would it make a difference in what happens tonight?"

"If I say it would, would you still tell me the truth?"

"Probably."

"But maybe not."

"Maybe not. I've had an ongoing relationship with the same woman for about a year. I can honestly say we have no agreements about not sleeping with other people."

"No *spoken* agreements."

"Right."

"One reason it doesn't make a big difference to me is that I'm going to be leaving for home next week. No matter what happens between us, I feel relatively certain that it won't go any further than the next few days."

"People get their emotions tangled up sometimes. How can you be so sure?"

"Because I'm married and I love my husband."

"Are you serious?"

"Don't married people have sex outside of marriage in Los Angeles? My, my. It happens all the time in Texas. My husband's the same way. I don't imagine he's sleeping alone every night while I'm gone."

"You know, I had you figured all wrong. I mean, when I met you, you wouldn't come home with me."

"Well, there was more to the story than I wanted to go into just then. But I made up my mind to tell you tonight. First of all, my husband was supposed to call me that next morning very early. I wanted to be at my sister's to get the call. Also, I have to admit that this—you and I—would be my first time being unfaithful."

"Nice choice of words. Hey, you know, I'm not real sure I want to spring for your maiden voyage. Sometimes it's like stepping off the fortieth story without a net."

"You're talking about feeling guilty and all that."

"Well, yes."

"Sounds like you've taken the plunge once or twice and didn't like the feel of hitting the ground."

"Let's just say that I know whereof I speak."

"Look, let's not make this a heavy thing, okay? I'm looking for a good time, a nice romantic evening. I like you, I'm attracted to you. Why don't we just leave it at that?"

"Why?" said Ace weakly.

"Yes. Why?"

"Well, I . . . I don't know."

"Neither do I. Here we are, the two of us. Let's have a good time."

Ace tried, but he couldn't come up with a strong, convincing argument. Things with Jenny were, if not *on* the rocks, edging pretty close to them. And he was attracted to Connie. Maybe it's just what the doctor ordered, he decided.

The waiter arrived with a Carpenter and an Absolut and set the drinks down between the two. "Would you like to order now?"

"No. Give us a few minutes," said Ace.

The waiter nodded politely, turned on his heel, and vanished into the shadows.

"To us," said Connie, lifting her glass and making a toast.

Ace got a resigned look on his face, raised his glass, and said, "To a beautiful evening."

"I LOVE DOGS. He's so cute," said Connie, on her knees playing with a frisky Marlowe as Ace locked up and fixed them each an Absolut on the rocks.

"Everyone says that. He *is* kind of cute. But our relationship—his and mine—is based on more that superficial looks. We like the same kinds of music, the same kinds of liquour, and, as you can see, the same kinds of women."

Connie walked over to the couch and sat down. Marlowe followed her and jumped up in her lap. Connie picked Marlowe up and set him just next to her, but Marlowe still managed to get his head on Connie's thigh. He seemed content with that, licked his lips, and his eyes started to flutter closed.

Ace handed Connie her drink and sat down at the piano. Connie had crossed her legs to take maximum advantage of the slit in her dress. She had great legs, Ace had decided by now, and the black stockings and lavender dress made a perfect museum to show off the masterpiece.

"Play me something," she said.

Ace smiled and began to tickle the ivories. He played three or four mellow tunes, occasionally glancing over at Connie, making eye contact.

"Very nice," Connie said after the fourth song. "I don't recognize them, though. Who does them?"

"I do."

"You mean you wrote them?"

"Yes."

"That's quite impressive."

"I was hoping you'd say that."

"You're used to impressing women, aren't you?"

"I'm used to trying."

Ace got up from the piano, walked over to the couch, and extended his hand. After carefully setting Marlowe's sleepy head gently aside, Connie took Ace's hand and followed him into the bedroom. Ace lit a candle by the bed, then turned and stood facing Connie. He reached around in back of her and undid her dress's zipper. Then he slipped the thin shoulder straps gently down over her shoulders and slowly pulled her dress down over her unfettered breasts, over her hips, and let it fall like a whisper to the floor. He could see through her panty hose that she wasn't wearing any panties. She stepped out of her dress and stood illuminated by the candlelight. She slipped off her shoes and peeled down her stockings. Ace noted that she must have spent a lot of time in the sun because she had a very distinct bikini line in the appropriate places, while the rest of her was tanned and, in the candlelight, seemed even darker, more exotic.

She unbuttoned his shirt, slipped it over his shoulders, undid his belt. Then, her eyes smoldering with sexual heat, she got to her knees. She untied and removed his shoes, then his socks. She unzipped his fly and pulled his trousers and briefs down. Ace did his part, stepping out of his garments.

The mirror on the wall next to the bed allowed Ace to watch the beautiful Oriental girl from another angle as she took his aroused penis *all* the way into her mouth.

After several blissful moments of this lovemaking, Ace gently disengaged Connie and led her to the bed. They were now both on their knees facing each other. Ace reached forward and hooked his arms under Connie's knees.

"Put your arms around my neck," he said softly.

She did so. As she did, Ace lifted her onto him, cupping his hands around her smooth, round buttocks. They looked deeply into each other's eyes. Then into the mirror. Into each other's eyes. Into the mirror.

ACE WAS AWAKENED the next morning by Marlowe's cold nose. It was time for a walk. As he came to, Ace looked at where the candle had once been. It was now just a pool of hardening wax. Connie's head, her hair mussed wildly, was on his shoulder, her left arm sprawled across his chest. He got up without waking her.

Over breakfast she looked totally composed again.

"You're a good cook," she said, finishing off his scrambled eggs with Mornay sauce.

"Thanks. I don't get a lot of practice. It's not much fun to cook for one person."

"This is great. Really. Better than I could do. I'm not much of a cook."

They both ate in near silence for a few moments, politely passing the salt and pepper to each other without much comment.

"I . . . I really liked last night," said Connie finally.

"Me too."

"It really was all I hoped it would be."

"How do you mean?"

"Well, I just wanted it to be something nice, something beautiful and satisfying."

"You don't ask for much."

"But I got lucky. I found you. You were the perfect person to have this experience with. A married woman's first affair ought to be something wonderful."

"You know, it's hard for me to talk to you when you say things like that."

"Like what?"

"Like 'a married woman's *first* affair.' I guess it's just semantics, but some words rub me the wrong way. Like 'ex,' for example. When someone refers to their old boyfriend or husband as their 'ex,' it sounds to me as nauseating as someone scratching a blackboard with their fingernails. In some ways, I appreciate your total honesty. In other ways . . . hell, I don't know. It feels like so much emotion and raw feeling corked up inside a test tube. I'm just kind of an experiment to you. Don't get me wrong, I'm not saying we ought to get serious or heavily involved, but it seems to me, sitting across from you now, that I can hear you thinking. And you're analyzing your reactions *to* our lovemaking—the experiment—rather than savoring the lovemaking itself. It just seems strange to me, that's all."

"I'm sorry. It was wonderful. Really. I'm not just saying that. But as funny as this is going to sound, I still feel that I've been faithful to my husband. I was with *you* last night. But it was all done within the context of my relationship with my husband."

"I wish I could be like you," said Ace sarcastically. "Your

life is compartmentalized. Something happens here, an emotion is felt there, and it stays there, never overflowing into a compartment into which it doesn't belong. Most people can't stop the flow of emotions, feelings, events into other aspects of their lives."

"I wish you wouldn't be angry."

"Hell, I'm not angry. I'm just confused. I was confused before last night and I'm still confused. It's not your fault.

"More coffee?" he said, changing the subject.

"No. I really had better be getting back."

"Fine. I'll just be a few minutes," he said, getting up from the butcher-block table and taking his half-finished plate to the sink.

Some people sang in the shower. Ace thought in the shower. With hot water pulsating on his neck, and the rest of the world drowned out, thoughts came. The day could be planned, even some problems solved. This morning he was filled with thoughts about Jenny. What had *she* done last night while he was making love to Connie? And what right did he have to be even the slightest bit ruffled, had she done the same thing he had chosen to do?

Things lately with women had become so serious. So heavy. He longed for some of the carefree, light-hearted fun that could be had in relationships. Hell, now even a casual one-night stand had forced him to be introspective. And he realized that in some way he felt slightly rejected by Connie. He had given her his best and gotten what he had considered at the time to have been the maximum response from her. Only to find the next morning that she had unemotionally placed the experience neatly on the shelf—a trophy to her sophistication to be hung over the mantle next to her husband's accolades. Why couldn't she have at least hinted that he *could* have swept her off her feet, made her do something she wasn't prepared to do? He liked to control things. Or at least enjoyed believing he was in control. Some women were good at that, he thought. That is, making a man *think* he was in control. It was part of an act, this fine balance, that made good relationships even better.

The water went cold.

"Damn," he said, almost leaping out of the shower.

Connie came to the door and peered inside. "Did you say something?"

"There's no hot water."

"Sorry. I must have used too much when I took my shower."

"That's okay. I was done anyhow."

"ANY MESSAGES?" asked Ace after he'd walked into his Hollywood office.

"Eddy Price called," said Bunny Aguirre, tearing off a piece of paper from her message pad and handing it to Ace. "He said it was important and to call if you got in before ten-thirty."

"What time is it now?"

Bunny looked at her watch. "Ten-fifteen."

"Anybody else call?"

"Like Jenny?"

"I didn't say that."

"I know. I did. Hey, Ace, you know, you've been looking like you're carrying the weight of the world around on your shoulders lately. Lighten up."

"Did you get that prescription from a doctor or out of a Cracker Jacks box?"

"No need to be nasty."

"Sorry."

"Life's too short to go around being sad all the time. And if it's woman trouble, that's no big deal. There's lots of fish in the sea."

"Have you been taking a philosophy class at night school lately?"

"You can be condescending if you want to be, but what I'm saying is true. Think about it. What you need is someone to take your mind off the heaviness of love. You need to go have a nice, light, fun time."

Ace started to say something but recalled his philosophical musings in the shower earlier in the morning, when he had come to a similar conclusion. "You might be right, but . . ."

"I'm available."

"For what?"

"To show you a good time. Take in a movie, have a few laughs. Nothing heavy. Just a good time."

"I'll have to think about it, Bunny. But thanks. Right now I've got to get hold of Eddy before ten-thirty."

"Remember what I said."

"How could I forget?" he said, and went into his office.

"EDDY?"

"Ace. You're at work and it's only ten-twenty. You run over the milkman to get in so early?"

"Don't give me a hard time, okay? I usually get here long before now and you know it. I was busy."

"Say no more."

"Don't worry. What's up?"

"We're going out to bring in Maddie Paxton. Thought you might like to join the party."

"Sure. What did you find out about the prints on the gun?"

"Her prints were on it all right."

"I hear a 'but' in your voice."

"Well, the handle's been wiped clean. Maddie's prints were found elsewhere on the gun."

"If it was her gun, that's not too unusual, is it?"

"We might not have anything more than a lot of circumstantial evidence, but we've got enough to bring her in and ask her a few hard questions. I think she'll give it up."

"She's a tough cookie. So, where should I meet you?"

"Meet me in the lobby of NBC. Then you can walk in with me. Can you be there in about thirty minutes?"

"I'm on my way."

"Good. See you there."

AT EXACTLY 11:00 A.M. Eddy Price walked through the double doors of the NBC lobby and flashed a badge to the guard. Eddy made a motion toward Ace, the guard nodded his head, and Ace followed Eddy down the maze of carpeted hallways to Studio C, where *Doctors and Lovers* was supposed to be taping.

"I thought they were going to close things down for a few days," said Ace.

"Apparently they're quick mourners," said Eddy over his shoulder.

Studio C looked like a medium-sized airplane hangar, though

not as well kept. Cameras, mike booms, and endless miles of cables were strewn wall to wall. Two sets were visible—the living room of one of the main characters and the hospital set and elevator of Simon General Hospital. By moving slightly to his left or right, Ace could see that the rooms that looked so real on TV were one-dimensional. The opposite side of the sets were just unpainted boards and nails supported by unfinished two-by-fours. It reminded Ace of a dollhouse. Then it occurred to him that watching soap operas was the natural extension of playing house, trying hard to have grown-up problems, secure in the knowledge that those problems were not real.

The set looked empty, but voices could be heard coming from the back of the set. Eddy, two plainclothes cops, and Ace followed the sound to a half-torn-down set, where Helen Clark was holding court.

Helen, her red hair coiffed to perfection, sat on the edge of a desk around which some twenty-five or thirty people sat, either on folding chairs, living room set chairs, or simply the floor. The foursome entered the scene to Helen's right, so that she did not immediately see them.

"I simply want there to be no misunderstanding about who is in charge now that Owen is gone. Since I am the chairman of the board of the corporation that created this show, nursed it into being, I know more about running it than anyone besides Owen. Therefore, since there is no time to seek out and train someone on such short notice, I will act as the show's producer, at least on a temporary basis."

"Martial law is usually imposed as a temporary measure," said Ace softly to Eddy.

"Shut up."

"Are there any questions?" asked Helen.

A young man Ace recognized as Jerry Russo raised his hand and said, "Do you foresee any major changes in the show's format or personnel?"

"For the immediate future, until I get my sea legs, things will remain status quo."

"What about the director's chores?" asked Maddie Paxton.

"I understand Owen made a change in that area recently, and I believe he knew what he was doing. So we'll stick with it."

Maddie took a deep breath and expelled her obvious disgust in a large, audible sigh.

"Anything else?"

No one raised a hand, so after about thirty seconds, Helen clapped her hands and said, "Okay. Let's get to work."

Everyone got to their feet and slowly made their ways down the hall to their appropriate stations. Eddy stopped Maddie Paxton, who was the last to leave. He withdrew his wallet and flashed his badge.

She didn't look too surprised. "That thing from the prop department or are you really Joe Friday?" she said glibly.

"Neither one, Miss Paxton. It's the real thing and so am I. My name's Eddy Price. I'd like to ask you a few questions. Are you free?"

"I'm available, but never free."

"That's an old gag."

"You looked like the kind of guy who'd like to hear it again."

Eddy looked a little flustered and turned his gaze toward Ace, who said, "I told you she was fun."

"Can we talk here?" asked Eddy.

Maddie paused a moment, put a cupped hand to her ear, and said, "It sounds like it."

"Okay, okay. Where were you the night Owen Clark was killed?"

"Let me see. I remember hearing about it as a news bulletin on TV while I was watching *Family Feud.*"

"So what does that mean?"

"I'm just trying to backtrack a little and give you a truthful answer. That means that I was home. I had been home since about five o'clock. I went for a swim, fixed a little dinner, did my aerobics exercises to the new Earth, Wind and Fire album—side one—then sat down to watch TV. I caught the last few minutes of the NBC national news and settled in to watch *Family Feud*. There, you satisfied?"

"Were you with anyone during this time?"

"No."

"Did anyone see you during this time? A delivery boy, a neighbor?"

"No."

"Did you talk with anyone by phone during this time—that is, did anyone call *you* during this time?"

"No. Not that I know of. Someone might have called while I was doing my exercises. I unplug my phone while I do my exercises. It's got to be continuous exercise to do any good, but I can see that you're a man who knows that."

"I wouldn't be so cute if I were you, Miss Paxton. From what you've told me, you don't seem to have an alibi for the time of the murder."

"So what? I didn't kill Owen. Isn't that more important than an alibi?"

"Do you own a handgun, Miss Paxton?"

Ace and Eddy could both tell that that threw her a little, but it only knocked her slightly off balance. "Yes. And it's legally registered. So?"

"Do you know where that gun is right now?"

"Yes, I do. It's in the drawer next to my bed."

"I'm afraid you're wrong about that. Your gun is down at police headquarters. It was found close to the spot where Owen Clark was murdered. It's got your fingerprints on it, and it has been identified as the weapon that killed Clark. It is also known that you were demoted by Clark recently. So, as you see, an alibi would be pretty handy for you right about now."

That took all the play out of Maddie. She turned slowly and moved over to a large, overstuffed prop chair and sank down into it. She stared straight ahead, trying to grasp her situation.

Eddy followed her over to the chair. When he arrived, she turned, looked up at him, and said, "I'm not answering any more questions without my lawyer."

Eddy nodded to one of the plainclothesmen, who walked over to Maddie and read her her rights.

Eddy walked back to where Ace was still standing away from the action. "Well, what do you think?" asked the cop.

"I don't know. Tell you the truth, she looked extremely surprised when you told her about the gun."

"I should say so."

"No, I don't mean shocked that you found her out. Just totally overwhelmed—like it was the first she'd heard of it."

"Trouble with you, Ace, is that you just don't think women can commit heinous crimes."

"No. I know better than that."

"Forget it. I'd write this one off if I were you."

"I'll be in touch. Thanks for asking me along."

"No sweat. Let me know if you hear anything about that Ashford thing you're working on, okay?"

"Will do."

ACE HAD LUNCH at a health food store in Glendale and put away what he considered to be some fabulous vegetarian spaghetti. He stopped by a Hollywood spa at which a good friend of his was the manager and took a sauna and Jacuzzi. But he still felt like a knot that couldn't be untied when he walked into his office.

"Hi," said Bunny Aguirre.

"Hi, Bunny. Any messages?"

"Cynthia Walcott called. She said you could reach her at her studio all afternoon, till about five-thirty."

"That it?"

"Jenny didn't call."

"Thanks, but that's not what I meant."

"Sure."

Ace started to walk by Bunny's desk and into his office.

"Hey."

Ace turned, and as he did, he got another full dose of Bunny's well-turned tanned right thigh. "Yeah?"

"You busy tonight?"

Ace thought for a second and said, "No. Why?"

"I'd like to ask you out on a date."

"I don't know, Bunny. . . ."

"Look, you need something light in your life right now. Something to take your mind off Jenny. What else would you do tonight?"

"I don't know," he said weakly.

"Probably just go home, have a few drinks, watch some TV, and fall asleep, right?"

"Maybe."

"Pick me up at eight. Here's my address," she said, handing him a piece of paper on which she'd already written her address and phone number. "I know a movie theater near my house that shows risqué foreign films. The sex is the draw, the culture the excuse. It'll be fun. You'll see."

"I don't know. . . ."

"I won't take no for an answer. It's settled," she said, turning her attention back to work.

Ace lifted his eyebrows in acquiescence and stood there, paper in hand, as Bunny began to type. He went into his office, sat down, and tucked the paper into his pocket. Things could be a lot worse, he told himself. Not a day went by that Stephen Kagy didn't hit on Bunny, or that somebody, usually one of Kagy's friends, didn't try to put the moves on Bunny. After all, she was a good-looking woman. What the hell, he finally decided. Things *could* be a lot worse.

He dialed Cynthia's number. "Hello, Cynthia?"

"Yes."

"This is Ace."

"How are you?"

"Fine."

"So what's new?"

"You heard about Owen Clark?"

"Yes. That's shocking."

"Murder often is. But I'm not convinced one way or the other that it has any bearing on what happened to Barry."

"Quite a coincidence."

"True. But I haven't figured out a way to make it all add up straight. And I don't like to be taken too far off the *real* scent by hunches and guesswork."

"I understand. So what *are* you up to, then?"

"I talked with Maddie Paxton yesterday. By the way, the police are questioning her as a suspect in Owen Clark's murder."

"That's ridiculous."

"Not when it was her gun that killed Owen."

"My god."

"I'm going to talk to Helen Clark this afternoon."

"Helen? But why?"

"I'm just trying to grab hold of any loose thread, Cynthia. Remember, I told you that I might not be able to find Barry's killer. It really might have been just a hit-and-run driver who never saw Barry before in his life; you know, some drunk. That might be the explanation. But I'm trying to talk with people who knew him. I'm trying to piece together some kind of picture that would give me something to go on. To be honest, even though I've come up with a grocery list of suspects and motives, I'm not on to any hot leads. So far, lots of people wanted him dead, but I can't pinpoint anyone who would actually do it.

"Of course, there are a few more people I'd like to talk with before I throw in the towel. That's why I want to talk with Helen. If this tack doesn't work, I've been thinking about something else. But it's kind of out of left field. I'd rather not mention it until I'm sure I want to go with it."

"You know, I was just thinking about Maddie."

"Yes?"

"I know she didn't kill Barry because I talked with someone I trust who was at the party that night who said Maddie never left the house all night."

"So what does that have to do with her being arrested for Clark's murder?"

"Just this. Her house was full of people—maybe a hundred guests—the night of the party, just a few days ago. Anyone could have taken the gun then."

"That's true."

"She kept it in her night table next to her bed."

"How do you know?"

"Barry told me. He told her that she ought to hide it better or at least put it away when she was having one of her parties. I mean, that's the most logical place to keep a gun—in a drawer right next to the bed. That's the first place anyone would look."

"You're right. But I'm afraid it doesn't help Maddie very much right now. Only her prints are on the gun."

"Well, I still don't think she did it. What do you think?"

"I don't know. She's a gutsy lady. If she would kill somebody, I don't think she'd be stupid enough to leave the gun lying around to be easily found."

"It doesn't make sense to me."

"But then a lot of things that happen don't make sense. Doesn't make them stop happening. I'll be in touch," he said, and hung up.

ACE SWUNG HIS white Celica, top down, into the semicircular driveway of the Encino Hills palatial estate of Helen Clark. The house was a sprawling one-story white structure. Ace's shoes made a pleasant sound as they scraped across the marble steps leading from the black asphalt to the front door. He pressed a lighted bell and a Japanese man wearing a white coat and black trousers answered the door.

"I'd like to see Mrs. Clark."

"Do you have a card, sir?"

"I've got a whole deck—and chips, if you can get two other players."

The man's face remained impassive. Ace withdrew a card that identified him as a private investigator, handed it to the man, who didn't ask Ace in while he delivered the card to the mistress of the house.

While he stood there, Ace recalled what Cynthia Walcott had told him about Helen Clark's sadomasochistic sexual tendencies. He didn't know anyone who had a real dungeon in his basement. The family room of the eighties? Probably not, he finally decided.

The man in white reappeared and said, "This way."

The marble continued into the foyer and disappeared shortly thereafter, replaced by carpet that felt to Ace like velvet quicksand. The detective was led down several long hallways that were adorned with paintings, each of which had its own lamp poised flatteringly above it.

"You got a souvenir shop on the way out?" asked Ace.

"I beg your pardon, sir?"

"I say, a guy could get lost in here."

"Don't be alarmed, sir. I know the way."

"Great," said Ace, and made a mental note not to ask this guy to perform any stand-up monologues at his next party.

Presently Ace was led into a fully equipped gym by the man in white, who left immediately. Three walls of the room were covered with floor-to-ceiling mirrors. Ace recognized several Nautilus machines lined up in a row. Two Exercycles sat next to the machines. And there, next to the Exercycles, was Helen Clark. Or at least that's who Ace thought it was. He couldn't tell because she was upside down.

"Mrs. Clark?"

"Yes. Mr. Carpenter. Come over here so I can see you."

Ace walked over to the contraption into which Helen Clark was strapped. Her head was pointed toward the floor and her feet toward the ceiling. She was dressed in a black dance leotard and turquoise leg-warmers. Her hair fell down so that it actually touched the floor.

"Good for the back."

"I wouldn't know."

"You ought to try it sometime."

"Yeah, well . . ."

"I saw you today with those policemen, didn't I?"

"Yes."

"See, I do observe things. I also remember seeing you at our party a few nights ago."

"That's *very* observant."

"Therefore, you probably saw the incident between myself and Arlene."

Ace thought about the proper comment, but none came. So he said, "You looked pretty tough."

"I *am* tough, Mr. Carpenter—when I have to be. But I don't like to be tough. Should I be tough with you, or do you like being the aggressive one?"

Ace had visions of Helen Clark spinning out of her back-fixer machine and leading him down to the dungeon. It was a bizarre image. "I'd just like to ask you a few questions."

"Why don't you tell me why you're here first, so I can figure out whether or not I want to answer them. I mean, it isn't every day a private eye comes into my home and wants to ask me questions."

"I'm investigating the death of Barry Ashford."

"Oh, really?"

"Yes. So I'm talking to people who knew him, trying to get a feel for why someone might have wanted to kill him."

"Well, Mr. Carpenter, if you've been doing your homework, you must already have a lengthy list of possible suspects. Barry Ashford was not a very nice man."

"How so?"

"Most of it I'm sure you already know. He was rude, hurtful for no reason, he often caused scenes with people, and he never hesitated to use whatever position and power he had for his own purposes. Personally, I'm glad he's dead. I didn't kill him, if that's what you're thinking. But it would be hypocritical of me to pretend that he was a better man than he was, simply because he's dead."

"Mourning the dead doesn't seem to be your strong suit."

"I imagine that's supposed to be a subtle reference to the fact that I'm not crying my eyes out because my husband just died. Well, Owen was the world's champion philanderer, an egomaniac, a terrible businessman, and we couldn't talk for more than two minutes at a time."

"Sounds like the perfect marriage."

"Oh, in some ways it was. And in our own way we loved each other very much and were quite happy."

"In other words..."

"In other words, I had the money and Owen had a fabulous imagination and a big cock. Simple enough?"

"I don't think I'll need my Apple Two to figure that one out."

"Good."

"Getting back to Barry Ashford, do you know anyone who— more than anyone else—might have wanted to kill him?"

"Hmmm...Oh, it's so hard. It's like going into Saks Fifth Avenue with two million dollars cash that you've got to spend in half an hour. There's just too many choices."

"Take your time. I don't have a meter running."

"Maybe *you* don't, but I've got to get in some tank time before a three o'clock appointment."

"Tank time?"

"My isolation tank, of course. I float for at least half an hour every day. I try to get in an hour, but sometimes it's just not possible."

"Yes." He was going to say he understood but stopped himself.

"Willy Dodd," said the upside-down mouth.

"Willy Dodd?"

"Yes. That's as good a guess as any. After all, some people carry the torch forever."

"What are you talking about?"

"Really, Mr. Carpenter. I shouldn't have to do all your work for you. Barry supplanted Willy as my husband's lover."

"Really."

"Yes, really. Not that it meant a great deal to Owen, simply that he had a new number-one boy. Believe me, the list was long."

"I didn't think your husband was gay."

"Owen gay? Are you serious? I didn't say he was gay.

Saying that Owen was gay would be like saying a baseball player throws to only one base. Owen was a multifaceted sexual being. He reveled in the myriad ways there were to get his rocks off. No, like I say, it's just that Willy Dodd wasn't number one anymore. That hurts a lover sometimes—or so I'm told. Anyhow, Willy bit his tongue for a while, but I'm sure the constant humiliation at the hands of that asshole Ashford weighed heavily on him. By the way, it was Willy who put the shit in Barry's hat."

"Really," said Ace, feigning ignorance.

"Seems to be quite a list of things you don't know. Here's something else you don't know. My husband was embezzling heavy sums of money from the company."

"Really."

"You've got a snappy repartee, Mr. Carpenter. You should read some Sam Spade or Philip Marlowe books. A better patter might make points with some of the people you talk to."

"I'll remember that. You don't seem too upset by the news."

"I'm never surprised by my husband's incompetence and bad taste. And I suppose it doesn't upset me because I'm the only other partner in the company, and though he embezzled several million dollars, it really means very little to me."

"Would he think it would mean something to you?"

"Oh, yes. Indeed he would have. In fact, I'm sure he was scared shitless that I'd find out. Owen was an easily controlled man. Money was the only thing that motivated him more than sex. Perhaps because he was aware that if he were to keep apace with his sexual appetite, there would have to be a constant flow of capital into the project. He also knew that I knew that my money was my only control over him—all you need is one good one. I might have threatened to cut him off had I discovered his crime. Certainly I would have made life miserable for him for a while."

"I wonder what he needed the money for?"

"I'm not going to sit here speculating about that with you, Mr. Carpenter. However, I will say that it's a great deal easier to spend a couple of million dollars than most people who don't have such money realize. One bad market transaction, a bad land development deal, a poor business venture. It's easy. And like I said, Owen was a notoriously poor businessman.

"What time is it?"

Ace looked at his watch. "Ten till two."

"I'm sorry, Mr. Carpenter, but I'm going to have to wrap this little visit up and float for a while."

"Okay. I appreciate your cooperation."

"No problem. Think you could find your own way out?"

"I left bread crumbs behind me."

"Good. Now that's the kind of thing you should say more often. It's not there yet, but you could be a real private eye with a little more work."

"Thanks," said Ace, turning away from her. "Happy floating."

BACK AT THE office Ace scanned the message pad for messages but found none. Apparently Bunny was running an errand for Kagy.

Kagy's door opened just as Ace had his hand on the handle of his own door. "Ace," said Kagy.

Ace turned around to see Kagy ride through his office door on a pink ostrich. The detective did a double take and said, "Stephen, you're riding an ostrich in the office."

"Right. Isn't that something else? It's great. You ever ride one of these suckers?"

"Not inside."

"It's a lot more comfortable than it looks."

A woman dressed in a light blue dance leotard cut up high in the crotch and in the back, so that three-quarters of her buttocks were exposed, appeared in the doorway just behind Kagy.

"Don't hold him by the neck," she instructed Kagy. "He won't be able to breathe."

"Sorry," he said, and let go his grip on the bird. Kagy gingerly got off the ostrich, relinquishing what passed for control to the woman in the leotard. "Want to try it?"

"No, thanks," said Ace. "It's one of my personal rules never to ride an ostrich on an empty stomach."

"So what do you think?" the woman asked Kagy, gently brushing back her dark hair off her forehead.

"It's interesting. Very interesting. I think Bob might go for it, actually. Yeah, I really do. I'll give him a call this afternoon and get back to you after I've talked with him. Okay?"

"Fine."

"And remember to wear that costume if I get you the audition. It's just naughty enough to start a few pulses racing, and enough of the right parts are covered up so that there shouldn't be any problems with the censors."

"What about cable?"

"Let's try that only if we don't get the spot on Bob's show. Cable's less money. Also, less clothes."

"Are you sure the cable show would want me to ride Hector in the nude?"

"Cable's looking for flesh—at least, the guy whose ears I've got is looking for flesh. But, like I say, let's talk about that *after* you see Bob."

"All right. You know," the woman said in a totally sincere manner. "I'm not ashamed of my body. I'm willing to do the act in the nude. No problem."

"That's good to know, Hildy. Really. I'll keep it in mind if I come across something where they need a beautiful girl to take off her clothes."

"Thank you, Mr. Kagy. Come on, Hector," she said, guiding the large bird out of the office.

"Where do you find these people?" asked Ace after Hildy had left.

"They find me. I know from the outside it must look like a crazy business, but really it's just a business like any other business."

"You seem to be getting a lot of animal acts these days."

"Yeah, well, there's a new syndicated show kind of like the *Gong Show,* but with pets. Pet owners bring on their 'gifted, talented pets' and perform with them."

"Sounds ridiculous."

"I know it does, at first. But it's a big hit, actually. Rating points in the Midwest have been really encouraging."

"It still sounds ridiculous."

"Maybe so. Hey, Bunny tells me that you two are going out this evening."

"Don't give me a hard time, okay?"

"*I* won't. But I'll bet you anything Bunny will—give you a 'hard' time, that is."

"That's just the kind of thing I'm talking about. Ease off, okay?"

"Sure, sure. But I don't mind telling you that I'm more than a little envious. I've been trying to get between those beautiful legs for two years now. And nothing. I mean, nothing. How did you do it?"

"She asked me out."

"Oh, come on."

"I don't care whether you believe me or not. She saw that I wasn't feeling too good about Jenny, and I guess she's just trying to cheer me up."

"Oh, that explains it. She took pity on you. Hey, now I never thought about that. Nice angle."

"Stephen, you're too much," said Ace, and walked into his office.

Just then the door opened and Bunny Aguirre oozed sensuously through the door, into the office, and sat down behind her desk.

"Hi, Bunny."

"Hi. Here's your stamps, Stephen," she said, handing him a roll of twenty-twos.

Kagy got a sad look on his face and sat down in one of the chairs in the reception room. He exhaled deeply and slumped down in the chair.

"Something wrong?"

"Oh, nothing, really."

"Okay," she said, and started typing.

"It's just that life's been dealing me a pretty rotten hand lately."

Bunny stopped typing and turned her attention to Kagy.

"How so?"

"Ah, it's not worth talking about."

Again Bunny resumed her typing.

"What the hell, it might do me good to talk about it," said Kagy in a voice that could be heard above the typewriter.

Again Bunny stopped typing and turned her attention to her boss. "What's the problem?"

"Women, Bunny. Women."

"Women?"

"Yes, women. I don't know whether you knew this or not, but I've been seeing this one special woman lately."

"No, I didn't know."

"Well, I have. I took her home to meet my folks—"

"I thought your parents lived in New York?"

"Yes, well, actually I took her to meet my aunt and uncle. They've been like parents to me since I moved out here. And they liked Sarah—that's her name. Yes, they liked Sarah very much. But then who wouldn't? She's a lovely girl. I gave her everything I thought I could never give a woman. I trusted her with my heart."

"And?" said Bunny with only polite interest.

"And she hurt me, Bunny. Hurt me like I've never been hurt before in my life."

"Really?"

"Really."

"I haven't noticed any change in you until just now."

"It just happened. While you were at lunch."

"What happened?"

"She left me for another man," said Kagy, nearly choking on his words and at the same time searching Bunny's face for the reaction of sympathy he was trying so hard to evoke.

"That happens," she said flatly.

Thinking quickly, Kagy tried, "But I talked her into coming back and she . . . she died."

Bunny stopped, a puzzled look frozen on her face. "All this happened while I was at lunch?"

"I'm sitting in the middle of the most traumatic moment of my life. Do you understand what I'm going through?"

"A little."

"Can you sympathize with me at all?"

"Sure, Stephen. That's one hell of a dose of reality for one afternoon."

"I knew you would understand. You're that kind of person."

"Thanks. Oh, by the way, I'm going to be leaving a little early tonight. I've got something to pick up at the cleaners."

Kagy closed his eyes in utter frustration, clenched his teeth, said, "Yeah," got up from the chair, went into his office, and slammed the door behind him.

"HAVE A SEAT, honey," Bunny said to Ace after she had let him into her Los Feliz high-rise apartment. "I hope you don't mind me calling you 'honey.' I call lots of people that. And we *are* out of the office now."

"So we are," said Ace, sitting down on a white couch. Bunny's apartment was decorated in a rustic style with lots of darkly varnished wood furniture: coffee table, end tables, the frames of two chairs, a clock with bronze hands and numbers, a large piece of driftwood in one corner. "Nice place."

"Thanks. Can I get you a drink?"

"Sure. What do you have?"

"I've got your favorite."

"Oh?"

"Absolut vodka."

"How did you know that?"

"I've heard you tell other people what you drink. Also, you sent me out for some a couple of months ago for a little party you were throwing. You told me then how good it was and that it was the only thing you drank."

"Very good. Sure, I'll have some."

Bunny retreated into her kitchen and Ace watched her go. She was wearing tight black slacks and a maroon blouse that tied at the waist, under which, he had noticed when he came in, she was free of encumbrances. She returned in a minute or so with two short glasses filled halfway to the top with clear liquid, each glass containing a couple of ice cubes apiece.

"Those are pretty healthy portions."

"We missed the early show. We've got about an hour to kill before we have to leave. I feel like getting drunk. How about you?"

"Oh, I don't know."

"Come on, honey, loosen up. Let's have a good time. Relax. You've got to learn to relax."

Ace took a sip of his drink. The first sip, as usual, burned a little going down. Still, it was smooth. "You had the bottle in the freezer. Now I didn't tell you *that*, did I?"

"No. But I know a few things on my own."

"I'll bet you do."

"Let's drink to happy times," Bunny said.

"Happy times," said Ace, and raised his glass toward Bunny.

NEARLY AN HOUR later Ace was just finishing up his third hefty glass of Absolut. His head was not spinning, but he knew the effects of the alcohol were hard at work. Still, he felt good. Real good.

"I guess I better get ready," said Bunny. "It's almost time to leave."

"Ready? What's wrong with what you're wearing now?"

"I just want to change; slip into something more comfortable. I'll just be a minute."

"Okay. I'll save your place." Bunny got up from the warm place on the couch she had just occupied and walked out of the room in a way only she and a few other sexual adepts could do, or so Ace was thinking at that moment. "Happy times," he said softly, and raised his glass to Bunny as she disappeared into what he figured was her bedroom.

When Bunny reappeared a few minutes later she was wearing a trench coat.

"What's this all about?" said Ace, surprised at Bunny's new apparel.

"You mean the coat and the high heels."

"Yes. I thought this was casual. You said you were going to slip into something a little more comfortable."

"I did. I don't think I'd be very comfortable walking into the theater without it," said Bunny, and opened her coat to reveal the body of a *Playboy* Playmate. Her breasts were just as he had imagined they would be—firm, round, slightly pointed with petulant, upturned nipples. Her pubic hair was neatly trimmed so that she could wear the kind of bikini that started wars.

"My God!" said Ace. "You look . . . great."

"Thank you. Ready to go?" she said as she closed her coat and reached to turn off a light behind her.

"What?" he asked incredulously.

"We're going to be late if we don't leave now."

"I don't understand."

"Okay, let me explain. You like fantasies, right?"

"Sometimes."

"Well, I do. But fantasies have no real charge for me unless I really think I might be able to live them out."

"Okay. I follow you there, but . . ."

"When I get a little drunk I lose my last remaining inhibitions, and that's when I act out my fantasies. How 'bout you?"

"Well, I've acted out a few fantasies when I was drunk. Or at least I think I have."

"I have a fantasy that you could help me with—if you want to."

"I don't know, Bunny."

"I've tried to cheer you up tonight, right?"

"Yes, but . . ."

"Look, a lot of guys would kill to get a look at what you've just seen. I trust you. You're not a borderline pervert like Kagy. The guy's only a step and a half from adding a few jackets to his wardrobe whose sleeves tie in the back, if you know what I mean."

"He's not that bad."

"It just bugs me how he's been hitting on me for two whole years and won't take a hint. Anyhow, there's been this one fantasy I've been wanting to try for a long time, and I just haven't gotten the right circumstances together to pull it off. If I'm really trying to impress a guy, I don't want to appear to be too off the wall. But you and I, well, we're just good friends, you know? I trust you. I watch you and I see how you act with people. You're a pretty mellow guy and pretty nice-looking."

"So, your fantasy?"

"Don't try to make me feel strange about this, okay?"

"I won't. Don't worry."

"I mean, it isn't that strange, really. Not in comparison to—"

"Bunny, just tell me."

"All right. I want us to go to the movie. We'll sit down front in an unoccupied aisle. Shortly after we arrive, I'll take off my coat and lay it on the seat next to me. You'll put your arm around me, so from the back nothing will seem out of the ordinary. Then, a little while later, you'll get up and walk out of the theater, taking my coat with you. We'll synchronize our watches. Exactly five minutes after that, I'll get up and walk down the main aisle, up toward the front of the theater, and out one of the exits near the screen that will lead directly into the alley, where you'll be waiting with the car and then we'll speed away. Now, how does that sound?"

"That's incredible."

"You like it?"

"Can't you get arrested?"

"Maybe if I did it at a PTA meeting. But this theater has a more sophisticated audience, mostly men. Do you think one of these guys is going to get offended at seeing this body?"

said Bunny, once again pulling back the coat to reveal her gorgeous, perfectly toned body.

"No, I guess not. Bunny, you're an exhibitionist."

"Could be a lot worse. Look, I'm not hurting anyone. If anything, I'm bringing a little cheer into the lives of those who see me. You know what I mean?"

"Yeah, I guess."

"So, are we going to do it or not?"

"I'd be committing a misdemeanor as your accomplice."

"If we get caught."

"It could happen."

"How? We're out and away in a matter of five to ten seconds. Come on. I'm just tipsy enough to finally do it. Come on, Ace. Please."

Bunny sat down on the couch next to him and let the coat fall apart so that it opened up far enough to remind him that she wasn't wearing any panties.

"Oh, what the hell. You're right. There really isn't much of a chance that anything could go wrong. Sure, I'll do it."

"WHERE DO YOU want to sit?" Ace whispered as they walked down the aisle. The movie had just started.

"About the fourth row from the screen on the right-hand side."

Ace walked to the fourth row, let Bunny walk in first, then sat down next to her. She sat low in her seat so that her shoulders were just below the top of the seat.

"Ready?" she said.

"I guess."

Bunny slipped her coat off, folded it, and handed it to Ace, who set it on his lap.

"How long do you want me to sit here?"

"Give me about ten minutes."

The movie was a French film about a rich man who was always trying to get his maid into bed. Polite laughter occasionally filtered throughout the theater.

Finally Bunny said, "Okay, now."

"Five minutes. You'll be outside in five minutes, right?"

"Right. And you better be there."

"Hey, I'll be there. Don't get uptight. Are you all right?"

"Yeah, yeah. I'm just a little nervous. It's all part of the excitement. Now go on. I'll see you out back."

Ace got up, tucked the coat under his arm, and walked up the aisle, through the lobby, and out to his car.

When he got into his car, his heart was beating fast. He was nervous, too. He turned the key over and the engine didn't catch hold. "Oh, shit!" He tried it again. Same result. He tried it again, this time thinking about Bunny running out into an empty alley totally nude. This time the engine turned over. He breathed a sigh of relief and pulled away from the curb. Within a minute he was parked at the back door to the theater. He checked his watch. "Two more minutes," he said to himself. He reached over and unlocked the passenger door so that Bunny could just jump in. He was starting to have second thoughts about his participation when headlights from another car pulling into the alley lit up his car. His heart began to beat faster. The car pulled up in back of Ace and stopped. He looked in his sideview mirror and recognized the black-and-white design of the car. "Oh, shhhit!" he said, and pounded the steering wheel with the palms of his hands.

Ace rolled down his window as the uniformed officer walked slowly up beside the car. Ace put both hands on the steering wheel. He knew the routine.

"Good evening, sir," said the officer.

"Hi. Something wrong?"

"You tell me."

"No, there's nothing wrong. Okay?"

"What are you doing parked in the alley by yourself?"

Ace searched his mind for a single answer that wouldn't bring down the house, but none came. "I came here to think," was the one he finally settled on.

"To think. You parked your car in a dark alley to think."

"That's right. Anything wrong with that?"

"Probably."

"I mean anything illegal."

"Would you mind stepping out of the car for a moment?"

"Sure, but I hope this isn't going to take too long; I've got to be somewhere shortly."

"What's that?" asked the cop, pointing to the coat on the front seat.

"A coat."

"Bring it out with you."

Ace got out of the car and brought the coat with him. The officer unfolded the coat. "You wearing this coat?"

"Yes. Earlier."

"Looks a little small."

"Did you ask if I was *carrying* or *wearing* the coat?"

"Wearing."

"Ah, I thought you said 'carrying.' You see, that's my girl-friend's coat. I was carrying it for her. I'm going to see her a little later on. She left her coat at my house last night. You understand."

"Yeah. Let's see your license."

Ace withdrew his wallet, took out his driver's license, and gave it to the officer. "There ya go."

"Look, you could save us a little time here if you just told me what the hell you were doing back here. You doing some-thing sexual back here? Be straight with me."

"Sexual? Like what? Definitely nothing sexual."

At that very moment the theater's back door burst open and Bunny Aguirre flew through it wearing her high heels, a watch, and a big grin. The officer dropped Ace's license on the ground and grabbed for his gun. Ace closed his eyes. Bunny Aguirre had her hand on the car door handle before she realized that the cop had a gun on her.

Bunny screamed and covered what she could of herself with well-positioned hands. The cop put his gun back in its holster and looked at Ace for an explanation. Ace just tilted his head and lifted his eyebrows the way people do when no explanation, especially the truth, could possibly set things right.

Bunny's screams had aroused the attention of the people in the house right behind the theater. Those people happened to be a troop of Boy Scouts, who, led by a large balding man with glasses, poured into the alley, scout knives drawn, to defend the woman who had screamed.

Ace picked up the coat, which was now lying on the ground, and tossed it to Bunny, who had taken refuge in Ace's car. The Scouts were yelling and looking for someone to put their knives into when the cop finally said, "I still don't get it."

"You know Eddy Price?" asked Ace as calmly as he could.

"Yeah?"

"He's a friend of mine."

"I REALLY APPRECIATE this, Eddy," said Ace as he took another sip of coffee while sitting on the side chair next to Eddy's desk.

"The coffee or keeping you off the deviate's dean's list?"

"Look, it's not so bad. I mean, we weren't molesting children or anything like that."

"Maybe, but from what I hear I don't think some of those Boy Scouts will ever be the same."

"Big deal. I spent my entire adolescence just looking for *pictures* of nude women. I don't think anyone saw anything that will keep him in analysis very long."

"Yeah, I must admit things have changed a lot since we were kids."

"I remember we had a contest, my buddies and I, to see who could find a picture of a naked woman, full frontal view. That contest went on for almost two years."

"What about *National Geographic?*"

"That didn't count. In fact, *National Geographic* went a long way toward warping my sexuality. For a long time we didn't think *white* women even had breasts at all. Finally, after nearly two years, one of the guys found some pornography in his father's drawer. Unfortunately it was a nudist magazine with all the genitals air-brushed out. But since none of us had seen real female genitalia before, we still weren't sure what it was supposed to look like. Finally we figured out what was happening. Another one of the guys had a sister who was about ten years older than we were. He had seen her taking a bath and assured us that whatever was down there, it had hair around it. That meant our nudist magazines were copping out on us.

"We were all just about to go crazy after all this time in search of the Holy Tail when we came across something that changed our lives. You know those things like little periscopes you use to see over people? It's got a series of little mirrors in it."

"Yeah, I think so."

"Anyhow, the guy with the older sister said that his sister always took a shower at the same time every Saturday evening, around six o'clock—she was always getting ready for her date around that time. Anyhow, one Saturday night, periscope in hand, all us guys waited anxiously outside the bathroom window for this guy's sister to take her shower. We were so excited we could hardly stand it. Not only were we going to get to see 'it,' but it was going to be live, not a picture.

"Finally the light went on in the bathroom, the shower water started running, and we cautiously put the periscope up to the window. I can recall it now as if it were yesterday. Seeing that naked body, every inch of it from head to sweet, taut young nipples; to flat stomach; to round, smooth hips; to that glorious tuft surrounding those little pink lips; down to her long, freshly shaved, muscled legs. I'll never forget how I felt as long as I live. I had finally seen it. A ritual had been completed."

"When was this?"

"Last winter when I was home for Christmas."

"Come on," Eddy said, scowling.

"I was about twelve. Can you imagine how easy it is to see pussy these days? You can browse through the magazines at the checkout stands in the supermarket and see fiery-red pink."

"I hear this babe you were putting on the show with tonight was a real looker," said Eddy, changing the subject.

"It was Bunny, my secretary."

"Bunny! No shit!" the cop said with some enthusiasm. "If you ever want to play party games again, I'll give you my address. She could make a dead man sing."

"Yeah, she's kinda cute."

"Yeah, *real* cute. Cute enough to just about get you free room and board as a ward of the state for a few days."

"Hey, I appreciate your putting in a good word for me, Eddy. No foolin'."

"I put in a word all right. I don't know how good it was, but it did the trick. That's the bottom line."

"Maybe I can return the favor. At least a little part of it."

"I'm listening."

"I had a talk with Helen Clark this afternoon."

"The grieving widow. You know, she didn't look too upset this afternoon when she was addressing the troops."

"She isn't. She misses Owen's love club, but that's about it. Anyhow, she told me that Owen had been embezzling funds from the corporation."

"Interesting."

"I can't say I've got much more than that. I just thought you might like to know."

"How was she taking it?"

"Like she owned a mountain and somebody just made off with a bucket of dirt. She seemed to take it in stride. But she did seem to think that Owen would have done his best to hide his crime from her, afraid she'd try to put him through some tough paces."

"Or maybe cut off his allowance."

"Maybe. Anyway, there it is. It might be something, it might be nothing."

"Maybe your boy Ashford was blackmailing Clark about the missing funds and got killed for his trouble."

"Then who killed Clark? Which reminds me, how's your case shaping up against Maddie Paxton?"

"We've got enough to sink her in debt to her lawyers for a good while, but it's all circumstantial. While the only prints on the gun are hers, the handle's been wiped clean. Add to that the easy access any number of people have had to the gun recently and the fact that the gun was so easy to find, I'm just not sure we could make it stick. But right now she's the best we got."

"So what are you going to do?"

"We turned her loose a few hours ago. Told her to keep in touch, not to leave town, the whole routine. Tell the truth, her lawyer was making us look kinda bad there at the end. But I haven't given up on her yet."

"Maybe you should go back to the old standby."

"You mean the close relative?"

"In this case, Helen Clark."

"Sure, why not? From what you tell me, she's got a motive—her husband was embezzling company funds. How much money is involved, anyhow?"

"She said a couple of million."

Eddy blew some air out his lips that passed for a whistle. "Three mil. People get killed for a whole lot less."

"But remember I told you it was nothing to her. I'd be willing to swear that if there ever were a woman who wouldn't kill for money, it would be Helen Clark."

"Maybe. Maybe she's just a good actress."

"Maybe."

"You know that guy Corey Eastland you told me about?"

"Willy Dodd's alibi, the guy with the bookstore over on Hollywood Boulevard."

"Right. We ran a check on him. He's pretty clean."

"That's a strange way to put it."

"Well, he hasn't got a record. We talked to a few people who live in the same building he does and a few store owners who work near the bookshop, and they say the guy is weird."

"By all means, let's lock the guy up and throw away the key. Look, if being weird were a crime, this city would be just one solid jailhouse. Were any of these fine citizens any more specific?"

"One of the tenants in the building where he lives, an old lady—says she's lived there for forty years, right below Eastland's apartment—says she hears things coming from his apartment."

"Things? Cooking noises, a loud TV?"

"Screams, moaning, sounds of people beating each other up."

"Come on."

"That's almost word for word."

"Anyone else?"

"The building's manager says Eastland pays his rent on time, but admitted that tenants with apartments close to Eastland's sometimes complain about noises. He said loud parties; he didn't say screaming. And the owners of the store next to the bookshop—an incense and poster shop—said they thought Eastland was a psycho because he once dumped their garbage out into the alley when they'd put some of it in his bin by mistake. Of course, these two characters were dressed like Sonny and Cher and talked like they had listened to one too many Jimi Hendrix albums with the volume on ten."

"Any connection between Eastland and Dodd?"

"None that we're aware of."

"Now, this piece of news might fall into the category of simple gossip, but Helen Clark told me that Willy Dodd used to be one of her husband's many male lovers and that Barry Ashford eased him out of Clark's bed and favor. Yet my client thinks Ashford was as straight as an arrow."

"Sharp arrows find their ways into all kinds of holes."

"I just thought I'd pass it along. Look, I think I'll call it a night."

"You going over to Bunny's?"

"No."

"Jenny's?"

"Come on, Eddy. It's been a long day," said Ace, standing and downing the last bit of cold coffee from the Styrofoam cup. "Thanks again."

"No sweat. Only next time, let me know where Bunny's gonna do her thing in advance. Okay?"

"Right," said Ace, who already had one hand on the glass door that led to the street. He pushed it and took in a deep breath of stale air.

IT WAS ABOUT twelve-thirty by the time Ace put the key in the door, opened it, and saw Marlowe dancing around on the hardwood floor, wagging his tail like an out-of-control flamenco dancer. Ace undressed, put on his robe, poured himself a glass of Absolut over ice, and sat down at the piano. Marlowe curled up underneath the piano, resting his nose on top of Ace's bare feet.

The phone rang. Ace's heart skipped a beat. Pictures of Jenny sprang hard into his mind. He wanted it to be her.

"Hello?" he said, his heart beating rapidly.

"Inspiration Tower?"

Ace let out a sigh of pent-up tension. "Nope. You've got the wrong number." It happened once every few months, usually late at night. His number was similar to the Inspirational Tower's number. Maybe people needed help more late at night than during the day.

THE SMOG WAS thick the next morning. It looked to Ace as though someone had placed a piece of wax paper over the city's skyline. The freshly ground coffee, which had been whipped in the blender and sprinkled with nutmeg, tasted good. Ace took a swig and then dialed the phone.

"Hello," came the weary voice on the other end.

"Hello. Julie?"

"Yes."

"Hi, this is Barry Lyndon," said Ace.

"Oh, yeah, the writer."

"Right. Look, I'm kind of interested in getting in touch with

Jerry Russo. You know how I might be able to reach him?"

"I don't have his home number on me," she snapped. "And you shouldn't call so early on a Saturday."

"I'm sorry," he said, knowing he was being pushy calling her at home for a favor.

"Look," Julie sighed. "Normally I'd have no idea how to get in touch with Jerry on a weekend. Except today."

"Where is he today?"

"He mentioned he'd be over at Neil Hamilton's studio in Hollywood."

"Neil Hamilton?"

"He's the guy who does the posters for the stars. Neat guy. He took some pictures of me one night."

"Really."

"Yeah. Guy really knows what he's doing."

"Yeah, I'll bet. Look, I'd really like to see Jerry today. Can you tell me how to get to Neil Hamilton's studio?"

"Okay. It's at the corner of Sunset and Gardner, right next to the Russian restaurant. Can't miss it. His name's on the front door in turquoise neon."

"Yeah, that'd be hard to miss. Thanks, Julie. I owe you another lunch sometime."

"Yes, you do," she said, and hung up.

THE JUICE TO Neil Hamilton's neon sign was turned off, but the name could still be clearly read on the wooden door. Ace Carpenter used the handle and walked inside.

Hamilton's reception room was a gallery of recognizable faces, bodies, and images all displayed in the most commercial manner possible. A redhead behind the desk looked up from her magazine when Ace walked in. She put the magazine aside and said, "May I help you?"

"Is Jerry Russo here?"

"Uh-huh. He's inside with Neil."

"Think they'd mind if I went inside?"

"Uh-huh. You a fan or something?"

"I'm a reporter," he lied.

"That's worse."

"Than what?"

"Than just about anything," she said, twisting her cute little overly lipsticked mouth into a sign of disgust.

"You ever have leprosy?"

"Yuck. You mean like in *Ben Hur?*"

"Yeah."

"No. That's gross."

"It's not worse than that," said Ace. "Look, do they ever come up for air in there?"

"Yeah. Neil should be taking a break in a few minutes."

"Mind if I wait?"

"It's a free country," she said, then picked up her magazine, turned to a makeup layout, and alternately read and looked at herself in a desk mirror she had carefully placed next to the telephone.

The wait wasn't too long. The magazines in the reception room weren't the usual *Field and Stream* or *National Geographic*. They were colorful and filled with lots of flesh, much of which had been captured for print by Hamilton. Ace recognized the face of Barry Ashford on the cover of a woman's magazine. Checking inside, he was able to ascertain that Hamilton had indeed been the photographer.

The door opened and Neil Hamilton stepped into the waiting room. The receptionist regarded Ace as she would something she had spilled on her Danskin and couldn't quite get off. "This guy wants to see Jerry," she said. "He's a reporter."

Without missing a beat, Hamilton, who stood just under six feet, wore jeans, tennis shoes, and a light blue T-shirt upon his lean, muscled, tanned body, turned and said, "For whom?"

"I beg your pardon?"

"You're a reporter for what magazine?"

"American Teen," said Ace, glancing down at the magazine with Barry Ashford's picture on it.

"He's inside," said the photographer, tilting his head toward the doorway to his studio. "It's his decision whether he wants to talk with you or not. We're taking ten. I don't know what you can do in ten minutes, but be my guest."

"Thank you," said Ace, and stood up and walked into the studio just as the redhead was lighting Hamilton's cigarette.

The studio was about thirty feet square and housed three strategically placed photo umbrellas, a camera on a tripod, and a large roll of white paper that descended from about ceiling height to the floor, where it eventually curled and rolled out onto the floor like a magic carpet.

At first Ace didn't see Russo, but then he spotted him sitting toward the back of the studio off to the right of where the white paper splashed onto the floor. Russo sat making faces at himself in a bulb-ringed mirror.

"Hi."

Russo spun around with a look composed of equal parts of embarrassment and surprise. "Yes?" he said tentatively.

"Barry Lyndon," said Ace, and extended his hand. "I'm from *American Teen* magazine."

"Barry Lyndon? Isn't that the name of a movie?"

"As a matter of fact it is. That way people always remember. Artists are always using pseudonyms. I'll bet Jerry Russo isn't your real name, is it?"

"Well, actually Russo isn't my real last name. *American Teen*, eh? I talked with someone from that magazine a few weeks ago."

"Tell the truth, I'm not actually on staff or anything. I'm a free-lancer. I figured that since you're so hot right now," said Ace, using all the hot-buttered praise he could spread over Russo, "that even if *American Teen* didn't use the piece—which they still might—someone would pick it up."

"Makes sense. Hey, haven't I seen you around the set? Yeah, weren't you on the set when Maddie Paxton was arrested?"

Ace coughed a little, giving himself some time to come up with a good reply. "Yes, I was."

"You're not a cop, are you?"

Ace laughed his best laugh and said, "No. I was just there doing a piece for one of the local trades about what was going to happen to the show after Owen Clark's murder."

"Okay," said the actor, satisfied. "Ask away." Russo turned back to the lighted mirror and started mugging again.

"Things are really going well for you now that you're the primary male lead on the show. Your whole career seems to have taken off. What was the real breakthrough for you?"

Not bothering to look away from the mirror, Russo said, "This may not be . . . hey, can I speak off the record first, then have you phrase it some nice way?"

"Sure, Jerry. You can trust me." This kid *is* new in town, Ace thought.

"Fact is, my good luck came from the worst possible luck

for someone else. I mean, Barry's death changed everything for me. I was supposed to be written out of the show. Then, just at the right moment, Barry gets killed, he's written out, and I'm sittin' here posing for posters. Life's crazy, you know?"

"Yeah, I know," said Ace. "Did you know Barry Ashford very well before his death?"

"Nah. But then I don't suppose anyone else did, either. He wasn't the kind of guy who opened up easily. He and I had a few drinks together, but that was about it. Which side do you like better?" asked Russo, turning both sides of his profile toward Ace.

"Do it again."

"You can be honest. I'm just curious to see if your opinion matches mine," Russo said, showing off his two profiles again.

"The left side," said Ace positively.

"Yeah, that's what I think, too."

"Wasn't there a party the night Barry was killed?"

"Yeah. Over at Maddie Paxton's place. Nice place."

"I understand someone put a pile of shit in Ashford's hat."

"That's right. Can you imagine that? And he fell for it. Shit in his hair. It was a mess. Of course, everyone knew that Willy did it. Willy Dodd; he is—or was—the head writer for the show. But no one was going to say anything. You know how it is."

"Sure, I know how it is. So, you were the person to most directly benefit from Barry's death."

"I know. I readily admitted it."

"So you did," said Ace with no accusation in his voice. "You think he was murdered, or do you buy what the papers say—just random hit-and-skip?"

"I don't know. I try not to think about negative things like that too much. I know *I* didn't do it, if that's what you're trying to get at."

"No."

"Jerry," paged Neil Hamilton as he came into the studio.

"Over here," said Russo.

"Time to go back to work," said the photographer, checking his tripod-mounted camera.

"Look, I've got to go," said Russo. "Best time to catch me is late in the morning on the set, say eleven-thirty, just before we break for lunch."

"Great. In the meantime, I'll check with the magazine and

see if they still want me to do a piece so close to the one they've apparently assigned to someone else."

"Whatever. Nice to meet you, Barry," Russo said, extending his hand as he stood up.

"Thanks," said Carpenter, and shook Russo's hand. Russo returned to the white paper backdrop, and for a moment Ace was alone with the lighted mirror. He looked at himself from a few angles, then back at Russo, who was now being posed by Hamilton. The detective laughed a little laugh out his nose as he thought about how easily some people can make a buck.

"HELLO?"

"Jenny?"

"Yes. Hi, Ace."

"What's up?"

"Two things. First of all, I've got two tickets to see Alvin Ailey tomorrow at Royce Hall. Secondly, I think we ought to talk."

Ace hesitated. "You might be right about needing to talk. I'm not sure about my schedule. If something happens . . ."

"I could leave the ticket at the box office for you," Jenny quickly added.

"Okay. What time does it start?"

"Two."

"Fine. I'll be there. If anything comes up and I can't make it, I'll call you at home tonight."

"Okay. See you tomorrow."

"Right," said Ace, and hung up. He'd just poured a shot of Absolut when the phone rang again. It was Cynthia Walcott.

"Just checking in to get a progress report."

"No real changes, Cyn. I'm kind of feeling like I'm just taking your money. Sure, I'm working, putting in the time, but I don't feel any closer to any results that are going to make you feel any better."

"You let me worry about that. Money is no object at this point."

"Let's get together for brunch Monday and I'll tell you what I've found out. Also, I might have an idea about an entirely different tack to take with this thing. But I'll need your approval."

"Fine. Let's say the Old World Restaurant, eleven-thirty Monday morning."

"You saying it is good enough for me. See you then," said Ace, and hung up.

Ace needed a little break to get his mind off of things. He took the phone off the hook and tried to play the Baldwin, but he couldn't sit still. A long walk with Marlowe didn't help either. Ace was restless.

He hopped in his white Celica and began making his way through afternoon traffic. He found a parking space across the street from a bookstore on Hollywood Boulevard. Ace turned off the motor, tuned into the all-jazz station, clicked his seat back a notch or two, and waited for Corey Eastland to close up shop. Ace didn't know exactly why he wanted to tail Eastland, just that his curiosity was aroused by Eddy's *"pretty clean"* description of him.

Shortly after six-thirty Corey Eastland, dressed in beige corduroy slacks and matching jacket, flipped the Closed sign around in the window and pulled the door shut behind him, checking it once to make sure it was locked.

Ace propped his seat up again, pulled away from the curb, and followed Eastland to a parking lot a block and a half away, where the bookstore proprietor got into a metallic blue VW and pulled into the boulevard's thinning rush-hour traffic.

The ten-minute drive took Ace east on Hollywood Boulevard, past where it intersects with and becomes Sunset, a few more blocks east until they hit Morehead, upon which both cars turned left and drove down a commercial street that snaked along the foothills. A few body shops and car-painting establishments set the tone for the neighborhood.

Finally Eastland pulled his VW onto a short cul-de-sac, parked, got out, walked back to Morehead, and went into the entrance of a blue building that was lighted by a simple white bulb.

Ace pulled on past the building by about a half a block, parked, and went to the entrance Eastland had just disappeared into. A small hand-painted sign read "Gordon's Spa," and an arrow pointed up the steps to the right. Ace climbed the stairs to a small landing, where he was confronted by a man sitting behind a small desk reading a paperback book, the cover of which was folded under. He was wearing a white tank top, yellow sweat-suit pants, and green sneakers. He was balding, and the overhead light glistened off the top of his head.

"Ten dollars," said the man.

Ace took out his wallet, found a ten, and slid it across the desk to the man, who had turned around to a peg board upon which hung about fifty keys. The man took one off a tiny hook and exchanged it for Ace's picture of a dead president.

There was only one door to go through, so after returning the bald man's smile, Ace opened the door and went inside.

It was another world. The building's front, the unpretentious steps, and the man behind the desk did nothing to prepare the detective for what he found awaiting him inside.

The place was immense, probably a converted warehouse. As Ace descended the steps, loud music throbbed in his ears and the eyes of at least a dozen men scrutinized him from head to toe—and in between. To the left of the bottom of the steps was a large Jacuzzi filled with naked men. To the right was a snack bar, where several men, some wearing towels, some wearing nothing more than a friendly smile, sat on stools sipping soft drinks or eating sandwiches. Beyond that Ace could just make out a room in which a large TV screen was filled with the picture of two men necking. By the time he arrived at the bottom of the steps a tall black woman with large breasts and a towel wrapped around her waist was waiting to greet him.

"Hi," said the woman in a throaty voice.

"Hi."

"First time here?"

"Yes," said Ace somewhat uncertainly.

"Let me show you to the lockers."

"Thanks," said the detective, and followed the black beauty past the Jacuzzi, up a flight of stairs, past about a dozen rooms marked Private, and finally into a locker room that also contained a large shower room and sauna.

Ace found the locker number that matched the one on his key and changed into the towel that he was given by the black woman. As he wrapped the towel around him, he looked for Corey Eastland but couldn't find him.

"You're kind of cute, in a rugged sort of way," said the black girl.

"Thanks. You're not so bad yourself." Ace felt somewhat lucky to have found not only what seemed to be the only woman in the place, but also one who looked pretty sexy. Her breasts were, in fact, quite beautiful.

The black girl moved closer to Ace until they were so close that only a volume detailing the ethical code of a politician could have slipped between them. It was then that Ace could tell. She might have had great breasts, but she also had some excess baggage down below.

"Shit!" said Ace, and pulled away, trying to minimize his total shock.

"You didn't think..." said the half boy, half girl. "Why, you sure did. You thought I was a woman." He/she smiled sympathetically. "It's cool. Nobody here makes anybody do anything they don't want to do. My name's Bernice," she said, and extended her hand.

"Barry. Barry Lyndon," said Ace, shaking Bernice's hand and composing himself.

"Isn't that—"

"Yeah. Quite a coincidence."

"Well, nice meetin' you, Barry. I'll be around if you need me," she said, then winked and slinked away.

Just outside the locker room was a sign that read Maze. Ace followed the arrow, and immediately he was plunged into near total darkness—at least, it was that way until his eyes adjusted to it. After they did, he followed a carpeted path through what was quite literally a maze of carpeted walls. Occasionally he would come across a naked man standing alone, trying to make eye contact. Once, a man put his arm on Ace's shoulder, but Ace just smiled and shook his head as though he'd just passed up a second helping of potatoes.

Farther into the maze, more activity was taking place. Off to the right of one of the paths, a large square room was filled with naked male bodies orally copulating each other. One thing that had puzzled Ace earlier on during his mystical trek was that occasionally he would see a hole in the wall. Its purpose finally became known to him when, near the end of the maze, a penis protruded through a hole and it was given the attention it sought by an anxious man who dashed toward it like a football fan to a two-dollar Super Bowl ticket.

Having reached the end of the maze, Ace started to wind his way back out. The thought occurred to him as he did that he might be stuck in there forever. It wasn't a pleasant thought. He passed the room with the half dozen or so men in it. This time Ace got a glimpse of several faces. One of them was

Corey Eastland's. Following the hirsute contour of Eastland's body, Ace discovered the head of Willy Dodd connected to it in a rather intimate fashion.

In a matter of a few minutes Ace was able to find his way out of the maze and back to the locker room, where he changed back to street clothes. He had reached the top of the stairs when he turned around to take a last look at Gordon's Spa. Bernice was sitting in the Jacuzzi looking up at him. She smiled and waved. Ace smiled back. But he didn't wave.

As he pulled his Celica back into the light traffic on Morehead, Ace now knew that Eastland and Dodd were willing to do things for each other. He wondered if they were willing to lie for each other.

Ace showered when he got home, and warmed his insides with a cold shot of Absolut. He called Eddy Price and informed him of the heretofore unknown connection between Corey Eastland and Willy Dodd.

THE HOUSE LIGHTS were going down when Ace walked quickly down the aisle to his seat. Jenny looked happy to see him and whispered, "Hi, honey," and kissed him on the cheek.

The dance concert was excellent—lithe, muscled bodies, a liquid, living monument to the human form, bathed in pastels and animated by an innate genius as much akin to the spirit as to the flesh. Ace had seen Ailey's troupe perform several times, and Sunday's show was a combination of old numbers and new. As he sat and watched, occasionally he caught a glimpse of Jenny out of the corner of his eye. She sat entranced, all reality suspended but for the one she shared with the artists on stage. He knew that she ached to be up there. That was her goal, to feel those magic moments where the spiritual electricity passed between artist and audience.

And just when he was certain that Jenny was lost to any other reality, without taking her eyes from the pulsating stage, she took his hand and held it tightly. Maybe it was his imagination, but he thought that he could feel a surge of energy fill his body.

•   •   •

"I PARTICULARLY liked the first solo," said Jenny, sipping on a Baileys in the Westwood Inn, a small restaurant just a few blocks from the UCLA campus in Westwood Village.

"The piece where he initially appeared to be running against the wind."

"Yes. It took my breath away."

"It was lovely," said Ace, smiling. How could he do anything else? he thought, looking across the table at her glowing face.

"I've got some news," she said, after sipping again from her tiny aperitif glass.

"I'm listening."

"Cynthia and I have decided to form our own company."

"That's wonderful," said Ace, genuinely happy for her.

"Not only that, but we have an angel. Cynthia knows a man who is willing to fund the company and has connections so that we can stage several legitimate shows here in California over the next year, starting in about four months."

"That's great news, Jenny. Really great. Your dream is coming true."

"It's a step in the right direction. I've met with the backer, and since I will be the principal dancer, I'm going to be paid enough to live on—at least for the next year. So . . . I'm going to quit my nightclub dancing job and work on this thing full-time."

"Sounds like your whole life is changing . . . for the better."

"I think so, Ace. I really think so," she said, her excitement dancing on her face.

"I'm genuinely happy for you," he said, and slid a hand across the table and placed it on one of hers. "You said you wanted to talk."

Jenny took a deep breath and the look of gaiety was washed away by something that looked more serious. "I think we're at a crossroads in our relationship," she said, her eyes just now focusing on Ace.

"I agree. What road do you want to take?"

"I love you."

"That doesn't answer my question."

"It might be a place to start."

"Maybe. But loving each other doesn't stop a lot of people from going their separate ways."

"Do you love me?"

"Yes, Jenny, I *do*. But things seem to have changed between us recently. I admit that I was hurt by the fact that you didn't want to move in with me, solidify our relationship more, make some commitments. I was just ready then. Apparently you weren't."

"It's not too late to reconsider, is it?"

"Moving in?"

"Yes."

"Is it just because you need somebody to share the rent now that you're quitting your job?"

Jenny withdrew her hand from under Ace's. "That's not fair," she said angrily. "That has nothing to do with it."

"I'm sorry. But this whole reversal leaves me a little confused."

"I was confused for a while, too, after you asked me to move in. Very confused. I'd never lived with anyone since I moved out from my parents' house, and that was more than ten years ago. The idea of moving in with you scared me. It had all the wrong connotations in my mind. I wasn't ready to abandon my dreams and become half of a *couple*. To me, it was like taking myself out of the game—puttering around the house, doing twice as much laundry, twice as many dishes, whether I wanted to or not; having my plans be contingent on fitting in with what someone else wanted to do. I hadn't given my dream all the chances it deserved. You know what I mean?"

"Yes, I know. But I never asked you to sign up for KP duty."

"I know that I was just looking for the worst aspects of things and magnifying those. But that's what happened to my mother. She was a dancer when she was young. She had offers and could really have done something great. I know it. But my father gave her an either/or deal and she was madly in love with him at the time, so she gave up dancing. She tries not to regret anything in her past, but I know she wishes she had called my father's bluff and at least given her career some more time. She told me the story so many times that it's become a part of me. Today she lives through my accomplishments. Whenever I tell her about my dancing—at the studio—and the plans I've got, her eyes light up and for a moment she sees herself there on stage living out her potential, her dreams."

"How does your father feel about your career?"

"He wants me to get 'this dancing thing' out of my system and get married."

"I guess I presented, or at least represented, a pretty undesirable choice to you."

"I just panicked. I felt closed in, like I was settling. You know what I mean?"

"I think so."

"Like I was settling for something less than my ultimate dream. It's real hard to explain, but I've never done that before. Most people drop their dreams and any chance of obtaining them as soon as they get out of school, or soon after. Me, I've stuck in there even though my father and lots of other people said I was just fooling myself. Sometimes I felt so foolish and it would have been so easy to take the path of least resistance. But I didn't.

"When you asked me to move in with you, I was really torn in two. I loved you—as I love you now—but all these other things were going through my mind and I felt like I was spinning out of control."

"Like with that guy who went to your place a few nights ago?" Half of him wished he hadn't said it, the other half was glad the words had finally found their way out.

Her eyes met his and for a moment she did not speak. "I was confused, honey. I felt backed into a corner and it was just a crazy way to try to break away; to try to see what it was like to be away from you." Jenny put her hand back on Ace's hand. He had thoughts of pulling it away but didn't. He couldn't blame Jenny too much. After all, he'd felt some confusion himself and had bedded Connie during that time. But he had found no answers there. As apparently Jenny had found no answers, either.

"So how did it feel—to be away from me?"

"I'm here, aren't I?"

"Yeah. But I'm still not sure what that means."

"You asked me to move in with you. I think I'd like to give it a try."

"Why? Why the change of heart?"

"Several reasons. My love for you is an important one. Another is that I realized that what you offered and what I feared most were not necessarily the same thing. After all, you're *not* my father and I'm not my mother. That scene was played out a long time ago."

"How does what just happened with the dance troupe affect things?"

"Well, I don't know how to explain it, except that when I heard about it, I felt wonderful. But something was missing. I wanted to have someone to share it with. Someone who knew what it meant to me, someone I loved. That's you. It's a turning point in my life. It's a new chapter. It's an achievement that no one can take away from me. I guess it makes me feel a little less desperate, less defensive about trying to keep all the demons away from my little dream so that it won't shatter or be sacrificed to some man trying to subordinate them to his own desires. I wasn't ready to get swallowed up. But I don't feel that threat anymore. Especially not from you."

"How would you feel if this golden opportunity of yours fell through? Would our relationship hang in the balance?"

"I'm not sure I understand what you're getting at."

"I mean a good relationship should be held together by trust, love, commitment, not on how well the breaks of life seem to be going. Because they won't always be going in your favor."

"I didn't mean that the major reason I decided to change my mind was because of this break. But it helped. It's an achievement; something that can never be taken away. I may go further, I may not. But it's mine, I earned it. In a way it's like a giant weight being lifted from my shoulders. I don't have to prove myself to my critics—and to myself—any longer. I wasn't a fool for sticking with my dancing this long."

"I'm happy for you, Jenny. Honestly I am. But I'm going to need a little time to think things out. I mean, I was all ready to write our relationship off. Now this. I need some time to think about it."

"That's fair," she said, squeezing Ace's hand a little tighter. "I never meant to hurt you. You know that, don't you?"

"Sure, I know. I'm going to be out of town for a few days, so let's talk when I get back."

"Where are you going?"

"I've got to check with Cynthia first, but I think I'm going to Boulder to follow up on a lead I got when I searched Barry Ashford's house. If Cynthia wants to spring for the expenses, I'll go. Just a hunch."

"Sounds like fun."

"Yeah, being a PI is a lot of fun. You know that. Good

thing I'm a real fun guy or else I might get worn down."

"You follow me home?"

"How far?"

"All the way."

"Sounds like fun."

ACE CARPENTER and Cynthia Walcott were seated in a booth near the back of the no-smoking section of the Old World Restaurant. A waitress in tight black slacks and a sweater that seemed to be in a tightness contest with the slacks handed them menus and left.

Across the aisle from where they were sitting, a man looked furtively around, got up, and walked briskly toward the front door. Immediately a waiter dashed to the table and scooped up a handful of change. A disgusted look screwed up his face. Arms akimbo in a threatening stance, the tall black waiter announced to the restaurant, "Oh, sir! You forgot your *change!*"

The cheap patron in question, branded by all within earshot for life, bolted through the door, his face as red as the catsup bottle still standing beside his empty plate.

"Some people can be so cruel," said Cynthia, taking a sip of her coffee, which had just been poured by the waitress in the black body paint.

"Waiters expect so much nowadays," said Ace, pouring some cream into his coffee.

"I *mean* the customer."

"Oh," said Ace, and let it ride.

"So, what do you have for me today?"

"I've discovered a great deal about the private lives of the cast and crew of *Doctors and Lovers,* but I haven't really gotten any closer to finding out anything about who killed Barry."

"You mentioned taking another tack—I believe that was the word you chose."

"Did Barry ever talk much about his days in Boulder?"

"No. Very little. Maybe once or twice, nothing significant."

"I seem to be coming up against dead ends here in L.A. Maybe I can get a feel for who Barry was, what he was about, by talking to some people who knew him back in Colorado. Maybe there was another side to Barry that had nothing to do with his being an actor. I'll admit it's a long shot, but I'm willing to give it a couple days if you are."

"We've come this far, why not? How long do you think you'll be gone?"

"Like I say, a couple days ought to do it. Maybe three. I know a reporter there who can open a few doors, rattle a few skeletons in closets—if there are any to rattle. He'll also be able to save me a lot of time doing legwork."

"Well, go ahead. When will you leave?"

"I've got a tentative reservation for a flight late this afternoon."

"Fine. Then you'll be wanting a check for expenses."

"It can wait."

"Don't be silly." Cynthia took her checkbook out of her purse, wrote out a check for a thousand dollars, and slid it across the table as though she'd just signed for coffee and doughnuts for one.

"Thanks," said Ace, folding the check and tucking it away inside his wallet.

"I understand Jenny told you about the new company."

"Yes. That's great."

"She and I talked a little this morning before she took her first class. You know, she really cares for you."

"Jenny's a great girl," said Ace noncommittally.

"I won't meddle. But—"

"I'm glad you feel that way. Good policy."

AFTER BRUNCH ACE went to the office.

"Any messages?"

Bunny Aguirre looked up sheepishly at Ace. "Connie called to say good-bye. She said she had to go home early. Jenny called to tell you to have a nice trip. You going somewhere?"

"Boulder."

"Hey, that sounds like fun."

"Purely business. I'll be gone a couple, three days. I'll be calling in for messages every day. If somebody really needs to get me, I'll be staying with a friend of mine there, Tom Fenton. Here's his number."

She took the slip of paper without meeting Ace's eyes. "Is there something wrong, Bunny?"

"I'm sorry about Friday night," she blurted out. "I'm so embarrassed."

"Forget it," Ace said. "It's no big deal."

"But if it hadn't been for your friend, we would have gone to jail."

"We didn't. That's the important thing to remember," he said, and started to walk into his office. Ace wanted to make Bunny feel better. He turned back toward her. "Bunny?"

"Yeah?"

"You *do* have one hell of a great body."

Bunny smiled for the first time.

PART THREE

EVEN IN DENVER'S STAPLETON Airport it was hot. Ace had expected it from what Tom had told him the night before when they'd talked. He knew the routine by now, since he'd been to Boulder at least once a year over the past five years to visit his old friend. Ace spotted the Airporter van, paid his $7.50, and settled back for the half-hour ride into Boulder. The country was as different from L.A. as animals from vegetables. Both existed on the same planet, but one was a whole lot meaner than the other. The mountains seemed so . . . visible was the only word Ace could think of. He was used to mountains on the West Coast, but not used to actually seeing them. In L.A. you knew from seeing old pictures that the mountains were there, not from personal experience.

The Airporter dropped him at the Boulder Inn, from where he took a cab the last mile and a half to Fenton's condominium. The key was under the bicycle seat of the ten-speed Fenton had parked on the second-floor landing. He used the key to let himself in and put the key on his key ring. This was Fenton's spare. This was the routine. Ace noticed the screen door was missing. Apparently the landlord still hadn't put it back on since the huge winter windstorm Fenton had described in great detail in an article he had published and sent to Ace.

Ace poured himself a glass of Absolut from the fully stocked liquor cabinet. It was a fresh bottle. Fenton aimed to please. A picture hung above the fireplace depicting Fenton and his championship softball team, a team that had placed first in the local league four of the last five years.

Ace took his single suitcase into the extra room, turned on the light, and set his bag on the twin bed. There on the pillow was a yellowed newspaper clipping of Fenton and Ace when they were both ten years old, each wearing a uniform just about a size too big. Each was smiling proudly ear to ear. The caption read: Dynamite Duo. Fenton had played second base, Ace shortstop, on the Columbus, Ohio, American Legion team. Although they were only ten years old in a league whose maximum age was twelve, they were universally considered to be the best double-play combination the city had seen in some time, easily the best in the league at the time. They went on to play Knothole ball together and high school ball, at the same positions. It was then that Ace discovered music and opted for playing in a rock and roll band, shunning the Traveling Legion tryout.

Fenton went on to get a partial baseball scholarship at the University of Colorado, where, after giving up serious hope of playing pro ball, he majored in journalism. After receiving his master's from the same university, he bounced around between a couple of local papers, finally getting his present position as features editor for the *Boulder Bulletin*.

Ace and Fenton had kept in loose touch over the years. A few years ago, when Fenton was in L.A. for a newspaper convention, the two old friends renewed their friendship in a big way. Since then Ace had come east to Boulder to ski once a year, and Fenton occasionally came to L.A. to take in some ball games and the local bars, and to rehash the same old stories, which sounded just as good each year.

Ace was watching Dan Rather on the network news when Fenton came home.

"Hey, Ace. You're looking good," said Fenton, a tall, broad-shouldered, dark-haired, trim man.

"You too. You don't have a baseball game tonight or anything, do you?"

"No chance. Let me just change and we'll get out of here and go grab a bite to eat. By the way, I've got most of the info for you," he said as he disappeared down the hallway into his bedroom.

Five minutes later Fenton was back, dressed in freshly washed jeans, tennis shoes, and a bright green sport shirt. "Let's go," he said, and already had his hand on the door. Fenton was always full of energy, and Ace literally had to walk faster than usual to keep up with him.

"NICE PLACE," said Ace after they were seated in the Branding Iron Restaurant. Ace had a large chef's salad, while Fenton chose a sirloin steak.

"This guy Ashford was kind of interesting," Fenton said after he'd chewed his piece of meat long enough to politely open his mouth.

"Oh?"

"Yeah. You'd think in a little town like this there would be some kind of recognition of a favorite son hitting the big time. But there was nothing. It's big news to the neighbors. But in the neighborhood he came from, people come and go a lot and the ones who stay learn to look the other way. His folks are dead; been dead since he was a teenager. In fact, I didn't talk to anyone, *anyone* who remembered him."

"Who looked after him?"

"Just before I came home I got a call from one junior high teacher who one of the neighbors said knew all the boys in the neighborhood. The guy, Patrick Higgins, says that he remembered that Barry had a stepmother named Sophie. Higgins says she was a mean old bat. He says she used to live in a red brick house on the corner of Maple and Houston. She might still live there, might not. That's about as far as I've gotten. But the more information you can feed me, the more I'll be able to check out."

"Thanks, Tom."

"I've written down Higgins's name and number and the address of the house the wicked old stepmother was supposed to have lived in," said Fenton, and slid a piece of paper across the table. "So what's this all about? From what you told me on the phone it sounds like a simple hit-and-skip to me."

"Probably is, but I'm just playing a hunch. You ever see this girl?" asked Ace, taking the picture he'd taken from Ashford's house out of his wallet and handing it to Fenton.

Fenton gave it a quick perusal, handed it back, shaking his head as he did. "Nope. Who is she?"

"I don't know. Maybe nobody. Maybe the key to the case."

"Why is her face crossed out?"

"I don't know. I know she's not in the cast or crew, and no one seems to know who she is. Like I say, Tom, it's just a wild hunch. Back in L.A. I'm running on empty. Maybe this'll shake a few things loose."

"So, how's Jenny?" asked Fenton, taking a sip of his red house wine.

"Fine."

"Now there's a looker, pal. I'm a leg man myself, and let me tell you, those are legs you don't mind waking up between."

"You haven't lost your way with words," said Ace sarcastically.

"Maybe that was a little tasteless, but you know what I mean. How are things going with you two?"

"Hard to say. A little while ago I asked her to move in with me and she got a little crazy about that. Then she mellowed and changed her mind. A lot of emotional water under the bridge for me since then, though. I've got to work a few things out in my head. Actually I was hoping a change of scenery might help clear out the cobwebs."

"This mountain air can do the trick," said Fenton, who was just then shoveling the last bite of steak into his mouth. "Aren't you done yet? Am I eating fast or what?"

"Let me put it this way. If there were an Olympic event for speed eating, you'd have a hunchback from carrying all the gold medals around your neck."

"No kidding? I never noticed it. Oh, well, I've got a real speedy metabolism, I guess."

Fenton ordered a vodka martini while he waited for his friend to polish off his salad. Finally he said, "You want to drown in a few bars tonight or hold off till tomorrow night?"

"I'd need a life jacket to keep me afloat tonight. I'm bushed and I want to get an early start tomorrow morning."

"Gotcha. Hey, let's pick up some taco chips, cheese—I've got beer at home—and watch the *David Letterman Show*."

"That sounds like just about my speed."

Ace fell asleep after the first tray of chips covered with melted cheese and didn't make it past Letterman's monologue.

Somehow he had managed to put himself to bed and got in a good nine hours sleep before Fenton slammed the front door hard on his way out.

A shower and lots of juice made the detective feel like a new man. Within an hour he was being handed the key to his rented Toyota and getting directions from the Budget Rent-a-Car man to Maple and Houston.

Ace pulled the yellow Corolla up in front of the old, dilapidated, blue two-story-plus-attic house that fronted on Maple. The paint was peeling and looked to have been doing so for a long time. Ace followed the cracked sidewalk up to the creaky front porch and pulled the screen door, which was hanging by a single hinge, open and knocked. There was no response. He knocked again, a little harder this time. He heard footsteps coming toward the door and stopping right behind it.

"Who's there?" demanded a voice.

"Ace Carpenter. I'm looking for Sophie Ashford."

The door opened and a woman who looked old enough to have been on a first-name basis with Abraham Lincoln revealed herself in the doorway. "Nobody's called me that for a long time."

After she had spoken, Ace realized that she was older at heart than in body. "Are you Sophie Ashford?"

"Not for a long time. Sophie Montgomery after that. What's this all about?"

"I'm a private investigator from Los Angeles and I'd like to ask you some questions about Barry."

She got a wry look on what could be made out beneath the wrinkles to be her face, and her head started to bob in an acknowledging fashion. "Barry, eh?"

"Yes, ma'am. May I come in?"

"Suit yourself," she said, and stood aside to let him pass. The house was an inward reflection of the house's exterior. Papers were piled high in every corner of every room. Unopened mail lay scattered carelessly here and there. Cats sprang up like darting weeds whenever he passed by one of their hiding places. Finally he was led into a large living room with torn curtains draped haphazardly over the windows in a manner that seemed designed simply to keep out as much light as possible.

"Have a seat," she said, indicating a chair currently occupied by a large yellow cat.

"But—"

"Just brush him off. He'll move." Sure enough, as Ace approached the chair the cat jumped off and scampered behind a pile of paper in a nearby corner.

"So, what about Barry?" asked the woman. "He doin' all right? Didn't kill nobody or nothin' like that, did he? Didn't rob no banks?"

Ace looked carefully for a sign of partial humor in the old woman's remarks but realized that she was totally earnest. "No, nothing like that. I'm afraid I've got some bad news for you, Mrs. Montgomery."

"Then he's dead, ain't he?"

"I'm afraid so, yes. I'm sorry to be the one to tell you, but—"

"Don't be. Somebody had to. I mean, it ain't like you killed him or nothin', right?"

"Right. I'm surprised that you didn't read about it in the papers," he said, tilting his head in the direction of a large pile next to the chair in which he sat.

"Oh, I don't get the papers no more. I used to, but I didn't pay my bills. Most of those papers are from a ways back. But I get some of the free papers, ad sheets mostly, now and then. Had a great collection goin' for a while. But the news is mostly the same, anyway. Just different names doin' the same old crap. Only good thing in the papers used to be the puzzles, and I got so I couldn't figure 'em out no more. So, no great loss for me, not gettin' a paper. 'Cept maybe I woulda heard about Barry's dyin' sooner. How'd he go?" she asked without a great deal of passion. But then she looked to be a woman who had long since handed in her key to passion. It just wasn't there anymore.

"He was killed in a hit-and-run accident in Los Angeles."

"Los Angeles," she said, and coughed out what passed for a little laugh. "I remember he said he wanted to go to California. Always talkin' about California, that boy. Wanted to make a million dollars, be a rich somebody." A strange look washed over her face and transformed it for a moment into something quite real and capable of understanding, or at least wanting to. "How close did he get?"

"To what?"

"To bein' a rich somebody."

"He got rich," said Ace. "A lot of people knew who he was. He was an actor on TV."

A real smile creased the old lady's cheeks and a faraway look filled her eyes. Then it passed, she sighed, and she was ancient again.

"I wonder if you wouldn't mind taking a look at a picture for me?"

"Sure. Why not?"

Ace took out the picture of Ashford and the girl and handed it to the old woman. She looked at it for a long time, then a look of recognition started her head to nodding. "Yeah, I remember that girl. Sally Wayland."

"Sally Wayland?" repeated Ace. "She a local girl?"

"Oh, yeah. She and Barry were one of a kind. Neither one did too well in school and both come from real poor families. Nothin' wrong with that—bein' poor—but sometimes it makes people crazy. Made those two crazy. At least that's what I always thought."

"How so?"

"They was all the time talkin' about how much money they was gonna make. Sally used to be crazy in love with pretty clothes. She'd steal magazines out of the stores and look for hours at the clothes rich folk was wearin'. I mean, it's only natural that folks'd want to improve their condition some, but these two, they wanted it all and they wanted it yesterday. That's why they was always talkin' about goin' to California. It was like other folks talkin' about heaven."

"You know what happened to Sally?"

"Nope. Not for sure. Nobody much cared what Sally did, and maybe that was the trouble. Now I ain't makin' myself out to be no saint, but I used to see that Barry ate his meals, took a bath now and then, and went to school more often than not. But I admit I was drinkin' a lot in those days. Doctors say that's what caused the stroke. That's why I'm the way I am now. But after all, I *did* take the boy in after his real parents died."

"I thought you were his stepmother."

"No. I'm his aunt, his only surviving relative. People didn't know much about our family, didn't want to know much about us. We was poor trash to most. But I don't much care what people think. I've lived a pretty honest life, never hurt nobody severe, don't take from the welfare. More than most these days, I'd say."

"Yeah, more than most," said Ace in a way that was not at

all condescending. "You know if any of Sally Wayland's family
or friends are still in town?"

"I don't get out much these days. I seem to remember that
Sally's father had a garage in town. But that was some time
ago."

"Do you remember where she used to live?"

"Sure. Our families were joined in poverty. They used to
live not three blocks from here. Maple between Main and Third.
'Bout halfway up the block on the right-hand side. Little brick
house set back from the street a ways. Don't know whether
they live there now or not, though.

"Now I got a question for you," said the woman, sitting
forward a little in her chair.

"Shoot."

"How's come you're here askin' questions about Barry's
past?"

"I was hired by a friend of Barry's to find out if the accident
was really a calculated murder. I've come across absolutely no
evidence to support that theory, and to be quite honest, I'm
here grasping at a few last straws."

"I see."

"What kind of a boy would you say Barry was? How did
he get along with people?"

"Probably ain't nice to talk this way about the dead, but
Barry was a tough one. Now he treated me fine, considerin' I
was an alcoholic at the time and all. He didn't beat me or steal
from me or nothin' like that. But Barry was real mad about
bein' poor. Real mad—that's the only way to put it. He felt
that life had dealt him an unfair hand and he was out to square
things up. You know what I mean?"

"Yes, I think so."

"People say yes, but they really don't know. You gotta be
real poor to know that feelin'. It's a bad, achin' feelin', bein'
poor is. Barry and I tolerated each other there at the end. He
was gone most a' the time—didn't want to see me drunk all
the time, I expect. Don't blame him none, though. He was
civil to me. Didn't blame me for his bein' poor."

All of a sudden the old lady's voice began to trail off to a
whisper, then to nothing. The old house was still, except for
a cat licking its paw under the old lady's chair. After a minute,
she looked up and focused on Ace and said, "Barry's dead?
You're sure that it's my Barry?"

"Yes, ma'am, I'm sure."

She looked like she wanted to say something. Her face looked like a dam trying to hold back a tidal wave, but it didn't break. Her mouth started to quiver as the long-forgotten unspoken words tried to find their way home. A shattered life was breaking away just a little more. She stared through Ace now, looking at a private screen. Her head began a slow, rhythmic bobbing, like an ancient, instinctual ritual.

Ace made a movement to get up. Her dead eyes gathered some life, blinked, and she said, "You gotta go?"

"Yes."

"I got tea to make."

"No. I've really got to be going."

"I wish I coulda seen him one more time. Just once more. Some things that shoulda been said that wasn't. You know what I mean?"

"Yes, I know," said Ace. He walked over to where the woman was sitting, extended his hand, which she took weakly. "Thanks for your time, Mrs. Montgomery."

"Got a lot of that."

"I'll show myself out."

As Ace walked out of the house, he was gripped with the eerie image of the woman staring off into space, mourning a past she never had.

A FEW MINUTES later, Ace pulled up in front of a redbrick house, set off and away from the street just as Sophie Montgomery had said it would be. Slate-gray flat stones wound their way from the curb to the brick house. The front window was open and Ace could hear the sound of a soap opera on the TV. He knocked on the door.

A woman answered wearing a tattered blue housecoat over a flannel nightgown. She wore pink fluffy slippers and a scowl on her face. "Whatcha sellin'?"

"Nothing," said Ace, and flashed his PI identification.

"So what do you want with me?"

"I'd like to ask you a few questions about your sister."

"Oh, yeah? Well, I ain't got no sister."

Ace took out the picture of Sally Wayland and Barry Ashford and handed it to the woman, whom Ace now placed at about thirty-five years old. She looked older because she was mad at the world.

"Hmmph," sniffed the woman. "Ain't seen those two in years. And it's too soon by me."

"But you are Sally's sister?"

"We got the same last name. That don't make her my sister."

"Would you mind if I came in and asked you a few questions? I've come all the way from Los Angeles."

"That figures. That's where Sally wanted to go. That's where the money is. That's where the sin is."

My kind of town, thought Ace, but he didn't say anything. "Okay if I come in?"

"Sure, why not," said the woman.

She led Ace into a living room that was small, but neat. Everything was stacked nicely in little piles. Her *TV Guide* and note pads were on the coffee table, stacked neatly according to their sizes. The local paper was on a side table next to the TV-viewing chair. In fact, everything in the room had an aura of neatness about it except the woman herself.

Ace was waved to a couch, and the woman resumed her position in the chair opposite the TV. She used the remote control to turn the sound down, but not off. Looking at the remote-control box in the woman's hand, Ace reflected on the priorities of the poor.

"My name's Ada," said the woman after she'd settled in.

"Just call me Ace. When's the last time you saw your sister?"

"I would appreciate you not callin' her my sister. Call her Sally."

"Sally, then."

"Haven't seen her in years. Last I knowed she was whorin' around with that Ashford kid."

"You ever watch *Doctors and Lovers?*" asked Ace.

"Never. It's opposite *The Edge of Night.* Why?"

"Just curious."

"You watch the soaps?"

"Nah. Prime-time soaps a little, but I'm usually working during the day. Could you tell me a little bit about Sally and Barry's relationship?"

"I don't know much about it. But people was always talkin' about Sally and that boy. Sally and me was like night and day opposite. Just like Dad and Mom. Sally was Momma's girl.

Me, most of the time, I'm like Dad. Sally was a whore, just like Momma."

"Do you mean that literally?"

"Momma run off with a sweeper salesman to God knows where. Near broke my daddy's heart, it did."

"Where is your mother now?"

"In hell, I reckon."

"She's dead?"

"Yep. Long time ago. Good riddance, is what I say."

"Have you ever kept in touch with Sally?"

"Nope. Wouldn't open one of her letters if'n I knew it was from her. An evil one, she is."

"Could you tell me anything at all you remember about Sally and Barry?"

"How's come you want to know about her and Barry?"

"Barry was killed in L.A. Hit-and-run accident. I'm just doing a little checking into his past."

"You think Sally did it?"

"No. That's not what I'm getting at. I'm just trying to understand more about who Barry Ashford was."

"He was a no-good piece of trash. Him and Sally both. They started hangin' around together, skippin' outta school together, and actin' like fools. They was like animals doin' it all the time. I even caught 'em doin' it in her bedroom one day. I come home early from my job down at the drugstore—the Rexall down at Maple and Main?—and there they were flailin' away, just goin' at it. It was disgusting. Now don't get me wrong, I'm no prude or nothin'. Sex has its place. The Bible says so very clearly and it outlines exactly where those places are. But my sister is a child of Satan. She was born that way, lived that way, and she'll die that way."

"What about your father? Or any friends Sally might have had?"

"You can be sure I don't associate with any of Sally's friends. Didn't have none 'cept for the Ashford boy far as I know. And my dad can always be found down at the church. Unless he's out preachin' the Word."

"He's a minister?"

"Yep. Got his own church over on Westlake just off Colorado. Got a neon cross just above an old Texaco sign."

"Okay, I guess that's about all I need," Ace said, and stood up. What he meant was that was about all he knew he was going to get.

Ada Wayland stood up with Ace and walked him the few short steps to the door, looking back over her shoulder at the TV as she did so.

"One thing," she said when Ace was already out the door.

"Yeah?"

"If you see Sally, tell her it's never too late to repent. Can you remember that?"

"I'll try."

"Ain't much to remember. Still, *most* people forget that," she said with a stern, righteous look on her face.

"Good day, Miss Wayland," said Ace, and turned and walked to his yellow Toyota.

Ace listened to some Steely Dan on the radio as he drove down Colorado, made a right—the only way he could turn— onto Westlake, which was a short two-block street in the middle of what could pass for a Boulder slum. In New York it would have been a place with a yard. In L.A. it would have been a $125,000 piece of real estate.

He pulled into what was once a Texaco gas station. The island with its pumps was still intact. The prices on the pumps read sixteen cents a gallon; they came from a time that was before Ace started to drive. These days, thought Ace, you could walk away with sixteen cents' worth of gas in an aperitif glass and not even have to walk carefully not to spill any.

The detective got out of his car, walked up to the front door and tried it. It was locked. The sign on the door said SERVICE TONIGHT AT 8 P.M.

"Hey Tom," said Ace into the receiver of the pay phone that stood at the corner of the lot occupied by Father Wayland's Haven for Lost Souls Church.

"Ace. How's it going?"

"Okay. I've got a name for you. Sally Wayland. See what you can dig up on her."

"That's W-a-y-l-a-n-d?"

"Right."

"Meet me back at the house about five-thirty. I've got a great place in mind for dinner. Then we can play it by ear. What would you like to do afterward?"

"Go to church."

"I MUST ADMIT that you really had me going there when you said you wanted to go to church after dinner," said Tom Fenton as he scooped up a spoonful of fried rice.

"Looks like it might be very interesting. You come up with anything yet on Sally Wayland?"

"No. Tomorrow for sure, though. I've got a friend searching the computer tonight as we speak. If there's anything there, he'll find it."

"Sounds like a strange family, the Waylands. Don't see that many church/service stations around these days."

"True. Seems to me I heard about this guy from some people a few years back. But I've never been there. Ought to be quite an experience."

"Should be. Tom, you might also try to get some info on Sally Wayland's mother and father. Seems the mother died some time ago."

"Shouldn't be a problem. Now, about this gas station/ church . . ."

TOM FENTON PULLED his olive-green Peugeot into the church parking lot and up beside a midnight-blue pickup truck. The lot was full, which meant about twenty cars snuggled around the antique gasoline pumps. It was about five minutes till eight when Ace and Fenton opened the door and were handed a photocopied sheet containing the evening's program and lyrics to a hymn.

Inside, the two first-timers took a seat on wooden folding chairs in an area that had obviously at one time been the service bay. There were still old oil stains on the floor.

Pictures of Jesus and the saints hung on the walls where fan belts and oil filters once took up space. A large hundred-watt bulb covered by what looked like a Tom Terrific hat swung lazily over the congregation.

The people appeared to be mostly farmers. Several chewed on tobacco, wore work boots, flannel shirts, work pants. The women wore little if any makeup and long dresses, no stockings. Ace noticed that the woman next to him hadn't shaved her legs for a long time.

Two boys who appeared to be barely into their teenage years sat, backs straight, hands folded in their laps, making little noises out of the sides of their mouths at each other. Finally a woman next to them shushed them into obedience.

"These chairs are uncomfortable," whispered Fenton.

"Maybe they're supposed to be."

Fenton was just about to ask his friend what he meant when things got under way.

The light overhead was dimmed with a dimmer switch and two spotlights came on, aimed at the ten-by-ten, slightly raised platform toward which all the seats were turned. The spotlights shined through revolving four-color plastic wheels, similar to those that get a metallic Christmas tree to turn colors.

Then the music started. Out of the shadows and onto the rear of the stage marched a woman who looked to be in her late fifties. Her hair was gray, she wore dark-framed glasses, a long dress, thick-heeled work shoes, and she was playing "Onward Christian Soldiers" on her accordion. This didn't seem to surprise anyone except Ace and Fenton, who simply looked incredulously at each other through the dim light.

Then the Reverend Wayland took the stage, Bible in hand, smiled, and raised his hands. The music came to a smooth halt. "Good evening, brothers and sisters," said Wayland.

In unison, all but two of the congregation answered, "Good evening, Father Wayland."

"Brothers and sisters, I come to you this night with good news. News that each and every one of you, from the lowest pitiful scumbag of a wretch to the sinners who aren't all that bad, can be saved."

Although it *did* sound like good news, it didn't seem to come as a bulletin to the congregation. They sat glassy-eyed and smugly reverent, as though they had already been saved.

Wayland made it through a few Bible passages, giving his own unique brand of interpretation to the scriptures, and the whole group sang a hymn whose words were printed on the photocopied handout. Then Wayland really got rolling.

"We have with us tonight a new member to our flock," said Wayland. Immediately Ace's and Fenton's hearts skipped beats. But Wayland was not referring to either of them.

"Step up here, Elmo Dawes," said the preacher to a man

sitting in the front row. A man wearing a shiny brown sport coat, which was probably the missing half of a cheap suit, over a green-checked flannel shirt, and tennis shoes that looked as though they'd been appropriated from the '49 Boston Celtics, stood and moved forward on uncertain legs. He had stringy red hair that hadn't seen the business side of a comb since Richard Nixon was a popular president.

"Step up here, Elmo Dawes," said Wayland encouragingly. Dawes looked at the twelve-inch step and appeared to be unconvinced that he could do so. But with the help of the reverend, Elmo was soon standing on the platform, wearing one of Wayland's arms draped around his neck.

"Not long ago, this man was a despicable sight," said Wayland. "I met Elmo in a strange, a *very* strange, manner."

Dawes screwed up a corner of his mouth at the memory and cocked his head to one side, then brought it back up straight.

"Brothers and sisters, I want to tell you that this was a disgusting man, a humiliated man, a man whom not one of us would demean ourselves to call a friend."

Dawes raised his eyebrows at that remark as though he didn't quite agree with the assessment, but still he kept quiet, hands folded in front of him.

"Brothers and sisters, I was walking the streets of our fair city down in Sinners Town, where the bars with their demon alcohol make foolish animals of us all. One night as I made my appointed rounds, this sorry piece of humankind leaped out from behind a garbage can—"

"It was an oil drum, Father Wayland," said Elmo weakly.

Wayland regarded the man in much the same fashion one would notice a mosquito at the beach while making love, but he managed a smile and said, "Thank you, brother Elmo. An oil drum." Wayland coughed to clear his throat and then gathered lost momentum. "Out from behind this oil drum leaped Elmo. He threw back his coat and exposed himself to me. He did not then recognize me as a man of God. He expected a big response from me, but received none. I said simply, 'Don't you have enough money for underwear, my son?' Well, let me tell you, brothers and sisters, that threw him for a loop. I mean, he didn't know what to say next. He put himself back inside his pants and he walked with me over to the all-night doughnut house, where I bought him some coffee and an orange-sprinkle doughnut.

"And I believe that this man's life was changed that night because he accepted the Lord. Do you believe, brother Elmo?"

"Yes, I do."

"Then that glorious time is upon you, my son. Take my hand."

Elmo took Wayland's hand and followed him off the platform to an area stage right. Another spotlight went on to reveal what looked like a Dodgem car painted blue with the sign of the cross painted on it in gold. Accordion music filled the air. Wayland led Elmo to the small blue compartment, helped him in, then stepped away.

"This is your day of glory, Elmo. Your baptism. Arise and be saved," said Wayland, raising his hands, which was the cue for a man standing to Wayland's right to throw a switch that made the Dodgem Car, with Elmo aboard, begin to rise off the floor. It wasn't until Elmo was halfway to the ceiling that Ace realized that the Dodgem Car was being lifted skyward by a hydraulic lift that had long ago been used to get cars off the ground to work underneath them.

"Am I dreaming?" whispered Fenton to his buddy.

"I think we're in the middle of a *Real People* nightmare."

Wayland said a few choice words that sounded a lot like incantations. Then the reverend lowered his arms and the accordion player started to play something that sounded like a school band march and Elmo began to descend slowly, presumably a changed and better man.

Taking Wayland's hand, Elmo stepped out of the car, off the lift, and back onto the platform.

"Have you seen the light, brother Elmo?"

"I have, brother Wayland."

"That's *Father* Wayland, my son," corrected the minister.

"Sorry, Father Wayland."

"Is the spirit in you, my son?"

"Uh-huh," said Elmo, and he began to nod his head affirmatively.

"Let's have a big hand for our new brother," said Wayland, and extended his hand toward the empty seat from which the convert had come a short time earlier. Elmo stepped off the stage and walked back to his seat.

"We'll be takin' the collection now," said the reverend. "I don't have to tell you that the work we do here and out in the slimy streets of this city is financed by your dollars. Treatin' sin is not a cheap business. No, brothers and sisters, it takes much time and much money. So think of me out in the streets at night when the bars close, trying to save the souls of those less fortunate than ourselves. Dody?..." called Wayland, apparently to the accordion player standing behind him on the stage. Accordion music pierced the air again as Wayland reached down under the small platform to produce a collection plate, which he set in motion in the first row.

"I know it's crazy, but I can't stop thinking of Lawrence Welk," said Fenton.

"It's the accordion."

"Right," he said, snapping his fingers in recognition.

Fenton and Ace each placed a dollar in the plate, a denomination the rest of the congregation seemed to be quite comfortable with, although Ace noticed some loose change and a few pieces of lint.

The meeting started to break up shortly after that. After scanning the plate with a not-too-happy look on his face, Wayland led the group in a hymn that everyone, except the two newcomers, seemed to know by heart. Then, with a flourish of inspiring accordion music, Wayland was gone. The spotlights were turned off and the dimmer switch screwed in the direction that made the whole room glow.

Fenton mingled with the crowd, getting ideas how he might turn this whole experience into a feature story for the *Bulletin*.

Ace went "backstage" and knocked on the door he had seen Wayland disappear into a few minutes earlier.

"Come in," said Wayland.

Ace entered to find Wayland sitting in front of a small makeup table smoking a cigar. He turned all the way around to face Ace, stood up, and said, "Do I know you?"

"No. My name's Ace Carpenter. I'm a private detective from Los Angeles—"

"Everyone in my congregation gives their money purely of their own free will. I will not have my reputation—"

"I'm not here to see you about your church."

"Oh?" he said, and motioned for Ace to have a seat in a stuffed chair that sat next to the door. He made himself comfortable by sitting back down in the chair in front of the makeup table but still turned toward Ace, feet up on a wooden crate that served as a makeshift ottoman. "So what *can* I do for you?"

"It's about your daughter."

"Ada? Why, I find that hard to believe."

"It's not about Ada."

"But you said—"

"It's about Sally."

Wayland looked away from Ace for a moment, chewed on his cigar as much as smoked it, then turned back to Ace. "So, what's this all about?"

"A friend of your daughter, Barry Ashford, was killed in a hit-and-run accident recently in Los Angeles. I've been hired to find out what I can about his background in case there was any foul play. To this point I haven't found anything to lead me to believe there was. I found this picture of Barry and your daughter among Ashford's things."

Ace handed the photo to Wayland. No emotion showed through on Wayland's face, although he did seem to nod his head almost imperceptibly.

"So I came to Boulder to find out who the girl was, and I found out it was Sally."

"I haven't seen my daughter in years," said Wayland, handing the photo back to Ace. "Not since she left town with Ashford. Those two were children of the Devil," said Wayland with less conviction than Ace might have suspected from the preacher.

"I was hoping you might be able to help me find her."

"You're askin' the wrong man. I'd probably be the last person on earth to know where she is. You see, Sally and I never got along. Like oil and water. I saw some letters from her just after she moved to L.A., but I never opened them. Then, after a while, she didn't write no more. It's sad. More than sad, really," said Wayland in his softest voice of the evening.

"Why's that?"

"Here I am in the business of saving souls, and I lost Sally. Well, she can't be blamed for the whole thing. It wasn't her fault, really."

"Don't be so hard on yourself. These are tough times for parents and children."

"Myself?" said Wayland, laughing as he spoke. "Myself? I don't blame myself. The blame rests squarely on the shoulders of her mother. Now, there was a sinner. She's rotting in hell as we speak. I have no doubt of it. In hell," he said passionately.

"What happened to Mrs. Wayland?"

Wayland turned a cold pair of eyes toward Ace and said, "She died."

"How?"

"God took her, blotted out the stain upon the tapestry of human dignity. She was scum, my friend. Scum. And that's all there is to be said on the matter."

Ace turned the subject back to Sally. "I'm trying to get a line on Sally, Mr. Wayland. Is there anyone you can think of that your daughter associated with besides Ashford who might still be in town?"

Wayland blew out a puff of thick cigar smoke as the anger at the memory of his dead wife seemed to drain from him. His face changed as he chased some old pictures around in his head. "One girl. I see her up at the McDonald's on Perry Street now and then. She works behind the counter. Got my eye on her."

"I beg your pardon?"

"She can still be saved. She's a good girl. I can tell by her eyes. Why couldn't Sally have been a little more like Terry? But then I know why. She was her mother's daughter," he said, the look of anger rising up again in his eyes like the manifest wrath of God.

"Well, I think I'll be running along," said Ace, getting up out of the overstuffed chair. The two men shook hands and Ace evacuated the smoke-filled room.

Ace was out into the garage area when he heard Wayland page him from the doorway. "Carpenter . . ."

"Yeah?"

"If you see Sally . . ." This was hard for him.

"Yeah?"

"Tell her I'd open her letters now if she wants to send any."

"I'll tell her."

Wayland nodded his head and walked back into his room and shut the door behind him.

THE NEXT MORNING the phone rang just as Ace was on his way out the door to try the McDonald's on Perry Street.

"Hello."

"Ace, I've got some interesting information on the Waylands. It's going to make your day. Meet me in an hour at the Cavalier, that's just across the street from the paper."

"In an hour."

ACE CHEWED ON a fish sandwich while Fenton carefully emptied a chili dog into his mouth. They split a pitcher of beer to wash it all down.

"We got lucky," said Fenton, setting his mug down after a hefty gulp. "Seems the Wayland family was big news about twenty-four years ago. The whole story is detailed in these articles," said the newspaperman, taking several photocopies out of his sport coat pocket and handing them across the table to Ace. "Those are for you. You can read them at your leisure, but I'll fill you in on the juicy parts.

"Seems you heard right about Mrs. Wayland dying when Sally was just a kid. Died of a fractured skull. Supposedly she fell down the stairs at home. But the D.A. thought it sounded fishy enough to put Mr. Frank Wayland, then owner of Frank's Texaco, on trial for murdering his wife. The jury eventually acquitted him. Not, according to the slant of the articles, because they thought he was innocent, but rather because they just couldn't prove it. There were no witnesses. Just Wayland's word that she fell.

"It gets better. It seems that there had been a running feud between the couple for a few years. Three years before her 'accident,' she had run off with a sweeper salesman for parts unknown. The best guess was someplace out west, probably California. When she came back a year later, she had a child with her."

"Sally?"

"On the button. You can imagine how that made Frank look and feel. Everyone knew the child wasn't his, and there was the wife back home expecting to be taken care of. To put it bluntly, Frank was thoroughly humiliated in front of his friends and neighbors. But apparently he bit the bullet—for a while, anyhow—and tried to patch things up. During this time he became the butt of lots of jokes. There were fights, lots of name-calling, and old Frank dove inside a bottle to try to hide.

"But then, to no one's surprise, that didn't work. He became violent and irritable. His business started to go down the tubes and the taunting became a part of his life, like getting up in the morning, brushing his teeth, and combing his hair. The humiliation never *stopped*.

"A few police reports indicated that Frank had begun to beat his wife every now and then. Finally, the inevitable—or what lots of people felt was inevitable—happened. Not surprisingly, Wayland had a great deal of public sympathy on his side. A lot of people thought the wife deserved what she got. So that sentiment, coupled with the fact that there wasn't any hard evidence to convict Wayland, led to his acquittal.

"It was then that Wayland went off the deep end. He closed down his gas station, stopped drinking, and started his 'Lost Souls' crusade. At first, people thought it was just something that would pass, an overreaction. But that was over twenty years ago. At the time, Wayland told one reporter that he had made a deal with God that if he were released from jail, he would devote his life to God."

"Incredible. What about the daughters?"

"Ada, who is about five years older than Sally, reacted to the whole mess by becoming extremely religious and, in fact, was often seen working with her father saving souls at the garage/church.

"With Sally, it seemed to have the opposite effect. It's understandable. One of the newspaper accounts told of how Sally was treated like an outsider in her own family. Her sister rarely spoke to her, and they never did sister-type things together. Apparently Wayland was pretty cool toward Sally, too. After all, she wasn't really even his daughter."

"Any idea who the real father was?"

"No. A couple reporters tried for a while to run it down, but didn't get anywhere."

"That's an incredible story, Tom. Can you imagine what it was like growing up in that house?"

"Luckily I can't."

"Life can deal some pretty strange hands sometimes."

"Yeah. You have any luck trying to run down Sally's friend?"

"That's where I'm headed from here. I *need* to get a line on Sally. She's becoming more and more real to me with every person I meet. I feel like I've *got* to find her."

"For the case or for personal reasons?"

"A little of both. I'm curious to see how this girl who lived in the middle of an insane asylum turned out. And there's just something about this whole thing that makes me feel that it's going to pay off for the Ashford case. Just a hunch. It's a feeling I get in my stomach when I'm on to something. Not very scientific, but I've found it works more than it doesn't."

"Good luck," said Fenton, raising his mug toward Ace.

"Thanks," the detective said, and they touched glasses.

"Look, I've got to be getting back," said the reporter, downing the last of his beer, taking out a five, and laying it on the table. "See you back at my place about six?"

"Okay. I'm thinking about heading home tonight. There's an eight-thirty flight on United. Could you take me to the airport if I decide to go?"

"Sure."

"Good. See you about six."

THE McDONALD'S was just the same as any McDonald's anywhere in the world, although the menu was not in Spanish like it was in Los Angeles. Ace noticed that right off.

"May I help you, sir?" asked a pimply-faced teenager wearing a blue-striped shirt and matching hat.

"I'm looking for Terry Summers."

For an instant the young man tried to find the name on his menu pad in front of him before he realized what Ace was really asking for. "She's in the back." He turned to a plump girl dressed in attire similar to his own, who was just then carrying a pile of medium-sized cups over to their appropriate place, and said, "Tell Terry some guy wants to see her."

"Okay," mumbled the fat girl. She deposited the cups in their rack, picked up a Hot Apple Pie, and was munching on it by the time she disappeared into the back.

"Stand off to the side, please, sir," said the boy behind the counter. "Terry'll be right up."

Ace moved a few feet to his left to a closed cash register and waited. About a minute later a blonde wearing brown jeans, a yellow blouse, and enough makeup to highlight what were genuinely pretty features walked up to the front counter. She looked around as if she were trying to find someone but didn't know who.

"Terry?"

The blonde turned toward Ace and said, "Yes."

"Hi. My name's Ace Carpenter. I'd like to ask you a few questions about Sally Wayland. Can you spare a few minutes?"

She thought about it for a second, appraised the stranger in front of her, and decided he looked okay. "Sure," she said, and lifted a portion of the counter up, walked through it, replaced it, and motioned for the detective to follow her to an unoccupied table.

"I don't want to get you in trouble," said Ace.

"I'm the manager. I just won't turn myself in. Why do you want to know about Sally?"

"I'm a private investigator. I was hired to find out if Barry Ashford was murdered or if he was simply the victim of a hit-and-run driver. I'm digging into his past, which led me here."

"Barry's dead?" Terry looked shocked and almost on the verge of tears.

"I'm afraid so. I'm sorry I was so blunt about it."

"No, that's all right," she said, recovering. "I haven't seen him or talked to him since he and Sally went to California about five years ago. But we were good friends back then. What does all this have to do with Sally?"

"Nothing directly. I'd just like to talk to her and find out some things about Barry."

Ace took the picture out of his shirt pocket and handed it to Terry.

She laughed and a very attractive smile filled her face. "I remember that picture. That was the summer before they left. It was taken out at Miller's swimming hole. Pretty scraggly-looking crew." She handed the photo back to Ace. "Why is Sally's face crossed out?"

"I don't know. You got any ideas?"

"No," she said, shaking her head.

"When was the last time you heard from Sally?"

"I got a postcard or two after they first went out to L.A. but that's about it."

Ace's heart sank just a little. He had been hoping for a lot more.

"But I'm still in touch with Turtle."

"Who?"

"Turtle Moynahan. The four of us were inseparable. Barry and Sally and Turtle and me. We were all four going out to the coast to seek fame and fortune, but my mother got real sick just before we were supposed to go. My father died when I was very young, so Momma just had me to take care of her. I couldn't leave. The other three went without me. Turtle and I still send Christmas cards to each other and an occasional letter."

"Did he stay in touch with Barry or Sally?"

"I got a card from him a few months ago telling me that his new group had just signed a record contract, and he said that Barry said to say hi. He's never mentioned Sally, though. I'm sure of that, because I always noticed that he doesn't."

"Do you have his address?"

"Not on me. But I've got it at home. You could call me later and I'll give it to you. I get home about five-thirty."

"Great. At least that's something. You say Turtle is in a band?"

"He's a guitar player. His group is new wave, I guess. I'm not that much into new wave music myself. I know that he manages one of those new wave clubs in L.A. called . . ." She searched the ceiling for the name. "It's something kind of disgusting, but I just can't . . . Balltrap. That's it. The Balltrap. Ever hear of it?"

"As a matter of fact, I do remember seeing it advertised in the entertainment section of the *Times*. But I've never been there. Guess I'll give it a try."

"Say hello to Turtle for me. Don't forget."

"I won't."

"This won't get him in any kind of trouble, will it?"

"No. Not at all. I'll just ask him a few questions and probably buy him a beer."

"Wow, that's incredible—about Barry."

"Yeah. It's always a weird feeling knowing somebody and finding out they're dead. Could you tell me a little about Barry and Sally?"

"Sure. They were like Romeo and Juliet. Kind of. I mean, they really loved each other. They had all their first times together. Childhood sweethearts and all that. But there was something about them, especially Barry, that was sort of—I don't know how to describe it exactly, except to say he was cold. Not toward Sally, Turtle, or me, but toward other people. He was an angry young man, a James Dean type of teenager. He was a rebel. He was loyal to his friends. But everybody else was his enemy, to be watched and beaten. I don't mean physically, but like in a game.

"Being rich, making it big, was an obsession with all three of them. Turtle told me that Barry was acting on daytime TV. Is that true?"

"Yes. *Doctors and Lovers*. He had a big part on it, too."

"Wow. He must've been making some heavy money from that."

"I would imagine."

"Funny. Barry made it—at least partially. Turtle's just signed a record contract. I don't know about Sally, but I'll bet she's doing real fine, too. And here I am managing the McDonald's in my hometown, not a mile from the house I was born in."

"You're alive. Barry's not."

"Maybe it isn't how long you live, but what you do while you *are* alive. Barry was famous, at least a little. He got to touch and taste his dream. That's a lot more than most of us get to do."

"Barry's dream killed him. And though I didn't know him, I know enough about him to tell you that he wasn't happy. People ought to be careful what dreams they chase. There are some pretty dark and lonely roads in dreamland."

"I've got to be getting back to work pretty quick," said Terry after she paused slightly to consider what Ace had said.

"Okay. One more thing. Did Sally ever talk about her mother?"

"Yeah. Sometimes. I suppose you know that Frank Wayland wasn't her real father."

"Yes."

"Well, Sally always thought that her father was some Hollywood celebrity. She had no reason to think that, but I think it made her feel better about the whole ugly mess that happened between her mom and dad. She figured that her father was in California. She had talked to a reporter who covered her father's trial, and the reporter told her that he thought her real father was in California. He told Sally that he'd done some snooping around and found some guy who worked at the post office who swears that Sally's mother had a post office box under her own name and that she regularly got mail from California with a Los Angeles postmark on it. No return address, though. No letters were found among Mrs. Wayland's personal effects. So the reporter could have been talking through his hat. But Sally hung on to the information like it was gold. In fact, that's one reason she wanted to go to California—to find her real father.

Maybe she has, for all I know."

"Thanks a lot. You've been very helpful. I'll give you a call around five-thirty to get Turtle's address."

"We're in the book. Under Myrtle Summers on Green Street. Myrtle—what a name, right? Okay, I've got to get back to work," said Terry, and stood up. "Make sure you tell Turtle I said hi when you see him. And Sally, too, if you find her. I'm really curious about what happened to her."

"Me too," said Ace. "Me too."

ACE GOT TURTLE'S address from Terry Summers by calling her just after five-thirty. He promised again to give her regards to her old cronies.

He took Fenton to dinner, and they were on the road to Denver's Stapleton Airport by about a quarter to seven.

"So, what do you think?" asked Fenton as he drove along the freeway leading up to Stapleton. "Was the trip a success or not?"

"I got a lot of information. Whether it pays off or not remains to be seen."

"Sort anything out about you and Jenny?"

Ace breathed out a deep sigh. "I don't know. Sure, I've thought about her. But I haven't come to any decision yet. I imagine I really won't come to any final decision until I talk with her again."

"Give her my best, okay?"

"Sure."

"You know, *I* even got something out of your trip."

"Oh?"

"I'm doing a piece on Wayland's church. I told the editor about what we saw last night and he wants me to do a story on it. In fact, I'm really looking forward to doing it. It's all so bizarre."

"Sounds good. Be sure to send me a copy of the story."

"Sure."

IT WAS NEARLY eleven P.M. by the time Ace rolled in, stopping first downstairs at his landlady's place to pick up Marlowe, who peed on the floor as usual when he laid eyes on Ace.

Ace unpacked, poured himself an Absolut, sat down at the piano and played a few original tunes before sleep claimed him.

BUNNY AGUIRRE seemed genuinely happy to see Ace the next morning. "Hi," she said with a big smile.

"Hi, Bunny. Miss me?"

"Yeah, as a matter of fact. It's boring around here when you're gone."

"I don't know how you can say that about an office where you can see people riding ostriches and armadillos."

"You know what I mean."

"Yeah, I'm sure I do. Any messages?"

"Jenny called. Cynthia Walcott called. Neither said it was urgent, just to call when you got back."

"Thanks," said the detective, and walked into his office. He decided to hold off calling Jenny for a while but got Cynthia Walcott on the phone and set an appointment for lunch at the Yellow Balloon, which was located near her studio. He tried Information for Turtle Moynahan but drew a blank.

ACE CARPENTER and his client talked over matching chef salads.

"So what do you make of it?" asked Cynthia after Ace had filled her in on what he'd learned in Boulder.

"I'm still not sure. But my curiosity is piqued. Before I write this case off to simple hit-and-run, I'd like to talk face to face with Sally Wayland."

"I wish I could be of some help there, but I can't. However, I do remember Barry talking about going to a new wave nightclub every once in a while. I never accompanied him, though. I'm not much into that kind of music."

"You're sure you never heard him mention the name Turtle?"

"No. I think I'd remember something like that."

"I'd like to nose around a couple more days if you're still interested."

"Certainly. My woman's intuition tells me that we're on the right track."

"Between your intuition and my stomach, maybe we've got something."

"I beg your pardon?"

"Nothing."

THE BALLTRAP WAS over on Olympic in West Los Angeles. It didn't look like much on the outside. It didn't look like much on the inside, either, but it was livelier. The girl at the door looked about seventeen. She was wearing tiger-striped pants that she had to have grown into because she could never have put something that tight on over her hips. She also wore a matching blouse, blue pumps, and green sunglasses, inside a place so dark that Ace had nearly fallen twice over people lying in the doorway.

"ID," she mumbled in the detective's direction. In a place like this, people were carded more to check species than age.

"Here," said Ace, handing the tigress his driver's license.

She held it close to her sunglasses, then squinted in Ace's general direction before handing it back to him, grabbing his hand, and stamping it with a fluorescent stamp depicting two large testicles caught in a bear trap.

"Is Turtle here?" asked Ace.

The girl tilted her head toward the main room, in which about a hundred people were either jumping around on the dance floor or sitting and drinking beer or wine.

"Could you be more specific?"

"You're looking for Turtle, right?"

"Quite a memory. Yes, that's right."

"He's the one wearing a shell on his head."

"A shell?"

"A turtleshell, dummy."

"Of course."

With that kind of a description, Ace didn't feel his job was going to be that hard. He made his way to the bar, behind which a man sporting a Pac-Man T-shirt was pouring the light alcohol.

"What'll it be, pal?"

"Just beer and wine, eh?"

"And soft drinks."

"I'll take a Heineken."

"Coors, Lite, or Bud."

"Lite."

The man ripped open a can of brew and set it and a mug on the bar. "That'll be two bucks."

Ace took out two dollar bills and a quarter and slid them across the bar. "I wonder if you could tell me where Turtle is?"

"If he ain't out on the floor, he's probably up in the sound booth or backstage in the dressing room."

"Where's the sound booth?"

"Just to the left of the stage."

"Thanks."

Ace poured the Lite into his mug and carried it around the main dancing and jumping area to a small booth near the stage and peered in. There on the floor were two hairy cheeks pounding up and down in between two thin, smooth legs adorned with green-and-white-striped knee socks. Apparently the girl caught a glimpse of Ace looking inside, because she screamed.

His rhythm interrupted, the male member of the duo turned around with an angry scowl on his face as though someone had just ordered him to shoot himself in the foot.

"Turtle?" inquired Ace.

"No, asshole. He's backstage. Now if you don't mind . . ."

"No. Go right ahead," he said, and walked briskly away. After spelunking through a labyrinth of hallways in the back, Ace finally came to a room marked "Dressing Room." He knocked and a voice said, "Come in."

It was like walking into a zoo. A woman was dressed in high heels, garter belt, torn black stockings, and a see-through bra, and her head was shaved. The guys in her band were dressed in Day-Glow jumpsuits wrapped in neon, which was even now blinking off and on. But they had hair—one bristly strip right down the center of each of their heads. In the corner sat a man dressed in metallic green running shorts, orange knee socks, a torn T-shirt, tennis shoes, and a hat made out of a turtleshell.

Ace walked over to him and said, "Turtle?"

"Yeah. Who're you?"

"Ace Carpenter. Terry Summers gave me your name."

The smile of a real person creased his five-o'clock-shadowed face. "Terry, eh? How do you know her?"

"I'm a PI looking into Barry Ashford's death. My investigation took me into his past, which took me to Boulder, Sally and Terry, and now you."

"Yeah, tough break about Barry," said Turtle, tightening the E-string peg on his Gibson solid-body guitar.

"So you know all about what happened to Barry?"

"Just what I read in the papers. But it hit me kind of hard. Barry and me go way back. He used to come in here at least a couple of times a week. In fact, he was in here the night before he died."

"He usually come in here by himself?"

"Sometimes. Sometimes he'd bring a chick."

"Anybody regularly?"

"Not lately. Up till a few weeks ago he'd bring in this chick named Arlene. A real hot piece of ass. Worked on that show he did. I only saw it once or twice when Barry'd just started doing it. I don't go for the soaps."

"What happened between Barry and Arlene?"

"I'm not sure, really. He just said it was getting too heavy."

"What did that mean? Too much commitment?"

"I don't think so. But I'm not sure. Barry went through a lot of women. She was just the last in a long line. I heard he was getting it on with some rich bitch recently."

"Yeah, that's what I heard, too," said Ace, thinking of his client. "What about Sally Wayland?"

"What about her?" For the first time, Turtle's senses seemed to come alive. He put his guitar on his lap and looked warily at the detective.

"Ever see her?"

"No. Not in years. Sally, Barry, and I all came out here together, but Sally was the first to lose touch."

"Any idea why?"

"No."

"How about a guess?"

"Look, what is this?"

"Did she find her father?"

"I wouldn't know anything about that. Nothing."

"Did Barry ever see her?"

"Not that I know of. He saw her for a while after we all came out. In fact, I think they used to share an apartment together for a while—maybe six months or so—but then he lost track of her, too. Least that's what he told me. If he was seeing her, he wasn't telling me about it."

"I'd really like to find Sally Wayland. I could make it worth your while."

"Look, man, I told you I don't know nothin' about Sally and even if I did, I don't sell out friends. So just forget it, okay?"

"Okay."

"Look, I've got to be getting ready for the next show."

"Sure," said Ace. "But if anything occurs to you that you might have forgotten to tell me, here's my card." Ace took a card from his pocket and handed it to the musician. Turtle took it and stuffed it into his open guitar case.

"You think Barry was murdered?"

"I don't know. That's what I'm trying to find out. Oh, by the way. Terry said to say hi."

Turtle just nodded his head and said, "Thanks," as he left the room.

"HI. MADDIE?"

"Yes . . ."

"Ace Carpenter here. How are you?"

"Fine."

"Yeah, that jailhouse food'll put you on top of the world."

"I didn't have time to acquire the taste. Thank God!" she said, a shiver in her voice.

"Maddie, I wonder if you could do me a favor."

"Maybe."

"You know that girl Arlene that had the catfight with Helen Clark a few nights ago?"

"Yeah."

"She works for *Doctors and Lovers*, right?"

"Yes. An underling till just a few days ago. Now she's got a bit part on the show. One of Owen's last great moves in this life."

"What's her name?"

"You'd have to take a number with her, honey."

"I'm not looking for a roll in the hay."

"And I believe you, honest I do," said Maddie in her sweetest, most insincere voice.

"Okay. Have it your way. I *need* her. Tonight, if possible. What's her last name?"

"Let me see now . . . Donahue. Arlene Donahue."

"I don't suppose you happen to know where she lives?"

"As a matter of fact, I do. Owen and I had dinner one night about a month ago. He was seeing Arlene afterward and I dropped him off at her apartment building."

"Could you tell me what apartment building?"

"Corner of Santa Monica Boulevard and Tanamera, on the northwest corner."

"Great. I know where that is."

"If she turns you down, or if you get tired of waiting to hear your number called, I've got a bottle of Dom Pérignon dying for a little attention."

"Thanks. I'll keep it in mind."

"You do that."

It was about 10:30 P.M. when Ace pulled up in front of the building on Tanamera. It was a modern West Hollywood security apartment building with a tennis court on the roof, saunas—coed, of course—Jacuzzi, mirrored entranceway, scanning cameras aimed at the front door. It had all the charm of a dead fish.

Ace ran his finger down the names next to the outside buzzers, looking for Donahue. It was possible, he thought, that Donahue wasn't her real last name. Or maybe she had a roommate whose name would be posted instead of hers. Or she might have refused to put her name outside. He was three-quarters of the way through the directory with no success when the lobby elevator doors opened and out strolled Arlene Donahue. She was alone.

Ace moved quickly away from the buzzers, down to his car, got in, and waited for Arlene to come outside. Presently she came out, got into a dark green Triumph, roared away from the curb, and turned left on Santa Monica Boulevard. Ace was right behind her.

She made a left on La Cienega, which she took up to Sunset, where she turned right, then left up Kings Road, which if covered with snow would be too steep for the Mahre brothers to ski down. It was just about straight up. Near the top of the mountain, which afforded a three-hundred-and-sixty-degree view of the city, Arlene turned right onto a short cul-de-sac. Luckily Ace saw the "Dead End" sign and drove past the road, parked his car on a shoulder, and doubled back in time to see Arlene walk through the open door of a house in which a party seemed to be in full swing.

Ace made his way to the front door just in time to see another couple enter. The couple, a short man and a large woman, said, "We're friends of Stan's." Then the short man took some money out of his wallet and handed it to a woman who was sitting behind a desk. She put the money inside a small metal box.

"May I help you?"

"I'm a friend of Arlene's," said Ace.

"You dominant or submissive?"

"I beg your pardon?"

The woman, whose hair looked as though it had been dropped in a vat of bleach, regarded the detective as something not too smart. "You like to hit or get hit?"

"Uh . . ." he stammered for a second, then said, "The former."

"Huh?"

"The first one you said."

"Okay. That means you're dominant. That'll be twenty dollars donation for refreshments and stuff."

Ace took out his wallet and handed the woman a twenty.

She took the money and said, "The bedrooms are to your right, down the hall there." She pointed without looking.

Ace nodded, looked around, and walked into the living room, which was filled with about a dozen people drinking cheap booze from plastic cups. He didn't see Arlene.

"Hello," purred a woman into Ace's ear from behind.

"Hello," said Ace, turning around to find a brunette, about twenty-five to thirty, slim, dressed in a white string bikini that showed up well against her tan, smiling at him.

"Hello."

"My name's Wanda Sue."

"Ace."

"Nice to meet you."

"Likewise."

"I don't believe I've ever seen you here before."

"No, no, that's true. I've been out of town for a while."

"Oh? I've been coming here for a year and I don't remember ever seeing you."

"That's how long I was out of town—just a little over a

year. My company sent me out of the country. Now I'm back."

"Oh, really. Sounds like you've got an important job. Tell me, what do you do?"

"I'm a visor salesman."

"Visors?"

"You know, like for the bills of caps. It's boring, really. You don't want to hear about that."

"No, actually I don't. But I would like to talk with you."

"Okay."

"Can I get you a drink?"

"Sure."

"Follow me," she said, and led him to a bar in the middle of the room. He scanned the sad choices of hard liquor available and said, "I'll have a beer."

Wanda Sue fixed them each a beer, and they moved away from the bar to a corner of the room and sat down on a couch.

"So," she said, "are you a dominant or submissive?"

Thinking back to his encounter with the girl at the door, he said, "Dominant."

"I knew it. I can tell," she said with a big smile on her face. "I'm submissive."

"Too bad," said Ace.

"No, that's good. That means we're compatible. Are you heavily into pain?"

"Huh?"

"Do you really get off on giving pain?"

"*Physical* pain?"

"Of course. Although I *could* get into a little verbal humiliation."

Ace felt like he needed a dictionary. "Good," he said because he couldn't think of anything else.

"I think we'd be good together."

"Maybe."

"I've access to my favorite dungeon in the back in a few minutes. Want to join me?"

"Well, I don't know...."

Just then Arlene came into the room leading a man on all fours by a leash. When they reached the bar, she commanded him to heel and he pulled up alongside her. Even though it was doubtful Arlene would remember Ace, the detective turned his head away from her.

"You know that woman?" asked Ace.

"Arlene? Of course. Everybody knows Arlene."

"So she comes here often?"

"Often? Are you kidding? Twice, three times a week. She's the star."

"Tell me about her."

"We're a pretty closed-mouth group of people."

"You could tell *me*."

"I could, but I won't. Unless..."

"Unless?"

"Unless you take me in the back room right now and beat the information out of me. I know your kind. You can be so persuasive."

"Wanda Sue, I'd rather just talk first if you don't mind."

"But I *do* mind. I'm hot, Ace. I'm really ready to roll, if you know what I mean. I need you. Now. I'll tell you anything you want to know. Back there," she said, tilting her head in the direction of the bedrooms.

"Come on, Wanda Sue, I just got here. I'm not really in the mood to beat you up."

"Just a little, okay?"

"You promise to tell me what I want to know?"

"Yes. I promise."

Ace heaved a heavy sigh, stood up, and followed Wanda Sue down a hallway to a bedroom outfitted like a dungeon with tin foil over the windows. The wall was covered with dildos and whips hanging from tiny hooks. There was also what looked like a mini-stockade.

"Well, what do you think?" she asked as she locked the door.

"Nice."

"Okay, how do you want me?"

"What do you mean?"

"You want me to keep my bikini on, or do you want me naked?"

"The bikini is fine."

"Okay," she said, her eyes radiating the heat in her body. They both just stood there looking at each other until the girl finally said, "Well?"

"Well what?"

"Come on. Hold up your end of the bargain. Dominate me. Choose something from the wall and let's get this show on the road."

Ace kept reminding himself that he wanted the information badly. He saw two handcuffs dangling from a metal bar that jutted out from what looked like an exercise machine with a crank. He put her hands in the fur-lined cuffs and cranked until her feet were just barely touching the ground. "Isn't this fun?" she said.

"Yeah."

Wanda Sue tilted her head toward the wall of dildos and whips, and Ace walked over to make his choice. Finally he hit upon something he could deal with.

"What have you got?" asked Wanda Sue when Ace approached her with his hands behind his back.

"A surprise."

"Ummm, I like that."

"Close your eyes."

She did, and when she opened them again she was laughing hysterically.

"A feather!" she screamed amid her giggling and screaming as Ace tickled her thighs, her underarms, and the bottoms of her feet. "I've never tried this before."

"You like it?"

"No," she said, and laughed loudly.

"Well, that doesn't make any difference to me. A deal is a deal."

"I like it when you talk that way to me."

"Great," he said, and continued tickling the girl. "Now it's your turn. Talk. You see the guys Arlene's been coming up here with lately?"

"Yes!" she screamed, her face dancing with laughter.

"Who?"

"I can't tell you that."

"But you know, right?"

"Yes."

"If I say the person's name, will you tell me if I'm right?"

"I don't know. . . ."

Ace began to tickle Wanda Sue more wildly.

"Okay, okay!"

"Barry Ashford."

"Yes. But not in a while. They had a falling-out."

"About what?"

"Wouldn't you like to know?"

Ace tickled harder.

"Okay, okay. They were doing a switch scene here one night—"

"Switch scene?"

"They'd take turns being submissive and dominant."

"All right."

"Anyhow, Barry comes bursting out of one of the rooms calling Arlene a maniac. I mean, he was angry. And he wasn't kidding."

"Why was he upset?"

"He said Arlene set him up, broke the rules."

"What rules?"

"You know."

"Pretend I don't."

"You sure you're a regular?"

Ace tickled her harder.

"Okay! She wasn't playacting. She brought her real hostility for Barry into the game and almost hurt him. I guess they were having some kind of fight and during their session she really put the screws to him. It scared Barry and he got real mad. I never saw Barry up here again. He said he never wanted to see Arlene again."

"Very interesting. Would you say Arlene is a dangerous person? I mean, really dangerous?"

"I wouldn't know. I've never been involved in a session with her. But if Barry was telling the truth, then yeah, she might be considered dangerous."

"You ever see Owen Clark up here?"

"Now and then."

"With Arlene?"

"Yeah, usually. Sometimes he'd come up alone."

"Do you have any idea why Arlene might have been mad at Barry?"

"Sure. I talked with Arlene about it. She said that Barry was going to stop seeing her because he was getting serious about some older chick."

"I see," said Ace, putting down the feather.

"Hey, come on. I'm starting to like it."

"I'm afraid that's about all I've got in me for tonight."

"Please?"

"No," he said. Ace cranked Wanda Sue down and let her

out of the handcuffs.

"Thanks. You've been really helpful," said Ace, unlocking the door.

"You going?"

"Yeah. I got to get up early tomorrow."

"You didn't stay very long," said Wanda Sue, pouting.

"Long enough."

Ace went home and was curled up with an Absolut and Marlowe in time to catch *Murder My Sweet* on the late show.

ACE MET EDDY PRICE at Ernie's for breakfast. The place was known for its mammoth home-fried potatoes and healthy portions of scrambled eggs. But Ernie's biggest draw was its coffee. It was strong enough to revive dead men. Ace had even heard of guys rubbing it on their bald spots with various results.

Ace and Eddy had worked their way through scrambled eggs, toast, and fries and were on their second cups of coffee by the time Ace had finished telling his friend what he'd found out in Boulder and in Hollywood since his return.

"Things are starting to heat up—at least, the possibilities are getting a little wider," said Eddy, slurping at the thick java.

"Yeah. There's Corey Eastland and Willy Dodd. Eastland probably held a grudge against Ashford for taking over his job and against Clark for firing him. Dodd obviously was angry with Clark for firing him. Dodd and Eastland are each other's alibis, but now we've got reason to believe they might be covering for each other."

"Maybe. We can't discount the guy's alibi just because he's sleeping with the person he says he was with."

"But it does make you think."

"Yeah."

"Then there's Arlene. She must have been pretty angry with Ashford and, for all I know, might have tried to kill him in one of those dungeons up in the Hollywood Hills."

"But she didn't have any reason to kill Clark. He'd just given her a part on the show."

"Maybe the two murders are unrelated."

"We still don't know that Ashford's *was* a murder—in the way *you're* talking about, at least," said Eddy.

"True. We don't want to forget Helen Clark. Her husband embezzling several million dollars from her company ain't a bad motive. Or maybe Ashford and Clark were getting it on and she was jealous."

"Maybe."

"And there's always Russo. He had a great motive to kill Barry. In fact, he admitted that his success is a direct result of Ashford's death."

"Don't forget Maddie Paxton. I had to turn her loose, but it *was* her gun that killed Owen Clark. All we've *really* got is two bodies and a carload of suspects."

"Don't forget Sally Wayland. I want to talk to her and find out what made Barry Ashford cross out her face on the snapshot."

"Personally, I think you're spending too much time thinking about that. But it's your business."

"True. I'd appreciate your running Sally Wayland's name through your computers and finding out what you can."

"Sure. No sweat. You want to go bowling tonight?"

"I think I'm going to see Jenny. Some other time."

"Sure."

"I'll be in touch," said Ace, standing up and taking a five from his wallet and laying it on the table.

THE BOOKSTORE COREY Eastland managed was about ten minutes from Ernie's. There was a parking space available about three doors east of the shop. Ace pulled into the space, parked, put a quarter in the meter, and walked the short distance to the store. However, when he got to the shop it was closed.

As he pressed his face against the glass, peering in for any sign of Eastland, a man came up behind him and said, "Damn."

Ace turned and said, "I beg your pardon?"

"I said damn. It's no way to run a business. That's for sure."

"This happen often?"

"It does," said the man angrily. "What's a person to think when a place is open or closed at the whim of its proprietor? But then, what can you expect on this street nowadays, right?"

Ace nodded his head.

"I'm a good customer, a damn good customer, of this store.

There's a lot of bookstores on this street that would be quite happy to have my business. I just don't know what gets into Corey sometimes."

"You know the proprietor well?"

"Oh, my, yes. We talk for hours about old movies and books. When he's in, that is."

"You wouldn't happen to remember whether or not he closed early the night Owen Clark, the TV producer, was killed, do you?"

"Oh, my, yes. I remember quite well, in fact. I heard the news bulletin on TV just before seven. I knew how much Corey disliked the man. And why not? Corey got a rotten deal, if you ask me. But Corey's a gentleman and acted quite well about it, all things considered. Anyhow, when I heard, I put on my tweed jacket and came around to see if I could catch Corey before he locked up—I just live around the corner. When I arrived, he wasn't here. In fact, I thought it quite odd at the time that a paper—a local Hollywood rag that's delivered in the mid- to late afternoon—was lying in front of the door. Apparently he'd been closed for some time."

"That's very interesting. Did you talk to Mr. Eastland the next day about Clark's murder?"

"Yes. Although we didn't talk *much* about it."

"Did he seem surprised or upset by it?"

"No. And I can't say I blame him. After all, it's quite hypocritical to feign sorrow for someone you despised while he was alive."

"That's true. You say you and Mr. Eastland are good friends; at least, you have a lot in common."

"Correct."

"You ever been over to his place?"

"Yes. I've made a habit of taking Thanksgiving dinner with Corey over the past couple years. One year it's at my place, the next at his. But I don't go over there any other time. Why?"

"I was thinking about swinging by there."

"Whatever for?"

"I've got a load of old books he might be interested in. Cinema biographies, some quite old and valuable. But I can't wait around. I'm leaving town this afternoon. I've heard so many good things about this place, I had my heart set on giving him first shot at the books."

"Of course. I wonder if I might trouble you for a preview of what you're selling?"

"I don't think it would be fair to the retailer—Mr. Eastland, in this instance."

"Certainly. And you're quite right."

"So, if you could tell me how to get to Mr. Eastland's house . . ."

"Of course."

EASTLAND LIVED IN a Silverlake six-unit apartment complex that was supported by what looked like stilts sticking up out of the side of a mountain. Hillside houses don't look that great from the street. All the money is usually on the other side, the side with the view. Eastland's house was no exception.

Ace rang the bell a few times and got no answer. He knocked hard a couple more times and got the same response.

He drove to the bottom of the hill to a gas station, where he used the phone booth to call Julie Wharton at *Doctors and Lovers* to get Willy Dodd's address.

Dodd's place in Studio City was about fifteen minutes from Silverlake via the Ventura Freeway. It was a bungalow set back from the street and fronted by lush trees. The small lawn was manicured, and a late-model Fiat sat in the driveway.

Ace parked on the street, brushed aside a few light-hanging branches, walked up to Dodd's front door, and rang the bell.

Willy Dodd opened the door. He looked tired. It wasn't that he had just been awakened. He just looked tired. "Yes?"

"My name's Ace Carpenter. I'm a private investigator. I'd like to ask you a few questions."

"About what?"

"About Corey Eastland and your alibi for the night of the Owen Clark murder."

Dodd was unaccustomed to trouble. The sophisticated criminals Ace often dealt with would have just shut the door in his face. But Dodd wasn't sure what move to make. "Okay. Come in."

He led Ace into the living room, which was strewn with crumpled-up paper thrown most likely from a chair in front of a typewriter that sat on a rolltop desk in the corner. "Sit down," he said, and waved Ace toward the couch. Dodd sat in the chair in front of the desk, turning it around to face the detective.

"You're in deep shit, Willy."

"What are you talking about?" He tried to act cool, but he was sweating.

"Your alibi is as full of holes as a piece of good Swiss cheese. And it smells as much, too."

"But I didn't kill Owen. I swear."

"Oh, that's going to carry a lot of weight."

"It should. It's the truth."

"The jury isn't going to be too sympathetic. Look, I followed Corey Eastland to the little hideaway club over on Morehead the other night. I know that you and Corey are, shall we say, quite intimate. I also know that Corey wasn't anywhere near his store at the time of Clark's murder. You told the police you were there with him. That doesn't look good.

"And try this on for size. Owen Clark used to swing any way the wind blew. I understand you and Owen were lovers at one time. Then Ashford moved in, took your place, and, well, it all adds up to a pretty unsavory business. Yeah, Willy, you're in deep shit."

"But I didn't kill anyone. I swear."

"Were you and Owen Clark ever lovers?"

"Yes. But that was long ago."

"Were you jealous that Barry took your place?"

"I don't know that he did. But I suspect he did. I mean, why else would Barry have such power over Owen? But Owen and I parted company for entirely different reasons. After all, Owen wasn't a one-woman *or* one-*man* type of lover."

"Okay. So where *were* you when Clark was murdered?"

"I was home sleeping. I'd had a very rough day—"

"I'll say. Clark fired you."

"Yes. I'd been drinking and I was to meet Corey for dinner. I heard about Owen's death on the radio as I was driving to dinner. It was Corey's idea, actually, that I use him for an alibi. I told him that I didn't think it wise to lie to the police, but he painted such a grim picture of what could happen if I told them the truth."

"It *is* a grim picture, Willy. It's going to be hard to swallow. Especially since you lied to the police to begin with."

"Dammit, it's true," he said, the frustration showing in his pained expression, his eyes beginning to fill with tears. "You've got to believe me."

"No, Willy, *I* don't. The police do. For what it's worth, I *do* believe you. But that's just instinct talking; not the facts."

"What should I do?"

"I'm not guaranteeing anything, but I'd go talk to the police about this thing, before they come to talk to you. Ask for Eddy Price. He's a pretty square guy."

"I remember him."

"Yeah, he talks tough, but he won't railroad you. But do it quick, Willy. It's not going to get any easier. And the longer you wait, the worse it looks."

"You're right."

"Yeah, I am," said Ace, getting up and letting himself out as Dodd began to cry, putting his head down on the desk.

"ANYTHING?" ASKED ACE as he walked toward Bunny's desk.

"Cynthia Walcott called. She said it was important."

"Thanks," he said, and walked into his office, closing the door behind him.

"Eddy?" said Ace into the phone.

"Yeah. Oh, hi, Ace. What's up?"

"I just talked to one of Corey Eastland's regular customers, and he says Eastland wasn't in the store at the time of Owen Clark's murder. I believe the guy."

"That makes Willy Dodd's alibi obsolete."

"True, but my gut leans more toward Eastland."

"Not me," said Eddy.

"Why not?"

"Just got a call a few minutes ago. Eastland's dead. I'm just about to head out there myself to take a look."

Ace hesitated, then said, "I think you'll be getting a visit from Willy Dodd pretty soon. He says the alibi was Eastland's idea. He sounds like the genuine article, but that's just my opinion."

"Okay. Gotta go. Talk with you later," said the cop, and hung up.

The buzzer on Ace's desk made its annoying sound. He clicked a switch and said, "Yes?"

"Jenny's here to see you," said Bunny.

"Send her in."

He met Jenny at the door and seated her in his client's chair opposite his desk and reassumed his own chair behind the desk.

"Good to see you," he said when he was settled.

"Good to see you. I left a message."

"Yeah, I know. It's just been a madhouse around here since I got back. I think a few things are starting to shake loose."

"That's good."

"But I was going to call you this afternoon. I thought maybe we could get together later tonight if you want."

"Sure."

"What brings you by here?"

"Oh, I was just in the neighborhood. I was picking up a Danskin over at Capezio and I just took a chance."

"I thought about you while I was gone."

"I thought about you, too." Jenny crossed one of her beautiful legs nervously, exposing her sleek left thigh through a modest slit in her dress.

"You still feel pretty much the same as when I left? I mean, you didn't recast me in the villain's role again or anything like that?"

"No. I love you. I think we ought to get this thing straightened out once and for all."

"I agree. But it's going to have to wait until tonight, okay?"

"Sure," she said, smiling. Then she stood up and moved toward the door. Ace followed her. Just before he opened the door for her, he took her in his arms and held her tighter than he'd held anyone in a long time. It felt good. He kissed her and felt her mouth open slightly, surrenderingly.

"This is a little distracting," he said, laughing a little and pulling slowly away. "Tonight."

"Tonight," she said, and left.

THEN ACE WENT back to his desk and dialed Cynthia Walcott's number.

"Ace, I'm so glad to hear from you. A man came by my house last night. He's a reporter for one of those scandal sheets they sell in the supermarkets. I started to send him packing— I thought he wanted to put together some gruesome piece about

Barry's death. But that's not it at all. He said that he and Barry had had two or three meetings about some blockbuster story Barry was going to give him. He said Barry wanted a million dollars for the story. He said Barry didn't tell him exactly what it was about because then the paper wouldn't need him anymore, but it was supposed to have something to do with George Harris."

"The actor?"

"Yes."

"All right, let's get together with him. Can you arrange it?"

"He's waiting for my call. I told him I wanted to talk to you first. How soon can you be at my house?"

"Twenty minutes."

"See you there."

CYNTHIA'S HOUSE WAS lush compared to Willy Dodd's. She had the living room decorated with lots of gray, white, and pink. Ace and Cynthia were seated on a long white couch when a man knocked on the front door. Cynthia got up and let him inside, offering him a seat on a big, white stuffed chair opposite the couch, where she sat back down next to Ace.

The man was tall, dark, about twenty pounds overweight, and didn't wear a sport coat to hide the fact. He was wearing a green Hawaiian print shirt, jeans, white bucks, and a fake gold chain around his neck. He was tanned and sweating.

"My name's Powell. Ray Powell. I work for *Nightside Companion*. You've seen it on the stands, I'm sure."

"Smelled it there, is more like it," said Ace.

"No need to get bitchy," said Powell, although he didn't seem offended. He appeared to have heard such remarks before. "After all, I'm doing you a favor. The paper doesn't know I'm here."

"And if any scum floats to the bottom as a result, you'll be there to scoop it up," said Ace.

"Look, it's a living. We wouldn't write this shit if people didn't buy it by the truckload. Give me a break, okay? Just lighten up."

"So why the call to Cynthia?"

"A few weeks ago Barry called the paper and said he wanted to talk with somebody about a juicy story. L.A.'s my turf, so we had lunch. I figured it was going to be about something to do with his soap opera, but he had other ideas. He said he had a story that was going to set the entertainment business on its ear, and that it had to do with George Harris. You can imagine how big a story that would be. I mean, after all, Harris is like a god, an untouchable. He was idolized by millions of people around the world for close to forty years. I mean, he was at the top of everybody's nice-guy list. Give you an idea of how well the guy was thought of, remember when he died?"

"Who doesn't."

"Well, there was a lot of talk he didn't die of natural causes like the papers said. Now, with most celebrities, that would have got a lot of ink. But nobody wanted to print bad things about Harris. No one wanted to be the one to desecrate the sacred shine. We couldn't get anybody to talk. Anyhow, the rumors were just that—rumors."

"Hadn't he just recently married?" asked Cynthia, speaking for the first time.

"Yeah. The day before, as a matter of fact. Some chickie about a third his age. One of the rumors was that she fucked him to death. Oh, excuse me, Miss Walcott."

"That's all right. I've heard the word before."

"Yeah, well, anyhow, if you're gonna go, why not go with a smile on your face? You know what I mean?"

"Did Barry give you any information at all that gave some idea what he had in mind to sell you?" asked the detective.

"No. He played his cards pretty close to his vest."

"So, why are you here?"

"Well, it occurred to me that maybe Ashford might have had some information that got him killed. It's happened before. I did a little checking and found out Miss Walcott had some private law for hire—you, Mr. Carpenter—and I just thought you might be interested. And naturally, if you dig up anything, you might return the favor. You know what I mean?"

"Exactly."

"Here's my card," said Powell, taking one out of his shirt pocket and leaning across the coffee table to hand it to Ace.

"If I get anything I think you should have, I'll give you a jingle," said Ace. He wasn't lying. But then there wasn't much he thought the man should have, anyhow.

Powell heaved a big sigh, stood up, and said, "Okay. I'll let myself out." The reporter nodded at Cynthia and Ace and left the house, pulling the door gently closed behind him.

"What do you make of it?" asked Cynthia, craning her neck to watch as Powell got into his bright orange VW and pulled away.

"Interesting. Did Barry ever mention this Harris matter to you?"

"Never."

"What do you know about Harris's death?"

"Well, like everyone else, very little. I understood that his death might not have been by natural causes, but the implication that I got was that he probably had a heart attack on his wedding night—if you get my drift. No sense digging up that kind of thing. Doesn't do anyone any good. That's what a lot of people I know thought. I never got the impression that there was anything sinister about his death, if that's what you mean."

"That's exactly what I mean. What about his wife?"

"I know absolutely nothing about her. In fact, I've never seen her. Their courtship was done primarily out of sight of others. In his later years Harris was a very private man. He didn't want the press to make much of the fact he was seeing such a young girl. You've got to remember that George was married to his first wife, Ilene, for nearly forty years. When Ilene died, he became somewhat reclusive, withdrawn. He wasn't the public personality he used to be. He was always very conscious of what other people thought. Also, he was quite proud of the fact that he didn't fit the typical mold of the Hollywood star. He never made a spectacle of himself at parties, rarely drank, and even more rarely dated. And he was very respectful of his late wife's memory.

"If I recall, he dated this young woman for a very short time, then they got married. It was a small ceremony; only very close friends. The press was not invited, although it was mentioned in the news.

"After Harris's death, the wife went abroad for nearly a year until things died down. I imagine she knew that's the way Harris would have wanted it handled. Since then, from what I understand, she just lives alone in his old house up on Mulholland Drive."

"Not a very visible person."

"Maybe that's what George saw in her. Because that's how he was toward the end of his life. She makes donations to charities in her husband's name now and then, but she doesn't give or go to parties or social functions. I mean, she wasn't actually in the entertainment business and didn't know anyone in the social circles besides George and a very few of his closest friends. I imagine she would feel out of place at most Hollywood gatherings. Maybe if they'd stayed married longer, she would have grown into Hollywood society."

"Yeah, maybe. Look, I've got to run. But I'll be in touch. I want to try something on for size," he said, and stood up. "May I use your phone before I go?"

"Certainly."

Ace picked up a nearby phone and dialed a number. "Bill?"

"Yes," said a voice on the other end.

"I'd like for you to check something for me. Pull up anything you've got down there on George Harris's wedding, his death and his widow."

"The actor?"

"Right. How long will that take?"

"About forty minutes."

"Great. I'm on my way," said Ace, and hung up.

"What are you trying to find out?"

"Just a hunch. I'll call you," said the detective, and let himself out.

Ace's mind was racing when he pulled away from the curb. Maybe that was the reason he didn't notice that he was being followed.

THE *L.A. Times* building had taken on a very clean, efficient look since the renovations. It looked like the perfect home for about a hundred computer terminals. The typewriter had gone the way of the quill. Reporters typed their stories onto their computer screens, edited with little green cursors, punched a button, and the stories were devoured by the next stage of the system.

"Hi, Bill," said Ace.

Bill Scranton turned around from his computer and smiled widely at his old friend. "Hey, buddy, how's it going?"

"Hangin' in there. Any word on what I ordered?"

"Just a sec." He picked up his phone, mumbled a few words into it, nodded his head, and hung up. "Yeah. It's ready. See that glass-enclosed room across the way?" he said, and pointed.

"Yeah."

"A guy'll be bringing it right up. He thinks it's for me. If he gives you any problems, just tell him to see me."

"Thanks, Bill. I appreciate it. I owe you a lunch."

"I'll add it to my list. Hey, what gives with this thing? This is old news. Or is it?"

"If I strike gold, I'll cut you in. Best not to say anything at this point. I might be way off base."

"Good luck."

"Yeah," said the detective, and strode through the ocean of computers to the room indicated by Scranton.

THE BOY WHO brought up the material didn't give Ace any problems. "I've got some stuff for Bill Scranton," he announced when he entered the room.

"Here," said Ace.

It was that simple. The boy handed Ace the articles and walked out.

Ace scanned the material, looking for any information that might prove helpful. It was all pretty much as Cynthia had said, no startling revelations about Harris's death and almost no information at all on his widow, except that she was young and had left the country following the private funeral service.

At the bottom of the pile was a photograph of the funeral taken from a distance with a telephoto lens. Even though there was a veil over the widow's face, there was something very familiar about it. Very familiar.

ACE LEANED HIS head inside a small office and knocked on the open door. A woman who looked to be in her mid-fifties, with recently coiffed gray hair, wearing dark-rimmed glasses and a smart-looking gray flannel suit, looked up from her work and put her pen down on her desk. "Yes?"

"Mrs. Whatley?"

"Yes."

"My name's Ace Carpenter, I'm a PI. Bill Scranton downstairs in the city room said you might be willing to talk with me."

"You and Bill friends?"

"For about five years."

"Come in," she said.

Ace took a chair opposite Whatley. "I wanted to ask you a few questions about someone. Since you're the society editor, I thought you might be able to help me out. Feel free not to answer if you don't want to."

Whatley got a big grin on her face, took off her glasses, and rocked back in her chair. She impressed Ace as a woman who had really been around, but who had retained a certain perspective on life that included a sense of humor. "Oh, I'll keep that in mind. Who are you interested in?"

"George Harris's widow."

"Hmmmm," she hummed, and rocked back and forth slightly in her chair. "The very private Mrs. George Harris. I don't know how much help I can be to you, Mr. Carpenter. Mrs. Harris is a woman who likes her privacy and has the money to keep it that way. If she had wanted to capitalize on her celebrity-by-marriage status, she could have quite easily, but she didn't. After a while, the gossip columnists and others in the press simply lost interest. People have a relatively short memory about such things."

"Bill said you were a friend of Mr. Harris?"

"In this business, one often says one is a friend of almost anyone. But in George's case, it's quite true. George and I became friends when I first started here in the fifties. I met him at a party where he and his wife, Ilene, took pity on me and introduced me to several of their friends. I never forgot their kindness. So yes, we were friends."

"Were you at his funeral?"

"Yes, I was."

"So you saw Mr. Harris's new bride."

"Oh, yes. I was even at the wedding, although I was made to promise not to give it much space. George made it quite clear that I was being invited as a friend, not as a reporter."

"I'd like you to take a look at something."

"Certainly," she said, and slipped her glasses back on.

Ace took the picture of Barry Ashford and Sally Wayland out of his pocket and slid it across Whatley's desk.

The newswoman studied the photograph, wrinkled her eyebrows, held it closer for a better look, and said, "Hmmm. That's quite interesting."

"How so?"

"That's Rebecca. Rebecca Harris, George's widow. Quite some time ago, of course. But that's her. And isn't that a young Barry Ashford standing next to her?"

"Yes. Did you ever hear her called by the name Sally?"

"You know, I seem to remember that Rebecca's real first name was Sally, but that she preferred to be called Rebecca. I've got a copy of the invitation in my files if you'd like to wait a second."

"Sure."

Whatley got up and went out of the room. About five minutes later she returned carrying a yellowing card in her hand. "Yes, here it is," she said as she sat down. "Sally Rebecca Wayland. Here, see for yourself," she said, and handed Ace the old invitation.

Ace took it, looked it over, and handed it back to Whatley. "That's a big help. I wonder if I could ask one last favor."

"Maybe."

"Could you give me Mrs. Harris's address?"

"On one condition."

"Which is?"

"You promise not to bother her."

"I won't *bother* her."

"Then what is this all about?"

"I just want to talk to her about Barry Ashford. She was an old friend of his, and I think she might have the missing piece of a puzzle I'm working on. No trouble, though. Honest."

"All right, then," she said. Whatley tore off a piece of paper from her note pad, wrote down Harris's address, and handed it to Ace.

"You know, that's quite a coincidence," said Whatley, her face wrinkled into a puzzled look.

"What's that?"

"Two of Rebecca's friends meeting their death so close together."

"I don't follow."

"I'm talking about Owen Clark. He was a good friend of George's. He actually produced the last two pictures George made. It was after George's prime, of course. But the pictures made money, and that was really what gave Owen credibility in the film community."

"Would you happen to know if Clark and Rebecca were close friends?"

"I don't know whether anyone was close to her, but I know

that Owen was one of the people at George's wedding and his funeral. I believe that Owen allowed Rebecca to use his house in France. Yes, that's right," said Whatley, remembering it all now. "That's where she went when she left the country for the year following George's death. Beyond that, I wouldn't know."

"You're a wealth of information, Mrs. Whatley. I really appreciate your taking the time to talk with me."

"Think nothing of it. If ever you come across anything I can use, please let me know."

"Will do."

ACE DECIDED TO stop by the West Hollywood police station to see if Eddy had anything new on Corey Eastland's death. On his way to the station, he tried to sort things out. So Sally Wayland had gotten her wish—she'd married money. But then why didn't she fla nt it, as her previous style would have indicated that she would? And what had happened between her and Ashford?

"Hi, Eddy," said Ace, standing before Price's desk.

The cop looked up. "Ace. Have a seat. I'm just looking over the info on Eastland's suicide."

"Suicide?"

"That's what it looks like. And there's more."

"I'm all yours," said Ace, sitting down in the side chair next to Eddy's desk.

"It actually ties things up pretty neatly. He left a note. I don't have it here because the boys upstairs are checking it for fingerprints, et cetera. But basically it goes like this. It looks like your boy Ashford really *was* murdered. Any guesses?"

"I'm not good at games."

"Owen Clark. It appears that Ashford found out about the money Clark was embezzling and was putting the screws to him. Finally Clark had enough and hired some pro to take care of Ashford in the most inconspicuous way possible. It almost worked. Tell you the truth, I thought it was a hit-and-skip all along. Tell me, did you have Clark pegged for this by now?"

"Not really."

"See, I'm making your job easy."

"So what about Clark?"

"Hold your horses. So, Eastland somehow became privy to the embezzlement information and decided to take his revenge that had been eating away at him since he was fired by Clark several years before."

"Why now?"

"Apparently he felt that Clark needed to be finally taught a lesson. Clark had canned *him* and he'd gotten away with it. Now he'd offed Ashford and was apparently getting away with it."

"The way I understood it, there wasn't any love lost between Ashford and Eastland."

"I wouldn't know. Anyhow, Eastland decided to get even. But how? From his friend Willy Dodd, he discovered what dozens of other people already knew—Maddie's gun was in the night table beside her bed. Now, Maddie Paxton wasn't very high on Eastland's list, either. Apparently they hadn't hit it off very well on *or* off the set while he was doing the show. In his note, he as much as says that her bad-mouthing of him to Clark was responsible for him being fired.

"So, one day Eastland allegedly broke into Maddie's house when he knew she would be working and took the gun."

"Impossible to confirm."

"I'm just telling you what the note says, okay?"

"Okay."

"So he took the gun and waited for Clark to get off work one night, did the deed, wiped the gun clean, threw the gun away, and that was that. Or so he thought. Apparently his conscience got the best of him. He said he couldn't live with himself anymore, knowing that he had taken another life. He finally became so depressed that he committed suicide. By leaving the note—so he says—he could maybe set some things straight and not be responsible for sending another innocent person to their death for a murder she didn't commit."

"Meaning Paxton, the person he hated."

"Yeah."

"The guy has pretty quick changes of heart."

"It makes sense. At least part of it does. We talked to Willy Dodd a little while ago."

"And what did he have to say?"

"He was scared. Plenty scared. He told us the same story he told you about the alibi being Eastland's idea. That would make sense. After all, it was perfect for Eastland. He convinced his friend Dodd that he was being big-hearted in providing him with an alibi, when it was Eastland's alibi all along."

"What about Eastland asking Dodd about the gun at Paxton's house?"

"Bingo again. Actually, though, Dodd says his recollection wasn't that Eastland had asked about the gun. He remembers telling Eastland about the fact that it was there. Apparently some people were getting high in Maddie's bedroom one night and someone was looking for some matches. They opened the drawer and saw the gun. Dodd remembers telling Eastland the story."

"I don't know, Eddy," said Ace, unconvinced.

"It plays pretty good from here. Come up with something else that fits all the facts and I'll listen. But for now, I'm willing to take this thing to the bank. Besides, you've got the luxury of working on one case at a time. See that," said the cop, pointing to a foot-high pile of folders overflowing from a wire basket on the corner of his desk.

"Yeah, I know. Okay. So, I think I'll be pushing on," said Ace, getting up.

"Look, don't get me wrong. If you get something that'll put some honest holes in this case, give me a call. Okay?"

"Okay."

ACE TURNED his white Celica up Beachwood Drive about five-thirty. In his rearview mirror he caught sight of the olive-green Chevrolet he'd seen pull away from the curb when he'd left the police station. He purposely made a wrong turn on Judson, then turned around in a driveway and headed back to Beach-wood. By the time he made his turn onto Belden, he saw the Chevrolet slowly making its way up Beachwood.

Ace parked his car and, without looking behind him, walked up the stairs to his apartment and locked the door. He quickly picked up Marlowe and put him in the back bedroom, pulling the door closed. Then he went out the back door and hid behind the bushes in the backyard.

About three minutes later a man wearing a gray suit came around the side of the house and stood at the back door. He looked at his watch and drew something out from inside his coat.

Ace stood up, gun drawn, aimed, and said, "Okay. Turn around and be easy."

The man in the gray suit jumped as if he'd just been shocked, then slowly turned around. He was holding a gun.

"Don't even dream about using that thing," said the detective.

Just then a loud explosion came from inside Ace's apartment. It sounded like a door being kicked open. It was enough to distract Ace for a second. The man in the gray suit lowered his gun and fired. The detective was falling and rolling away by the time the shot whistled through the bushes. Ace squeezed the trigger and fired. The gunman let out a howl and went down grabbing his knee. Ace raced to where the man lay moaning, straddled him, and landed an anesthetizing left to the gunman's jaw.

As he did, he heard footsteps doing a fast dance on the pavement out front. Ace got to his feet and ran around to the front of his apartment just in time to see the other man running around to the driver's side of the olive-green Chevrolet. Ace was about forty yards away from the other gunman by the time the man had his hand on the door handle. By the time the man was inside and pulling away, Ace was only a few yards from the car. He got down on one knee, and, grabbing his right hand underneath with a steadying left hand, he fired several shots at the right front wheel of the car. At least one hit the mark as the front tire popped and the car veered sharply to the right and into a telephone pole.

The gunman, who was a little shaken up from the collision, was out of the car and running by the time Ace tackled him from behind. The two men went sprawling. Ace grabbed his gun from his belt and shoved it between the gunman's legs. The man was breathing fast and was somewhat dazed. But the feeling of the gun barrel in such an intimate place brought his eyes into sharp focus.

"You can sing with a high voice, or you can sing with a low voice. Either way you're going to sing. Doesn't make any difference to me. I've got all the law on my side I'm going to need."

"Okay, okay, okay," said the man until Ace thought the guy was going to wear the word out.

"Who are you working for?"

"I'm a licensed security agent," said the man, his words

running together. "Bates Security Company. You can check my ID."

"Now, that's not what I want to know and you know it."

"I can't tell you. I've got my ethics," said the man, coughing a little as he spoke.

"That's about all you're going to have in a minute, pal," said Ace, and cocked his thirty-eight.

"Okay, okay, okay," said the man, repeating his favorite word again like a mantra.

"Give."

"Rebecca Harris."

"Good answer," said Ace, and relinquished his hold on the man. Ace stood up but still pointed the gun at the man. "Get up. We're going back to my place." He didn't get any argument.

ACE WAS HOLDING his gun on his two guests when the police arrived, in response to the call Ace had asked one of his interested neighbors to make.

"You think these guys have anything to do with the Ashford case?" asked Eddy.

Ace had decided not to tell Eddy that he knew the two guys were working for Rebecca Harris, alias Sally Wayland. He had tracked her down, and he wanted first crack.

"I don't know. I know they work for Bates Security Company."

"We've had some problems with them before," said Eddy. "Seems they're muscle for hire for a lot of the got-bucks types here in town. The bodyguard business ain't what it used to be. I'd like to take a look at their client list."

"Can you do that?"

"I'm going to try."

"You need me anymore? I've got something to do."

"Nah. I think we've got all we need from you. If we need you, I know how to find you. And don't forget, if you get anything else . . ."

"You'll be the first to know."

• • •

AFTER CALLING JENNY to say that he'd be a little late, Ace drove up Laurel Canyon to Mulholland and headed east through the hills that split L.A. and the Valley in two. Just before the Encino Hills, he came to the Harris estate. There weren't any guards or security cameras. Just a long driveway up through trees and bushes that totally obscured the house from the road. He parked in front of two pillars that made the house look like something out of *Gone With the Wind*.

He knocked on the door and a black woman wearing a black dress and a white apron answered the door.

"Yes, sir?" she said in a voice that was neither friendly nor unfriendly.

"I'd like to see Mrs. Harris."

"Is she expecting you?"

"No."

"Then I'm afraid I can't—"

"Give her this," said Ace, taking the photo of Sally and Ashford out of his sport coat pocket and handing it to the maid.

The woman took it and closed the door, leaving Ace standing outside on a welcome mat. A few minutes later the woman came back and opened the door. "Come this way." This time her manner was definitely not friendly.

Ace followed the maid to a large study with high ceilings and a real fireplace.

"Mrs. Harris will be down in a moment. You may help yourself to a drink if you like," she said, extending a hand toward a wet bar stocked with fine liquor.

"Thanks."

The woman gave him an extra-long silent look, then turned on her heel and walked out, shutting the study's double doors behind her.

Ace poured himself a glass of what he recognized to be one-hundred-dollar-a-bottle brandy and walked around the room. It was a museum. There must have been fifty pictures of George Harris with other famous movie stars, politicians, even a couple of presidents. And on the mantel over the fireplace was the special Oscar awarded to him, not for a picture, but for a lifetime of making America laugh. He had received it just a few months before he'd died. Ace was thinking what it would be like to actually touch an Oscar when one of the study's doors opened and Rebecca Harris walked in.

"Hello, Sally," said Ace.

"Who are you?"

"Ace Carpenter. I'm a private investigator looking into the death of Barry Ashford."

"So?"

"You used to be real tight with Barry back in Boulder."

"Are you getting to some kind of point?" said the blonde, lighting a cigarette with a lighter she had just picked up from the desk. She put it back down and heaved a cloud of smoke between her pretty lips. Ace realized that the picture hadn't done Sally Wayland Harris any justice. She was beautiful. Her blond hair had been recently done in a style that looked as though it had been invented for her. She moved gracefully, confidently, in a lavender dress that seemed to be caressing her as she walked. Maybe she wasn't trying to distract the detective, but it was working anyhow. But Ace got his mind back on track.

"The point is, I didn't come here to play forty questions. I know a lot. More than the police, but that's only a temporary arrangement. They're only one step behind me and moving fast. I just wanted to get here first. I think I've earned it."

"You're talking a lot, but not saying anything, Mr. Carpenter."

"I know about Bates Security." He let that missile hit its mark.

The woman turned away for a moment, then turned back; her face softened a little and she waved Ace toward a large beige couch, where they both sat down.

"Mind if I call you Sally?"

"No. It's been a long time since anyone has."

"Okay, Sally. I went to Boulder and I know a lot about you, your mother and father—who's still preaching, by the way, and he told me to tell you he'd open your letters if you still wanted to send any. I know about your relationship with Barry and what motivated you to come out here. There are a few things I don't know. But it's just a matter of time. The cops know everything I do, except that the guys from Bates were working for you. And they'll have that in a few hours. So we don't have much time."

"Why should I tell you anything?"

"You look like a woman with a story to tell. Besides, my guess is that Barry started this whole thing in motion. He was a son of a bitch and everybody knew it. See, I've got this idea that the murders of Ashford, Clark, and Eastland all have something in common. And I've got a pretty good idea it all leads back to you. But I don't know why. However, everybody— and I mean everybody—is going to know all about it pretty soon."

"But that can't happen, Mr. Carpenter. It just can't."

"But it's going to."

"You've got to help me."

"I don't. But I'm willing to listen."

Sally stood up and did her best walk over to the wet bar and poured herself some Chivas Regal, neat. "Can I get you a drink?"

Ace held up his glass. She nodded and came back to the couch. "It's all such a nightmare, Mr. Carpenter. I did what I did, what I *had* to do, to protect my late husband's name. And now it turns out that it was all for nothing. Nothing," she said, tears gathering in her eyes.

"Why don't you start at the beginning and tell me the story. And try not to leave anything out, okay?"

Sally nodded her head, swallowed hard, blinked away some of the tears, took a healthy sip of the straight Scotch, and began. "Barry and I came out here about five years ago with a friend of ours—"

"Turtle," said Ace for effect. He wanted her to believe she shouldn't lie to him.

"Maybe I should have hired *you* in the first place," she said, somewhat taken aback.

"Maybe," said the detective with a manner that appeared more smug than he had intended.

"Anyhow, we all had our reasons for coming out here. Turtle wanted to be a rock and roll star, Barry wanted to get rich, and I wanted to find my father. A reporter in Boulder gave me the name of a guy out here who might be able to help me find out who my father was. I went to see the guy and it was real 'welcome to L.A.' time. He said he could do the job, but it was going to cost. The three of us didn't bring much money with us, and I was working as a waitress down on Hollywood Boulevard at the time. So, I did what I had to do—if you know what I mean.

"A few weeks after he started on the job, he had come up with the address of a doctor's office where the records regarding the identity of my parents were supposed to be kept. At that point he'd kind of reached a dead end without taking some personal risks that could get him in trouble with the law. So he gave me the address and told me I was on my own.

"The address turned out to be a doctor's office in Beverly Hills. I made up a story to get to see the doctor. I made sure I had the last appointment of the day—I told them I had to work and couldn't get off till about five. I'd taken a look inside the office the day before and figured out what I was going to do. There was a big leather couch in the reception room. I figured that when the receptionist closed her little window after I'd paid my bill, I'd hide behind the couch. That's exactly what I did.

"So, about an hour after I hid, everyone was gone and the office was locked up. I went back to a large room with about a dozen three-drawer file cabinets. Luckily they were arranged by year. I went right to 1953. It wasn't hard after that. There it was. Mary Lou Wayland. Then I saw my real father's name and address. I didn't put a great deal of significance on it at the time because it was such a common name—my father's name, that is. I took down the address next to his name and drove there the next day. I couldn't believe it when I saw it."

"It?"

"This house."

"*This* house?"

"My father's house. My husband's house."

"My God! Are you telling me that George Harris married his own daughter?!"

"That's right. You can understand how this could change the public's perception of him."

Ace laughed and stroked his chin. "I guess *so.*"

"You're shocked, aren't you?"

"Yes, I am."

"Most people would be. And that's all they'd want to hear about it—that the famous Hollywood saint married his daughter. Oh, it would make great copy, that's for sure. But that's just not the way it was."

"But he was your father, right?"

"Yes."

"And you are his daughter, right?"

"Yes."

"And you married him?"

"Yes, yes, yes," she said, tears now starting to flow freely. After a minute or two, Sally composed herself again and continued.

"After I found out that George was my father, Barry and I decided on a plan that would make us a lot of money. Actually it was Barry's plan. You must understand that I was still pretty much under Barry's spell. He was a very persuasive man. He figured that if I could make a connection with George, start going out with him, get him to eventually marry me, then Barry and I could live off the blackmail money for the rest of our lives like a king and queen. I told Barry that the chances of getting that close to George were very slim. That's where I was wrong.

"Barry dogged George day after day getting to know his schedule. One night Barry knew that George was going to be eating dinner at a West Hollywood restaurant, alone. As you know, Barry is a good actor. He arranged for us to have a table very near where George was sitting. We spent all our money on clothes, so that we wouldn't look out of place in such a 'fancy' restaurant.

"Anyhow, Barry gave a masterful performance of a cad and left me crying at the table near where George was sitting. I looked up, trying to catch George's eye, until he finally came over and offered me his handkerchief. He was such a gentle and kind man. That's why this whole thing is so unfair," she said, her voice cracking.

"So that was the beginning. I told him that I'd just come to town, didn't have a job, and had been used by the guy who'd just left me sitting at the table crying. George was very sympathetic. I ate dinner with him that night and he drove me back to my cheap apartment. And he was the perfect gentleman. He didn't put any moves on me or try to take advantage of the situation.

"When I got home, Barry was ecstatic. I tried to share his excitement, but I couldn't. I mean, after all, I'd just talked to my real father for the first time in my life and I was setting him up to be conned. But you must remember that I still harbored some hostility about his responsibility in my mother's death, indirect though it was.

"The next day, George called me—I'd given him my number—and told me that there was an opening at his agent's office, if I could type. I said I could, so I started to work that afternoon. The next few weeks George and I saw a lot of each other. He'd stop by his agent's office on one pretense or another and we'd get to talking. He took me to dinner almost every night. We just talked. That's all. I really got to love the man— as a father, as a man, but not as a lover. He looked at me as his companion. He was a lonely man, really. But that's another story.

"So after about a month of this, George asked me to marry him. I was to be his companion. We would travel and live out the rest of his life spending money, traveling, talking, doing things he'd always wanted to do—but not alone, and not with someone who was just hanging around him for his money.

"This was just too much for me. I was stricken with guilt and told Barry so. But Barry felt that he was on the verge of a big score and wouldn't listen to reason. He threatened to go to George and tell him that we'd been scheming all along, if I didn't continue. I just couldn't allow that to happen. I decided to go through with the marriage. Then, on our honeymoon, I'd planned to sit down with him, tell him the whole story, and promise to make it all up to him for the rest of his life. As his daughter, as his companion.

"The night George and I were married, Barry called me to tell me that he'd found out George and I were leaving the country. He would not be double-crossed, he said. So I decided to sit down immediately with George and tell him the story. He was so shocked he couldn't move. I thought for a while that he'd had a stroke, that he was paralyzed. When he finally spoke he said, 'My entire life's work, my reputation, Ilene's memory'—Ilene was his first wife of forty years—'is ruined. I will be humiliated on the front page of every newspaper in the land. They will say that my entire life was a lie. I'll be portrayed as a monster.'

"I did what I could to comfort him, but it wasn't much. Finally, after an hour or so of holding him and trying to reassure him, he appeared to be all right. He said that he was tired and wanted to go to bed. The next morning I discovered him in the bathtub, his wrists slit. He was dead."

Sally dropped her head into her hands and wept.

After a minute Ace said, "How did Ashford take all this?"

Sally pulled herself together, sniffling, taking a Kleenex from a box on a nearby table, blowing her nose. "Barry was

a bastard, but he wasn't a murderer. Tell you the truth, it scared
the hell out of him initially. Then he calmed down and tried
to make the best of the situation. Things were hushed up by
George's friends, and I went away to Owen Clark's château in
France. I kept in touch with Barry by mail, but we didn't see
each other during that time. However, I did send him money.
When I came back a year later, things had quieted down. Barry
and I got together and talked. I'd lost my feelings for Barry,
and I believe he had for me. He asked me for a favor—one
last favor. I talked with Owen, who was a good friend and
who had taken care of things very well for me, and asked him
if he could give a friend of mine a job. I told him that Barry
was a friend of mine from Boulder and that he was quite
talented. I introduced them and they hit it off very well. In
fact, they may have had something sexual going on in the
beginning, for all I know. Anyhow, Owen was impressed enough
to give Barry a part on the show, which Barry milked into a
starring role by employing his usual tactics of back-biting and
clawing his way to the top.

"Things were going fine till a few weeks ago when Barry
came to me and asked me for a million dollars."

"What for?"

"Barry wanted out. He was dying in Hollywood from the
booze, the sex, the drugs, and the hate he inspired in everyone
around him. Things between himself and Owen had soured,
and Barry knew that Owen had considerable clout in the in-
dustry. Look what happened to Barry's predecessor, Corey
Eastland. Owen blackballed him. The next thing you knew,
the guy's managing a bookstore on Hollywood Boulevard. Barry
didn't want to wind up that way.

"Naturally I told him no. He then told me that he had another
way of getting the money, but that I might not like it. He said
that he'd been in touch with a scandal sheet and, without giving
all the details, had been offered a million dollars for the story
about George and me.

"Well, I just couldn't have that. But I couldn't have Barry
blackmailing me, either. I knew that he'd be back when the
money ran out. That's the way Barry was. I couldn't let him
know that I was willing to pay. I have dedicated my life to
seeing that George's memory is maintained in the high esteem
in which he left it. So, I had no choice."

"Other than what?"

"Barry wouldn't be moved. I was desperate. Barry had to be . . ."

"Persuaded."

"Exactly. Like I say, I was desperate. I had been told by Owen a couple of years ago about Corey Eastland, who had gone off the deep end when Barry had virtually replaced him in the series, and of the humiliating scene between the actor and Owen. I followed up on the lead—a man seeking revenge—and contacted him. From the little I was able to gather about Corey Eastland, he seemed like a time bomb waiting to go off. We met for lunch. He was such a sycophant. It turns out that he admired George as much as any fan could. When I told him what Barry was threatening to do, he got a crazy look in his eye.

"I asked him to try and persuade—and officially, you'll notice that I used the word 'persuade,' not murder—Barry to drop his plan. He said that he would take care of it.

"Naturally, I was as shocked as anyone to read a few days later of Barry's death."

"Naturally. So what about Owen Clark?"

"That's quite simple, actually. It appears that Owen—being the philandering, gambling, poor businessman that he is—got himself a couple of million dollars in the hole on a bad land development deal. He came to me one night and told me he needed money, that he knew that Barry had tried to blackmail me, and, unfortunately, that he was doing the same thing. It was all quite civil, really. He told me not to look at it like blackmail and that he would try to pay me back someday.

"Naturally, I refused. Then he became very disagreeable. He said that he had been George's best friend—which he actually hadn't—and that he had known George long before I arrived on the scene and that he was entitled to the use of some of the money; certainly more than I, since I'd only known George for about a month.

"Well, I knew what had to be done. Owen is not the kind of person to learn from his mistakes. I knew it would happen again and he would use me and George's money as a safety net from here on out. I just couldn't let that happen, nor could I let him take the story to the magazine, as he threatened to do. After all, a million dollars can be quite an enticement—especially to someone who owes a lot of money.

"The next step was quite easy, actually. I contacted Corey Eastland again and told him about Owen. He hated Owen even more than Barry, so he didn't need to be convinced to . . . persuade Owen to change his mind. I'm not sure how Corey actually did it, but I know he planned to make it look as though Owen had killed Barry and that Maddie had killed Owen. Quite a clever fellow, actually."

"The clever fellow's dead," said Ace dryly.

"Oh." The actor's widow winced. She tried to make it look as though it hurt, but it really didn't, and it showed.

"Police say it's a suicide."

"Really."

"Really. But I have my doubts."

"Why?"

"I just do. Are you going to tell me who really killed Eastland?"

"What do you mean?"

"Look, don't get cozy with me."

"Cozy? Mr. Carpenter, I've just sat here and bared my soul to you."

"I doubt it. My guess is, the same guys who roughed me up because I was getting close to the real story are the same guys who offed Corey Eastland. And I don't think Corey Eastland was as clever as you are."

"And what's that supposed to mean?"

"Read between the lines," said Ace, and stood up. "Thanks for the chat. I'm sure the police will be around to see you shortly, so I hope you're not planning to go out—like to Europe or any place like that."

"As a matter of fact, I was planning a cruise. But I don't see that it's anyone's business but my own. The police, I take it, are satisfied with the case as it is. At least, they haven't been in touch with me. And I did nothing wrong except tell my problems to someone who took it upon himself to help me out." Her face turned colder than it had been during the conversation. "And you can't prove otherwise," she said flatly.

"Maybe," he said, and let himself out through the double doors.

• • •

ACE PULLED OFF Mulholland onto a little gravel-covered area
where playful teenagers and adults went to play adult games
and look out upon the city lights under whatever stars could
filter light through the layers of pollution. From his vantage
point the detective could still see where the Harris driveway
emptied onto Mulholland. He didn't think he'd have to wait
very long. He was right.

About fifteen minutes later headlights lit the driveway. A
white Mercedes 450SL glided onto the main road and flew past
Ace with speed and purpose.

Ace followed the Mercedes to Laurel Canyon, then down
to the Sunset Strip, then west to Doheny, then south to Lake-
side, a small street running east and west just south of Santa
Monica Boulevard. The Mercedes pulled up in front of a one-
story white stucco. Sally Wayland Harris got out and walked
quickly to the front door. She knocked once and was immediately let in by someone who was apparently expecting her.
Ace didn't see who it was.

The detective pulled up behind the white Mercedes and
examined the right front fender. It looked okay. That is, it
looked okay until he got down on his knees and looked up
underneath. A new fender had recently been put on Sally Wayland's car.

Ace stood up, wiped off the pieces of grass from his pants,
and walked to the front door. He knocked once. No answer,
but he heard some scurrying around inside. He knocked again
and the door opened.

"What do you want?" asked Jerry Russo in a much less
friendly tone than when Ace had last talked with him as the
fan magazine reporter, Barry Lyndon.

"It's all over, Jerry. My only question is whether you or
Sally ran Barry Ashford down."

Russo's face turned white. He threw out a muscular arm
that grazed Ace's forehead and sent the detective falling into
the bushes. But Ace's reflexes were good enough so that the
blow hadn't done any damage. In an instant Ace was on his
feet and only about ten yards behind Russo, who was running
for his life. Ace chased the actor for a block and a half, where
he finally tackled him behind a bus stop bench. Two old ladies
waiting for a bus turned to watch the action as Ace rolled over
and over with Russo. The actor was big and in good shape,
but he couldn't fight worth a damn. He was a lover, not a

fighter. A well-placed fist to the solar plexus and to the Adam's apple took all the fight out of the young actor.

"That's Axel McGrew," said one of the old ladies.

"I beg your pardon?" said Ace, catching his breath.

"Alex McGrew from *Doctors and Lovers,*" she said with a straight face. "Are you filming this?"

"No," said the other woman almost condescendingly to her companion. "Alex is a hero on the show. He looks like a common thief here. This *must* be real life." With that, the two women turned and boarded the bus that had just stopped by the curb.

Ace got Russo to his feet and marched him back to his house. But by the time they'd returned, the white Mercedes was gone.

"SORRY I'M SO LATE," said Ace when Jenny Ling let him in.

"I'm sure you've got a good excuse," she said sleepily. It was about eleven-thirty by the time he finally arrived. "Absolut?"

"Sure."

Jenny went into the kitchen and came back a minute later with two glasses of chilled Absolut and handed one to Ace. They both sat on the couch.

"So . . ." she said, taking her first sip.

"I solved the case."

"You mean the Ashford case?" said Jenny, her eyes blinking into a concentrated focus.

"Yes."

"Well . . . who did it?"

"It appears to have been a joint effort. Sally Wayland, also known as Rebecca Harris, was being blackmailed by Barry Ashford. She and her current boyfriend, Jerry Russo, are responsible not only for running down Barry—Russo was actually behind the wheel at the time, in Sally's car—but also for killing Owen Clark and Corey Eastland."

"You're kidding!"

"No." After filling her in on the missing data regarding Wayland's marriage to her father and Owen Clark wanting money to cover up his embezzlement of company funds, Ace continued. "It was all rather simple, actually. They weren't

taking any heat for Ashford's murder. Then Owen started making noises. Russo had been Maddie Paxton's lover on occasion,
as had most young studs in town. He knew about the gun, took
it one night, and used it to kill Owen. Russo knew approxi-
mately what time Owen would leave. He just waited outside
the studio. He pulled up alongside Clark at a stop sign, waved
to Owen, who, recognizing his lead actor, rolled down his
window and ate a bullet.

"And Corey Eastland was made to order for the whole rap.
He had reason to want both men dead. Russo went to see him.
Eastland, being the Hollywood fan that he was, as well as
being a homosexual, welcomed Russo literally with open arms.
But Russo went to Eastland's apartment for just one reason—
to set him up. He left the typewritten suicide letter implicating
Eastland in the two murders. He wiped the typewriter keys
clean, then, using Eastland's dead body, put fresh fingerprints
back on the keys.

"They might have gotten away with it, too. Sally was planning to leave the country in a couple of days—a plan she
moved up to tonight after I talked to her and spooked her. She
was picked up at the airport about an hour ago. Russo was
getting ready to leave the show and take a vacation—with
Sally. With all the money he was about to have half of as Mr.
Sally Rebecca Wayland Harris, he could have lived pretty well
for a long time. And if he'd ever wanted to get back into the
movies, he could literally have written his own ticket by pro-
ducing his own films.

"Sally had some local muscle from Bates Security keeping
tabs on me since I got back from Boulder, in case I got too
close. I was so far off base for so long that I posed no real
threat. But when I pulled Sally's number with Mrs. Whatley
down at the *Times,* I became a threat for the first time. Things
were a little touch and go there for a few minutes, but those
two guys were no match for my thirty-eight."

"Ace!" exclaimed Jenny. "You didn't tell me there was a
shooting."

"I just did."

"Oh, my God! Were you hurt?"

"Nah. I'm too smart to get shot. Good thing for Marlowe—
he hates blood."

By the time Ace had concluded telling Jenny about chasing

Russo down and dealing Eddy Price into the game, it was almost an hour and two Absoluts later.

"You're a pretty smart guy, Ace Carpenter," said Jenny, who was now curled up next to him on the couch. She had on her turquoise robe. It was short and showed her long, tanned, supertoned thighs and calves to full advantage. "You're my hero," she said.

Ace took a sip of Absolut and said, "This town is full of heroes. And they're about as deep as a piece of celluloid is thin. And just as real. I'm no hero. I'm just a guy trying to do my job as well as I can. I try not to hurt anyone who doesn't ask for it first. I don't lie unless it's absolutely necessary— and then only about sex and taxes, or when I'm under cover. I'm never going to be rich, but I'm smart and willing to work, so I'm not going to be poor, either. I play the piano and guitar well enough not to be embarrassed to play at parties. But I'm a man with a problem."

"What's that?" whispered Jenny into Ace's ear.

"I love you. I honestly love you, Jenny. And I honestly *don't* know if you love me."

"Then you don't have any problems, honey. I love you. I've been thinking a lot about it. There's no doubt in my mind anymore. What I told you before you went to Boulder was true. It hasn't changed, it's only gotten stronger."

"So, you want to move in?"

"I started packing this afternoon."

"Now I've got another problem."

"What?"

"Where to put all your stuff."

But that was a problem Ace could put off till morning. Jenny stood up from the couch and slipped off her robe. She extended her hand to him and shook her long black hair so it settled airily over her shoulders. He looked into her sultry almond eyes and felt something in the pit of his stomach. He couldn't explain exactly what it was, but it felt like the closest thing he'd ever known to going back home.

The Bestselling Author of
the <u>James Bond</u> Thrillers

JOHN GARDNER
THE SECRET GENERATIONS

The Explosive New Novel of England's First Family of Spies

"*A master storyteller at the height of his power.*"
—Len Deighton

"*This is Gardner at his best!*"
—Kirkus Reviews

John Gardner, who carried on the grand spy tradition of Ian Fleming's incomparable James Bond, now presents an explosive novel of intrigue and suspense that sweeps through three turbulent decades—marking the beginnings of the British secret service. From World War I to the rise of Nazi Germany, a proud and aristocratic family discovers that a tradition of espionage leads to a desperate and decisive undercover game of loyalty...and betrayal.

_____ **THE SECRET GENERATIONS** 0-441-75760-X $4.50

Available at your local bookstore or return this form to:

C CHARTER
THE BERKLEY PUBLISHING GROUP, Dept. B
390 Murray Hill Parkway, East Rutherford, NJ 07073

Please send me the titles checked above. I enclose _____. Include $1.00 for postage and handling if one book is ordered; 25¢ per book for two or more not to exceed $1.75. California, Illinois, New Jersey and Tennessee residents please add sales tax. Prices subject to change without notice and may be higher in Canada.

NAME_____

ADDRESS_____

CITY_____ STATE/ZIP_____

(Allow six weeks for delivery.)   465

HIS MOST SENSATIONAL
THRILLER YET — Over 4 Months on
the *New York Times* Bestseller List!

Lawrence SANDERS

THE FOURTH DEADLY SIN

"The suspense never lags.
It is the entertainment novel...
near its best!" —Washington Post

The First Deadly Sin was the blockbuster that launched
his phenomenal success. Now, ten best-sellers later,
Lawrence Sanders presents his most compelling, most
suspenseful thriller ever. A celebrated New York psychi-
atrist—considered a saint by patients and colleagues—
is brutally beaten to death. There are no leads, no apparent
motives, and six suspects—the doctor's own patients.

— THE FOURTH DEADLY SIN
0-425-09078-7 $4.50

Available at your local bookstore or return this form to:

BERKLEY
THE BERKLEY PUBLISHING GROUP, Dept. B
390 Murray Hill Parkway, East Rutherford, NJ 07073

Please send me the titles checked above. I enclose _____. Include $1.00 for postage
and handling if one book is ordered; 25¢ per book for two or more not to exceed $1.75.
California, Illinois, New Jersey and Tennessee residents please add sales tax. Prices
subject to change without notice and may be higher in Canada.

NAME_____

ADDRESS_____

CITY_____ STATE/ZIP_____

(Allow six weeks for delivery.)